THE NEGLIGENTS

Kate Smith was born in Essex in 1974, and grew up on the Isle of Wight. After studying English Literature at Cambridge University, where she wrote and performed comedy sketches as part of Footlights' Smokers, she qualified as a lawyer. A short stint as a barrister was followed by a longer one as a solicitor.

Kate now lectures in Tort Law at BPP University in London and writes comedy with a partner for television and radio. She recently completed an MA in Creative Writing at Manchester Metropolitan University, obtaining a distinction and the Michael Schmidt Prize. She lives in Hove with her partner, their son, a chocolate Labrador and an angst-ridden cat.

The Negligents

KATE SMITH

Valley Press

First published in 2018 by Valley Press
Woodend, The Crescent, Scarborough, YO11 2PW
www.valleypressuk.com

First edition, first printing (May 2018)

ISBN 978-1-908853-59-2
Cat. no. VP0117

A CIP record for this book is available from the British Library.

Cover design by Fitzpatrick Designs.
Text design by Jo Haywood.

Printed and bound in the EU by Pulsio, Paris.

Supported using public funding by
ARTS COUNCIL
ENGLAND
LOTTERY FUNDED

For Mum.
See? We elephants never forget.
With so much love and thanks.

Also for Westwood, our very happy family home.

'They were careless people, Tom and Daisy – they smashed up things and creatures and then retreated back into their money or their vast carelessness, or whatever it was that kept them together and let other people clean up the mess they had made…'

F. Scott Fitzgerald, The Great Gatsby

'Negligence as a tort is the breach of a legal duty to take care, which results in damage, undesired by the defendant to the plaintiff.'

Attributed to Professor Sir Percy H. Winfield

LOSS/DAMAGE

'Why do we begin with loss?'

'Does it matter if we can't remember the whole case name?'

'If negligence means carelessness, why don't we just call it carelessness?'

They were as intimidating as judges, some of them. Polina sat on the front of the desk, ankles crossed. Had she been like this when she was a student?

'Good questions,' she lied. 'Why begin with loss? In the beginning is my end?'

'Do we need to know this for the exam?'

Something in the student's tone reminded her of Grace, the expectation that you'd furnish them with what they wanted, that that was your job. A hazy memory of Grace's garden rushed her, the feel of it, camouflaged as any other day, or a composite of days, and she saw her own body in silhouette, cross-legged and unsure of itself, her lips chewing words on their way out. What she'd always meant to say back then, and didn't, was don't speak to me like that. Don't say things about my mum.

'Why are you always going red?' Grace had said.

'Don't speak to me like … '

'Why? Are we under fire?' Grace quickly ducked her head down, searched the skyline with her eyes.

Their story started there, bang in the middle of nothing, over and over again.

Grace was in the grass, using her elbows to pull her along. You have to keep low, she was saying. And watch out for mines. These were games made up by Grace for Polina, who could not describe how special this made her feel, a spike of joy to stab all the bubbles that bubbled up inside her. Grace never said sorry, but she gave you something, and that was better than sorry, though more fleeting, her favours mercurial, quicksand. Polina couldn't ever stay the right way up in these games and it was she who always wanted to apologise although she couldn't fathom what for. Who else is going to play with you, Grace would taunt, which made something open up in Polina's belly, a gap she could fall through. So, she'd laugh in Grace's face as though she was deep-down confident that Grace liked her, (because she did?). And she wondered if Grace bought the true lie Polina told herself – I am liked, I am likeable – and whether it could shield her from the thoughts that crowded in like the girls in the playground. *We saw you riding your bike, Polina. You're weird. Do all the girls in Russia think they're boys?* My mum is half Serbian, she's not Rus ... Ignore them, her mother always told her, but she didn't tell her how.

She and Grace stamped on a strip of caps from Ed's gun, three pops. The air was delirious with farts and gunpowder. It made Polina rash. 'Let's be best friends for ever!' she said.

She wanted to go further and grab this chance to secure something from Grace, but she didn't know how to get what she wanted. And anyway, Grace had stopped to take an urgent telephone call. She put her hand over the imaginary mouth-piece like they did in films and raised her eyebrows at Polina: 'Did you say something?'

'Promise?' said Polina, her dark hair stuck to her forehead with sweat. It came out more like a plea than a question.

A student coughed. Twice. 'I'm going to be a corporate law-yer so I don't need to know negligence.' Good luck with that, Polina thought.

Grace would say their story began much earlier, before they were in it. If you want loss and damage, start at the beginning. Meet my parents meeting.

Polina glanced at the clock behind the students' heads. Half an hour left. I am here or there or elsewhere. She picked up the water bottle from the desk and drank. It wasn't water.

— ◊ —

EVIDENCE OF LOSS/DAMAGE

1.1: GRACE'S PARENTS MEET.

1.1.2: DOUG'S NEGLIGENCE (CARELESS DRIVING – CAUSING PI TO GIRL – WHO?) DISCUSS PSYCHIATRIC LOSS/DAMAGE RE DOUG?

There was no other sound, no scream, nothing to tell him he had just hit a little girl. But Doug saw her in his mirror as he drove away, lying on the ground with her white skirt ballooning up around her, one stick arm raised in the air as though she had a question. Zig-zagging up the road, the dog he'd swerved to avoid was grinning as it pulled an invisible owner on the lead flying backwards from its collar.

He'd braked, too hard, exactly what he told his learners not to do, and the relief of having missed the dog made him laugh until the laugh turned into a cough. High five! He held his palm up in the air and controlled the wheel with his other hand while screeching into reverse. There was a light thud, that was all.

A high-pitched mosquito whine bothered him close to his ears and he looked around jerkily for the insect even after he worked out that the sound was coming from him. 'Please,' he heard himself say.

In his mirror, he saw someone – the mother? Saw her sink to her knees. He didn't think she'd seen him but, just in case, he got faster. Sweat pooled in his armpits. I've been working too hard, he told himself, licking his lips. It's flu. There was no need to stop, he'd only get in the way, he'd lose his job, which he loved, and he'd be late for the new client he was due to meet right now.

When he pulled up to the house, she was already there on the pavement, waiting. She got in and smiled. She was very pretty, nervous.

Doug was shaking badly, his teeth chattering.

11

'Good news, Amy,' he said. 'The dog's OK.'

'The dog?'

And he burst into tears.

1.2: GRACE BORN – APPROX. 8 YEARS AFTER 1.1. NOTE ED.

1.2.1: THIS IS ALSO WHERE GRACE'S MOTHER MEETS POLINA'S MOTHER. DOES DAMAGE START HERE? LIMITATION PERIOD?

The shop in the maternity wing looked exactly the same as it had eight years ago when Amy's first baby, Ed, was born, still selling lavender bags made by the terminally ill, or for the terminally ill, Doug forgot which, and romantic paperbacks and mugs with blurred cats' faces all over them. He remembered the aroma in there too, how it caught the back of your throat like essence of Portaloo. He grabbed something quickly because he was in a rush, but the lady manning the till took a fucking age to scrabble her hand around in the pastel blue Tupperware box for change. He wanted to do it for her, especially when she picked up but couldn't keep hold of a five pence piece, like an arcade grabber. 'Butterfingers!' she said.

After some identical corridors and a wrong turn, the staff no help at all even when he'd slipped and almost twisted his weak ankle, finally, he found Amy, propped up on pillows second from the end. He tapped his top pocket and the cigar was still there, like an old man's finger pointing to his heart.

'Doug?' she said.

'They moved you!'

'She was breech.' Amy's voice sounded hoarse and distant.

'She's beautiful,' he said, before he'd even seen her.

It was already different this time around. When they'd put Ed in his arms, it was so bewildering he'd tried to hand him back. Not mine, he'd almost said. His new daughter was yeasty and suspicious, the skin on her arms all wrinkled and, as he picked her up, weighing so little he almost threw her in the air, she squinted back as though he was dazzling her, her eyes dark blue, searching his face for something she recognised. He couldn't remember how it had felt before he loved her. 'Grace?' he said as his tears blurred the view.

Ed stood up from the armchair he'd folded himself into. 'Daddy, I held her and she didn't cry!'

'Hello, son,' Doug said, pretending he'd known Ed was there all along.

Grace felt for the air with her fists as soon as he put her down and it was all he could do not to scoop her right up again. Instead, Doug started to go through his pockets and, with Ed smiling next to him, made a show of the not-being-able-to-find, tapping every pocket, then Ed's pockets. He pulled out the cigar, stretching the game, popping it into Ed's mouth still in its cellophane wrapping, as Amy laughed, lovely and low. This was easy, he was good at this. He sneaked a little peak at Grace ... but, wait a ... he actually had lost the present. Ed batted the cigar away, going along with it but starting to want his present for real.

'Our turn next. A girl, like you.'

The man sitting on the bed next to Amy's was not, as had first appeared, wearing a baseball cap back to front; it was hair pulled into a ponytail. Doug groaned on the inside.

'Aren't kids wonderful? Everyone should have one.' The man smiled, revealing buck teeth. He put a hand to his heart. 'Howard. And this is Maggie.'

On the floor next to Maggie's bed was the plastic bag Doug had dropped. He snatched it up, gratefully.

'What do you think of your new sister?' Howard asked Ed.

He was an unprepossessing, flimsy-looking man (did they call that a ninja's build?) and, with that dirty coat and the hair pulled back, looked like something dredged from a river. Those teeth? A beaver.

'She's alright,' said Ed.

'She's a beauty. What's her name?'

'Grace,' Doug said, before Ed could.

'We're calling this one Apple Pie. Right, Margarita? Or Faulty Clock because her timing's off.'

'We steered clear of hippy names,' said Doug.

Maggie opened her eyes to look at Howard and something passed between them that Doug couldn't grasp. Howard whispered to her: 'Remember the lunacy of the crust on that pie?'

She seemed to find this amusing. Doug raised his eyebrows but Amy wasn't looking.

'Daddy?' said Ed, with an edge to his voice.

Howard shrugged his little shoulders at Doug. Grinning isn't the best idea when you have teeth like that but Doug resisted the urge to point to his own teeth, like you point to your face when someone has food on theirs. Instead, he turned his attention full-beam on Ed.

'Here you go, buddy! My family's complete.' Doug handed Ed the toy from the hospital shop as he recited the lines that had sounded much better in the car on the way here. Something about Howard being there compelled Doug to give it more gusto than he'd wanted to.

The toy was a cheap-looking, bug-eyed, royal blue furry monster, about the size of a pint glass. It wore a badge depicting what looked like another blue monster, itself wearing a badge.

'Thank you,' said Ed, unimpressed.

'Let's have a look,' said Amy. Grace was making sucking noises.

Ed held it towards her, blinking.

'It was all they had,' Doug said to Amy, sighing as he tried to hide his irritation and the slight wave of resentment he felt as once again, whichever way you looked at it, Ed was making this all about him.

Doug didn't look at Howard. He hoped Amy would hear in his sigh that he was being the bigger man here.

—◊—

1.3: POLINA AS YOUNG GIRL WITH MOTHER, MAGGIE.
1.3.1: NOTE MAGGIE'S RELATIONSHIP WITH OWN PARENTS – LINK TO LOSS?
1.3.2: DAMAGED BY MOTHERHOOD/GENETICS/BOTH/OTHER?

Watching her daughter examine furniture in the doll's house was making Maggie light-headed with memories. Did all mothers catch occasional glimpses of their childhood shadows, trailing behind them or climbing the walls as they walked? She wished she could take moments of nothing and everything, like now as Polina chattered, and preserve them in a jar to enjoy when she was in the mood. Think of the luxury of holding the jar up to the light whenever you felt like it, giving it a shake. If somehow you could separate the clear from the murky, the way you could filter impurities, wouldn't love be so much easier to do?

Maggie's own doll's house had been perfect. Built by her father, who never made anything before or after, it had a real drawer in the kitchen containing a miniature knife, fork and two spoons. Spoons were much easier to make than knives and forks, according to Auntie Joan, who'd taken three days making one fork from a paper clip.

'Quality takes time, Margarita,' she'd said. 'You must never, however tempted' (she looked at Maggie's father, picked up a spoon and swung it disdainfully like a turd pomander) 'rush.'

Later, Maggie's father confided: 'Spoons are more complicated than they look.'

'Sometimes I call her Auntie Moan,' said Maggie, to make him laugh, though it wasn't true. And he didn't laugh.

When Maggie searched for happy memories from childhood, there was always the doll's house, illuminated by a shaft of sunlight, its wallpaper the same – there had been a little left over – as the wallpaper in their sitting room. She wished they'd not bothered with the wallpaper in the doll's house. On their real walls, artichoke heads as big as Maggie's face grew and swirled magically upwards, higher than she could trace on tiptoes, but when she peered inside the doll's house, the single artichoke head pasted on the slant looked like a jellyfish split open at the guts.

The trick with the doll's house was to make yourself small so you could fit inside it when you needed to (as long as you didn't look at the walls). You could eat soup with one of the spoons or hide under the miniature bed when your mother went on too long or your father raised his fist in the air like it had been jerked upwards on a puppeteer's string.

Polina had stopped playing, and it pulled Maggie back to the present. A painting she'd never liked of a dilapidated barn caught her attention, its interior dark behind the gap of a rotting door. Whose idea had that been?

'Mummy?'

Then, and it was a startling revelation, she realised the painting depicted perfectly the gloom of her own childhood. She wondered how she'd never noticed that before and felt so exposed that, if there had been other adults in the room, she'd have made an excuse to cover the picture or take it off the wall. Inside the barn's murky threat, she imagined a child like her, feeling about, searching for a means of escape. As an adult, the door of the barn was the place she peered out from, on the threshold, looking at the pink sky and swaying and not daring to believe it might be possible to take a step, while behind her the darkness got darker.

She used to think the black hole at the bottom of her fear was as bad as it got until she became a mother. That's when she discovered the hole was actually a portal to somewhere worse.

'Mummy?'

She opened her eyes. 'I'm not crying, Poli.' I cannot have her look at the picture and see what I see, Maggie thought. As lightly as she could, she asked: 'Do you like that picture?'

The fear was cut with other feelings, like the need to keep Polina safe, which was really just another kind of fear, to side-swipe her out of the path of the train that came for them and would not stop coming.

'Can I sit on your lap?' said Polina.

Maggie dropped gently to her knees and patted them. The freshly washed smell of Polina's hair was more than Maggie deserved. What if I'm driving the train?

One night after dinner, Maggie's father smashed up the doll's house. 'Poor Milan, not coping today?' Maggie's mother had said, as she smiled and reached across to ruffle his hair. Maggie had never seen her do that before. 'Other men manage. Look at Uncle Gleb. Wild horses wouldn't drag him away from that sorting office, withered arm or not.'

She should have stopped there. Maggie watched her father touch his nose. 'Perhaps I complain,' he conceded.

'All this Serbian pride: I am provider!' She banged her chest, gorilla-like. It didn't look or sound like Maggie's father at all. 'And yet here we are eating watery soup. Again!'

Maggie remembered her father had tried to put their three empty bowls together, to hand them to her mother.

'Don't trouble yourself,' her mother said. 'You must be so tired.'

'Are you stupid?' He was up, the word 'stupid' coming out higher than the rest. It made Maggie feel like giggling. One of the bowls cracked clean in two when it hit the ground.

To Maggie, her mother looked like a doll. If you wanted to push her over, you could do it, easy, one shove. But he didn't push her all the way over; the important part seemed to be that he had the power but hadn't used it. 'They broken my English in pieces!'

He stabbed her with stiff fingers in time with the words (broken, English, pieces) in her shoulder blades, or rather in the no man's land between shoulder blade and armpit. Maggie's fingers went to the same pouches on her own body.

'You mean they break my English in pieces,' Maggie said.

His neck turned towards her. 'What?'

She hadn't meant to say anything. 'Or, they have broken?'

'Go to bed, Maggie,' her mother warned, her eyes not leaving his face. 'Everything's fine.'

'It's not!'

Answering back was not allowed. Maggie of all people knew that. She had once presented her mother with a list when her father was out, just common sense, the answer to the question her mother had not been clever enough to work out for herself. Read it, Maggie had said, like a slap. She remembered the list, word for word, and the look on her mother's face.

Wrong Things to Say (Don't Do Them)
1. Auntie Joan, Uncle Andrei, Maria, Uncle Gleb.
2. Are you going to make her sit there all night?
3. Anything to do with fiddling with ring.
4. Don't answer back.
5. When is soon?
6. Wednesday evening is not a good time and crying because it is manipulative.

Her father looked at Maggie and raised his eyebrows questioningly. At first she hadn't understood. His eyes still on her, he pointed at the doll's house with his index and middle fingers flexed in what she took to be an attempt at a gun, although it looked like his fingers had got stuck together with glue. He made a little 'puff' sound as he rested the tips of his fingers briefly on the top of Maggie's mother's head. Would his fingers stick to her hair? He waited for her to choose. The drawer was the only thing that remained intact after he smashed up the doll's house. She kept it for a while.

Howard was completely different from Milan and that's why Maggie married him. Rocks and avalanches versus jelly and ice cream. Who doesn't love jelly and ice cream? She hadn't known men like him existed. He brought her presents like a lovestruck schoolboy, flowers from a graveyard, a pebble, a wonky heart he'd carved from wood. He was problem-free, he said; problems to him were water off a duck's back, and he didn't care about material things or his looks (although he did care about his looks. His mum never made him wear a brace). Once, they spent the whole day in a field and she told him things about herself, to test the water; not the big things (not the doll's house) and he didn't run away. In fact, he didn't react at all which at the time she took to be a good sign. He listened, hardly blinking, and when she finally stopped talking, he said: 'Look! I brought a picnic.' (Two apples.) They'd tried to make snow angels in the corn; she tamped him down with one bare foot on his chest like he'd asked her to, but he wasn't heavy enough. It's like lying on a bed of nails, he said, and she'd had to stop him lighting a cigarette there and then in a cornfield. You worry too much, he said. When he fell asleep – they'd done it in a rush, she couldn't get comfortable – she noticed a tiny field mouse watching her, wringing its tiny paws. 'You worry too much,' she told it.

Everyone loves jelly and ice cream. And that was the problem. When she'd finally had enough of the others, the telephone calls to the house at all hours, the trips away (he worked with wood, he didn't need trips away) the lies on top of lies, she told him, or tried to, and he left her for someone else, just like that, as though she was the one being unreasonable. The final insult, he'd said, was when she couldn't find tears to match his, but the truth was she was through and out the other side of tears. Tears were for people who'd only just realised that everything was lost.

'Look!' said Polina, fascinated, holding out a plastic doll she'd just pulled from a room inside the doll's house, forgotten from a previous game, its facial features blank and sticky like a burns victim.

Maggie tried very hard to pretend she didn't wish she were

anywhere else, but it was like fantasising about a cigarette, the pull of it, even after all these years, and pulling in the other direction was the pain in her stomach she knew she would have if she were somewhere else, missing her daughter with the intensity of a spasm. How could it still be so early in the day?

'Breakfast?' she said, brightly.

—◊—

1.4: POLINA/GRACE, GARDEN – FEW YEARS AFTER 1.3. LADEN WITH LOSS (BLAME GARDEN OF EDEN. AREN'T GARDENS ALWAYS PLACES WHERE THINGS ARE ABOUT TO BE LOST THANKS TO THAT ONE?)
1.4.1: ALTERNATIVELY, POLINA V GRACE/GRACE V POLINA?

'It needs more mud or it won't work,' said Grace. She dropped the wooden spoon and flapped her stirring arm, making her silver bangles clack. Tat, Polina's mother had warned her, when she'd pleaded for silver bangles of her own. Do you want people to think we're gypsies?

The girls' bottoms were raised as they knelt side by side, stirring sludge in the paint-stained bucket.

'You said we were going to share,' said Polina. Her fraying blue cardigan was tight on her arms where she'd pushed up the sleeves.

'We are sharing,' said Grace, grabbing the spoon back.

Polina could tell from Grace's proud face what she was going to say before she said it.

'In-can-ta-tion,' said Grace. It was Polina's word, stolen. Grace opened her eyes. 'It's not funny, Pauline.'

Polina picked up her shoebox with its homemade holes and held it at eye-level. She carefully poked her little finger in a hole. 'Hello in there.' There was a whip of air from Grace's spoon as it just missed her nose.

'Also, Marmite,' said Grace. 'Go and ask my mum for some.'

'I don't like Marmite.'

'If you want Caroline to suffer we'll need Marmite.'

Polina reluctantly got to her feet.

'I've done loads more potions than you!' said Grace, without looking up. Her voice scythed the air as Polina walked through the long grass, the shoebox under her arm. 'Or do you just want to make perfume?'

At the open kitchen door, Polina stood for a moment, intoxicated by the smell of burning jam, then checked the soles of her shoes for clods of earth, shining the tip of one with spit. The door was heavy and thick, the width of two doors glued together, and she touched its blue and yellow stained glass petals for luck. A door is a door, Polina's mother said later. But this one is beautiful, Polina replied. Her mother held her face: for going in and going out.

Grace's mum faced away, talking to the jam in the too-big saucepan, the size of a witch's cauldron. Polina wanted to tiptoe on the shiny floor tiles; her whole foot fitted inside the lines of each square. She wanted to close her eyes and slide in her socks from the door to the sink, a gap wider than her whole house. The surfaces glared at her as she stepped in. There were two microwaves.

'Mrs Mullin?'

Amy turned from the sink. 'Poli! Hello! It's Amy, how many times?'

Polina saw that Amy had been crying and instantly forgot what she'd come in for. 'Do you want to see our toad?'

'Sit down, let's have a look.'

Polina sat and picked at the sticky tape securing the lid of her box while Amy ladled hot jam into the flip-top bin. Some of it got ladled onto the floor.

Amy swatted the air. 'Something for Janet to do,' she said.

Janet wasn't a real cleaner, according to Grace; she was on a gap year.

'He's going in the potion then we're going to let him go,' Polina said, but inside the box, the dead toad had gone grey

21

and was crispy at the edges. She curled her toes tightly inside her shoes and then remembered what she was supposed to say. 'Have you got any Marmite, please?' Her chin quivered.

The bin smoked.

In the garden, Grace seethed; her arm was aching, she was too hot and her hair had come out of its band. She rested the spoon against the side of the bucket and slumped back onto her heels, casting a brief sideways look towards the kitchen. Picking up her notebook, she clicked her new biro from purple to green and scribbled over the name Caroline.

'POLINA' she wrote and then below that, neatly, 'Suffer.'

1.5: POLINA/MAGGIE FRAGMENT. LOSS – CHILDHOOD. (LOSS OF CHILDHOOD?) DISCUSS.

She was too tired to do alternate legs anymore, so she went right foot down the stair, left foot joins it, right foot down the stair, left foot joins it. The light coming from the fridge was exciting, like Christmas. Polina curled into the room and her mum was at the kitchen table, spooning up gloop from a cereal bowl and pressing a hand to her forehead.

'What are you doing?' Polina whispered, gruff with sleep.

Maggie looked up, quickly.

'Poli. Back up to bed.'

She loved Maggie best when she was like this, not quite cross and not on duty. It made Polina bold.

'Is it yogurt?' she said.

'Yes, it's yogurt. Now up.'

'Did you get hungry?'

'Come on. We'll both go.'

Maggie stood and pulled her dressing gown tightly around her. The question and answer game was fading and there was nothing you could do to bring it back, but Polina tried.

'Why were you sitting in the dark?'

It wasn't going to work. Maggie steered Polina out of the kitchen, walking behind her with both hands on her shoulders. Polina wished she could go back to just before she spoilt things, but you never could.

1.6: ED. LOSS OF IDENTITY.

1.6.1: NOTE – HE IS TEENAGER AND THEREFORE CANNOT BE INAU-THENTIC. CAUSED/CAUSES DAMAGE. LOST. LOSSED?

Ed spent most of the morning upstairs in his room trying to emulate the slap bass technique of Mark King from Level 42, which meant pressing a snooker cue to his chest like a bass guitar and whacking his thumb against it, but Grace kept messing things up by coming in without knocking to borrow things she didn't need.

'I don't like this song,' she said.

'You don't say song, you say track.'

'Mum says you've to go and help downstairs. Can I borrow your calculator?'

Ed carried a basket of bread rolls into the garden and put it on the picnic bench. They were having what they always had for lunch, what his mother called her assembly job, which just meant ready-made food bought from shops with the cling film removed. Doug had been digging some kind of trench in the garden all morning, which was why there was mud in the kitchen where he'd traipsed in and out. Ed didn't see why they had to have a celebratory lunch, or why they all had to orbit around Doug's mood just because he dug a hole, like digging a hole was so fucking hard and important.

They sat on the picnic bench, Ed between his gran and his mother, Doug on the other side next to Grace. Ed could just about see Grace's nose above the bench.

23

'She needs a cushion, Doug,' said Amy.

'She can get her own cushion, can't you, love?'

'She can't reach the food.'

Ed tensed. Amy was speaking slowly, which was a bad sign. Doug got up.

'Garden looks lovely,' said Gran, gesturing at it. It looked like a building site. The shed was completely obscured by a huge mound of earth and the washing line was lying at a funny angle on the ground as if recently uprooted by a tornado.

'I hope that wasn't too much trouble,' said Amy, as Doug came out of the house with a cushion.

'Voila,' said Doug, plonking Grace on the cushion. She giggled. Doug looked at Amy. She met his stare.

'Did you make all this?' said Gran, shaking her head as though overwhelmed by the food.

'What have I done?' said Amy to Doug.

Ed stopped eating. This was new territory. Amy put down her glass stiffly. 'Really, Doug, are we speaking in code?'

'He was always good with codes at school, weren't you, Doug?' said Gran.

'Did you enjoy your *lunch* with Marian last Thursday?' said Doug, doing little inverted commas in the air with his knife and fork.

Ed watched the puppet show with its awkward food-encrusted metal characters.

'Was it *fun*? Did you *reminisce*?' Doug seemed to be working up to something. 'Or did you, I don't know, skip dessert and just fuck like rabbits?'

For this part there were no inverted commas.

Amy went white. Ed had never seen that happen and he didn't know what it meant. Her answer sounded strange, quiet. 'I'm sleeping with Marian now, am I?'

'Are you?' said Ed. He couldn't help it.

'Fuck like rabbits!' said Grace.

Ed gulped to stop himself laughing. Gran looked at the sky.

Doug was sweating a lot, ramming crisps into his mouth like ammunition. Little bits shot out as he talked. 'Not Marian, necessarily.' He got faster. 'But for all I know, *Marian* could be code for any Tom, Dick or Harry. You could be, I don't know, screwing the butcher.'

'I think we need a machine to decipher all the crap you spout,' said Ed, looking at his plate. He had an idea that he should try and divert attention away from his mother, to buy her time, though he wasn't sure why.

'What did you say?' said Doug.

'Where's my real dad? Now there's a mystery.'

Ed tried a world-weary laugh that came out miserly, and when he reached for his glass, his hand shook. Now he'd started, he couldn't stop the thoughts; his real dad, his other life, just out of reach.

'If you enjoy a mystery, you'll love my library book,' said Gran, nudging him. 'It's about a Welsh woman trapped down a mine.'

'Right.'

'I'll get it. It's large print.'

She eased her way out from the bench inch by inch, so slowly it seemed perhaps she wasn't moving at all, or else was negotiating a very tricky three-point turn in an unfamiliar vehicle with a stiff turning circle. No one helped. Ed registered her groans and sharp breaths. He felt bad for not helping. Almost bad enough to help. Eventually, she disappeared into the house, which seemed to break the spell.

'Did you hear what he said to me?' said Doug, pointing at Ed, eyebrows raised. He looked at Amy as a footballer looks to a referee.

'I don't go to that butcher's anymore,' said Amy. 'I'm not sure it's even a butcher's now. I think it's flats.'

'Alright, butcher, baker, candlestick maker, who gives a shit? Maybe you're not that fussy.'

'Meaning?'

'I don't like this,' said Grace, pointing at the coleslaw, the only thing on the table that Amy had made.

'I need a drink,' said Doug.

He stood up sharply, as if he'd been bitten, but couldn't move any further because the bench had trapped his legs.

'Of course you do, darling,' said Amy.

You were doomed when you heard that voice.

'Is my real dad an alcoholic?' said Ed.

Doug thumped his fist on the bench. The glasses jumped. 'Fuck this! I've had it up to here with you.'

'I need to go to the toilet,' said Grace.

Amy started to clear the plates. 'Ed,' she said. 'Don't make it worse.'

'I haven't finished,' said Doug, grabbing a bread roll from the basket and lobbing it at Amy. It hit her shoulder and plopped to the ground. She looked at it.

'You weren't with Marian. I called her,' said Doug.

'Do we have to do this here?'

'You ruin everything,' said Ed to Doug, spontaneously gripped with wonderment at the sheer scale of Doug's ability to ruin everything.

'I'm sick of you carping on about your fucking father when you don't know the half of it.'

Doug tried to stand again, and failed again. His face was blotchy. The bench seemed to be restraining him for his own safety.

'No one tells me anything!' said Ed, swallowing hard.

His eyes met Doug's and for a moment neither could pull their gaze away. Ed felt his heart drop; he wanted to punch Doug but the moment to do it passed and he concentrated instead on not crying. Grace looked at Doug like he'd just slapped her as she climbed out from the bench, all knees. The cushion fell on the ground.

'I don't like you.' She pointed dramatically at Doug, her jazz hands flapping as she helter-skeltered towards the house in tears. Amy pushed a strand of hair behind her ear.

'Muuuummmy! Gran's stuck in the toilet!'

'Oh Christ,' said Amy, standing. 'She's done it again.'

'I'll go,' said Ed. But he didn't.

'I can't get her out!'

'You'll have to break the door down,' said Doug to Amy.

'She's your mother,' said Amy.

'Tell that to my blood pressure!'

'MUMMY!'

'Alright.' Amy moved quickly.

Ed caught sight of the bread roll and wondered whether it might sit there for ever.

1.7: CARELESS TALK/WHISPER. (SOON AFTER 1.6)

'I'll get the playing cards.' Grace's gran got up from the table and steadied herself.

Polina looked at the beetroot on her plate, the way it made the potatoes go pink as though the birds painted on the plate were bleeding. Grace quickly forked the last chunk of beetroot from her plate onto Polina's. They stared at each other.

'Rummy?' said Gran, from the other room.

'Yes, please!' said Grace. They hated rummy.

Gran glared at her cards.

'Ed doesn't like red food,' said Grace.

'Dead food?' said Gran without looking up.

'Red food. Like beetroot. Daddy loves beetroot.' She glanced at Polina. 'So do I.'

'Are we playing this round with a wildcard?' said Polina.

'There's a reason for that, Grace. What with Ed not being your father's and your mother still not saying who the … Who'd like a bonbon?'

Their heads snapped towards Gran, who was overheating as she rattled the sweet tin too vigorously.

Later, in bed, Polina wanted to replay what Grace's gran had said, but she couldn't get it to make sense.

'Are you scared of Gran?' Grace whispered.

'No.'

'Even though her teeth talk by themselves?'

'They do not.'

'They do,' said Grace.

They were sharing a bed that was bigger than a single but wasn't quite a double.

'Lavender makes me feel a bit sick,' said Polina, trying not to breathe in the smell of the room.

Grace farted in reply. Polina farted back. They went to high five in the dark and missed each other's hands, but Polina could tell that Grace was smiling. 'Do you sometimes think she's going to creep in and suffocate us with pillows?' Polina whispered, riding the good feeling of togetherness.

'That's stupid,' said Grace. She sounded put out. 'It's unkind.' She wasn't whispering any more.

The fun drained away. Polina burned. 'What I meant ... '

WHUMP!

'You first then the other!' Grace squawked, pretending to be her gran, smothering Polina with the full force of the pillow.

Polina fought back. 'I hate you!'

Grace lay back helpless with laughter. The bed vibrated.

1.8: POLINA FRAGMENT(ED).

When Polina couldn't sleep she stood outside her parents' bedroom. Sometimes when her dad wasn't there, she'd go in and her mum would cuddle her in bed. When he was there, she usually hovered outside the room until she got cold. Polina could see a little bit through the keyhole but couldn't hear what they were saying. Once, she saw her mum sitting in front of the mirror, brushing her hair, her head to one side and it looked as though she was smiling.

She turned to face Polina's dad and lifted her arms as if to say 'I don't know'. She wasn't smiling anymore.

1.9: GRACE MISSING; POLINA MISSING GRACE.

Her birthday present for Grace was a book, *The Secret Garden*. It was given to Polina as a present last year but she already had her own copy, dog-eared with two pages missing, so her mum took the new one and put it in the wardrobe before Polina could even smell its newness. She'd been allowed to walk to Grace's house on her own for the first time, her heart still thumping as she watched a swaying cobweb in the top corner of the porch. She rang the bell again but there was no sound from inside the house. She really needed the toilet. Last year, for Grace's birthday, Amy bought (bought!) sandwiches with no crusts and put them on a silver tray with crisps around the edge. They always played good games like Squeak Piggy Squeak and Electric Cushions.

Grace's dad opened the door and took a long time to notice she was there, or perhaps he couldn't see properly because his eyes were red. Polina waited for him to speak. Last year, he did magic tricks with a real rabbit. She felt silly in her party dress.

'Polina. Didn't Amy call?' he said, looking over her head.

'No,' said Polina, blushing. 'Sorry.'

'Why on earth are you sorry?' He scratched his chin. 'Grace has appendicitis.'

He squatted down to her level, a sudden movement that made Polina take a step back. She handed him the book.

'Will she be at school tomorrow?'

'Well, let's see, can you turn water into wine?'

He didn't move and she could smell his breath, like the

heat that wobbles from the side of a bus. If this was a joke she should laugh, so she tried but not too much in case he was being serious. She turned and walked away, forcing herself not to run. When she looked back, he was still there, talking to the ground. She waved. He wasn't looking.

1.10: GRACE POST-OP. STRAIGHT AFTER 1.9.
1.10.1: NO EVIDENCE OF ANY CLINICAL NEGLIGENCE THOUGH GRACE WILL TRY AND CONVINCE OTHERS THE OPERATION WAS 'BOTCHED'.

'I was awake for some of it,' said Grace, rolling up her jumper to show off her scar.

She was lying on her bed. Polina knelt on the floor.

'It looks like a mouth,' said Polina.

'What are you doing at school?'

'Romans. You don't actually need your appendix, Caroline's mum says. Can I see the poem now?'

Grace rolled her jumper down and let her head fall back. She looked at the ceiling, did a few big blinks, checked to make sure Polina had seen, then did a few more.

'I'm starving. It's because I'm post-op.'

'You haven't done it, have you?'

Grace carefully leaned over the side of her bed and pulled out a small packet of Wotsits. She tipped them all into her mouth.

'Can I have one?' said Polina.

'None left.' Grace's lips had gone orange. She reached down again and came back up with a crumpled piece of paper that she tossed at Polina. It had orange fingerprints on it. 'I actually prefer free verse now, so you might not understand some of it.'

Polina looked at their poem. It was supposed to be a joint effort, like the heads, bodies and legs game but with words. She sighed. 'Why do you have to spoil everything?'

If They Gave Us a Wish (At School)
by Poli West and Grace Mullin (who wrote all the good bits)

If they gave us a wish
I'd say, 'Only English'
(I'd say Caroline stop going on about your mum all the time = you are really annoying. PS Your mum has found Jesus? Where? You will not say. I shall investigate when completely better from my operation.)
Maths is so tricky (maths is fassinating)
And it might sound quite picky
(This poem is boring. Listen. I'm snoring = a ryme!)
But I don't like the way that Miss Marshall says "Bicky"
(She means Becky. People from South Africa do not have the letter E and some of them are poor which is completely terribal. No offense Poli or your – single – mum.)
Also I'd wish for a Wagon Wheel tree,
With Wagon Wheels, Penguins and Fruit Clubs – all free!
(Gross. You will be really fat like Nicola and catch Type 2 Direbeetis and then die. Orange Clubs are much nicer.)
THE END
(Or mint ones.)
(THE ACTUAL END)

Grace's mum called them from downstairs.

'Girls? That rabbit won't clean itself!'

They looked at each other. Polina tried very hard to stay cross.

'Think about Flopsy in a shower cap,' said Grace.

'Your spelling is really bad,' said Polina, but the image of Flopsy was already too strong.

'Doing this.' Grace scrubbed under her arms.

They collapsed with laughter until it was hard to breathe.

'Ow,' said Grace.

'Your stitches,' said Polina, alarmed.

They both stopped laughing like a switch had been flicked and silently stared at Grace's jumper as if awaiting a sign from the scar. They caught each other's look at the same time.

'Your eyes are really big,' Polina whispered.

'I know.'

'You know everything.'

'Yes.'

Which was so unexpected it set Polina off again. Then Grace.

—◊—

1.11: POLINA AND GRACE WATCH THE VIDEO. (SOON AFTER 1.10)

It must be a trick that adults play on children because Polina could not believe there was another reason they were being made to watch this at school. The lady was lying naked on her back on a wallpaper table, the same kind as the one they had in their lounge before they got a real table, and there were people standing round, not exactly looking at anyone else. You couldn't see their faces and the colour on the video was the colour of bad dreams, of purple and beige and things about to go wrong.

Grace said: 'I already know all this. It's gross.'

Next to Polina, Caroline sat cross-legged on the rug, jiggling her knees up and down. On the video a voice said, 'It's coming!', while the lady moaned so much she didn't even sound like a human. The other children were looking at one another or fixing their eyes on the screen, so Polina tried to block out their panic as she waited to be told what to do.

The teachers were cutting it fine. A doctor was peering up inside the lady's bottom, but the baby was much too big to come out. Polina couldn't wait any longer and began looking around for the teacher. It was Mrs Webster. What was the point if it was Mrs Webster? She was probably in on it. Polina could still see her name in Mrs Webster's book under A for 'Answering Back', which she had not done, and it made her ribcage burn.

'Flopsy died,' whispered Grace. 'We're getting another one. I'm calling it Flopsy.'

Polina looked at her, horrified on top of the horror she already felt.

'Her heart went really fast and the vet said she was probably engorged.'

A man on the video said 'vagina' and everyone giggled, so Polina giggled, even though she didn't really want to because vagina was the ugliest word in the human language apart from war.

'Push for me!' the doctor said, impatiently.

'Rrrrrrr!'

'Sounds like Daddy doing a poo,' said Grace, and nudged Polina.

'Gahhh!'

Then the baby slopped out along with blood and some gunk and a bag of spares. Polina felt something inside her close down. She thought about the lady who just nearly died but no one cared and about Flopsy's heart going really fast and she started to cry in secret because she'd just worked out that the adults were lying and children had to pretend they don't know. She barely noticed Caroline's hand going up, fast.

'Mrs Webster, Polina's wet herself.'

1.12: SOON AFTER 1.11 – POLINA RUNS INTO HER FATHER.
(NOTE TO SELF – IF NEXT SECTION FOLLOWS ON CHRONOLOGICALLY, NO NEED TO LABEL.)

Whatever went wrong now was Polina's own fault for going out of bounds. She noticed this newsagents looked even dingier than the first as she bent down with her hands on her knees to get her breath back. One of her laces was undone. Inside the window a tatty postcard taped to the glass said: STRICTLY NO MORE 3 MAX SCHOOL CHILDRN IN SHOP AT ANY TIME.

Grace had promised that dreams can't hurt you in the day, and that made Polina brave enough to glance over her shoulder as she pushed open the door. A bell tinkled. She scanned up and down the road but there was no sign of a white car, nor the lady with black and blonde hair in the passenger seat, the window rolled down: Your mummy asked us to come and collect you. I would never ask a stranger to come and collect you, Maggie said, as if that should be the end of that, but it wasn't because sometimes in the dream the woman in the car had Maggie's face.

She had trouble finding the magazines. Multi-packs of pickled onion Space Raiders, her second favourite crisps after Frazzles, were piled next to peach-coloured toilet rolls. The shopkeeper with polished black hair was chatting to a customer and shaking his head at a little girl who was holding the customer's hand.

'Always she will want more, Howie. That is the prerogative of the female.'

Cars, cars, cars. Polina scanned the magazines on the top shelf, where her eyes were drawn to a front cover of a woman wearing a red beret. She looked like she was about to lose her temper. One of her fingers touched her bright red lips and she'd pushed her breasts – with no bra – up towards the reader, the places where the nipples should be replaced with blurry squares. Polina almost tripped as she stepped backwards.

'What are you doing, please?' The shopkeeper's voice felt like a pinch.

'Nothing, please,' said Polina, as confused as he was by her choice of words.

'It looks like you are planning to rob me.'

'I'm looking for *Crafting for Beginners* featuring a pullout section on quilting.'

The two men looked at each other. The shopkeeper chuckled, a surprisingly high-pitched sound. 'I will go out the back to check if we have this *Crafty for Beginners*,' he said.

The other man turned towards Polina, still smiling. 'Poli?'

She looked at him and at the little girl, who was dressed entirely in pink, a pink finger wedged up her nose.

'Hey, Poli-Doodle! Come and give your old man a hug.'

He was nearly bald.

'I can't!'

Polina struggled with the heavy door of the shop and then ran with her hands over her ears to stop the rushing noise. When she got to the paving slabs she was running so fast she couldn't stay inside the lines, which was a year of bad luck, Grace said, or maybe less if she had a word with God for you.

'Where have you been? What's the matter?' said Maggie, as Polina ran up the stairs, salty snot tears dripping into her mouth.

'They didn't have it!'

Dinnertime. Grace came. Maggie put jacket potatoes in the middle of the table and they all looked like Polina's father's bald head.

'Thanks a lot,' said Grace, picking up a potato and dropping it quickly onto her plate. 'Hot!'

'You've helped yourself,' Maggie said. Her mouth was tight. 'Polina?'

'Your house is really great,' said Grace, her mouth ajar as she tried to chew a chunk of hot potato. 'It's like a museum.'

'I was just thinking about that chat we all had once about manners,' said Maggie, brightly.

Polina forked a potato onto her plate.

'Like the Natural History Museum,' said Grace.

'My mother always told me, daft as it sounds, that to be polite, if you wanted, say, a biscuit, you had to decline it when it was offered. But if you didn't like it or didn't want it,' Maggie laughed rigidly as though pretending to have taken herself by surprise, 'then you had to say, "Yes, please, what a delicious biscuit". Grace, will you stop wolfing down that potato.'

Grace closed her mouth and appealed with her eyes to Polina, who ignored her.

Maggie took a breath. 'So, you like museums?'

'Not really,' said Grace.

'Aren't you hungry, Poli?'

'At home we normally have something with a potato, like ham or something,' said Grace.

'I'm sort of medium hungry,' said Polina.

'Butter,' said Maggie, lifting the lid on the butter dish.

'You look like you've seen a ghost,' said Grace, leaning towards Polina. 'My brother sees ghosts.'

'Don't be silly,' said Maggie.

'Are you thinking about your dad?'

Polina shot a glance at her mother. 'No.'

'And your sister?'

'That's enough,' said Maggie, putting her knife and fork on the plate and wiping the corner of her mouth with a napkin. Polina eyed it distrustfully. They never had napkins. She longed for Grace's house where there were no napkins and it was noisy all the time and no one listened to anything you said.

'It may have been someone who looked like him,' said Maggie. Again. She was blinking a lot. 'Or someone having a joke.'

They let that sink in.

'So where do you think he lives?' said Grace, as she twirled her fork in a circle close to her ear. 'He could live literally five minutes away.'

'Let's run you home,' said Maggie, grabbing car keys.

'Does your sister look like you?' said Grace.

1.13: MAGGIE IS AT THE DOCTORS BUT IS NOT DEPRESSED.

Maggie put back an old ripped copy of *Country Life* and picked up *Let's Talk*, its pages thin and shiny like school toilet paper. She wanted to look inside but, wary of what people might think, she pulled a disdainful face as she flicked through, that she hoped conveyed a kind of despairing benevolence.

Last time, the doctor had written her a repeat prescription but that wasn't going to be possible again, according to the receptionist, who was sorry about that, with her hotline to the inside of the doctor's head.

'Can you please check with him?' Maggie had asked.

'I've checked.'

'It's very important.'

She heard the receptionist's hand go over the receiver like a gag, heard her call to someone who wasn't the doctor.

'… will need to see you, Mrs West. Wednesday at 9.30?'

No.

The gag again. And muffled laughter.

'… not for another two weeks.'

'That's too long.'

Doctors' waiting rooms have a smell. Children's flatulence and fresh paint. Maggie sighed as she looked around at the others, the genuines and the malingerers (mostly malingerers) thinking, my life is cling film stretched over that smell. *Let's Talk* was starting to make her skin prickle, like sunburn on the inside. "Does your daughter have an eating disorder? The tell-tale signs no mother should miss!" Signs like Wagon Wheel wrappers under cushions, perhaps? Was eight too young for an eating disorder? Maggie had waited until Polina left the lounge before going in, feeling like a burglar in her own home as she lifted each cushion and felt with one hand down the back of the sofa, agitating the cool dust there. Maybe she'd put Howard's letter to Polina somewhere safe, but it wasn't with the others.

The Wagon Wheel wrapper was a consolation prize. With perfect timing, Polina had bounced in just as Maggie was examining the wrapper.

'When does a liquid become a gas?'

'What's this?' Maggie held it up. 'We don't hide things.' She felt her face redden with the hypocrisy.

Later that evening, Maggie found the letter, minus its envelope, on the bookshelf, tucked inside *Fantastic Mr Fox*.

In the waiting room, Maggie clicked open her handbag and dug around amongst mints, a chewed pen lid and a lipstick, *All Shine* (never worn). A couple of old to do lists, now thin as tissue paper, fluttered to the floor. She bent to pick them up.

To Do
1. *Colic NOT soothed by attending baby's needs.*
2. *The books are wrong.*
3. *STOP THE CRYING.*
4. *Disappears by 4 months. Howard: Me too!*
5. *Laugh when he laughs?*

'Mrs Western?'

She stood and smoothed her skirt down. 'It's West.'

The receptionist, unrepentant in her ill-fitting bra, called across to her: 'Take a seat, Mrs Western. All our doctors are very busy this morning.'

A child with mucus for eyes kicked his seat while his mother leaned over a crying baby in a pram, her vest top riding up over her belly. Maggie caught sight of part of a tattoo on her white blue stretched skin. DAR … Darren? Darling? Dartford Tunnel? She tried smiling at the child. Today's list said: 1. Ask Bob for more hours; 2. Buy glue; 3. Stick plate together with P. A game? Maggie added: Check P for tell-tale signs.

At the reception desk, she tried to reason with them.

'Everyone's in the same boat, I'm afraid.'

'Yes, but I'm supposed to be at work.'

'Do you want to make another appointment?'

Maggie pictured her pills, all punched out.

'Three o'clock next Tuesday?' said the receptionist.

'Alright.'

She waited for her legs to stop shaking and started the car.

—◇—

'You raaaaang?' Ed said in his ancient butler's voice that sounded like a creaking door.

They were in B&Q, an echoey shop that sold things you already had in your house. Its ceiling was so high you couldn't even see it.

Grace pressed the bell again and this time Ed sighed as though he was cross. 'You rang agaaaaain?'

She was laughing so much it was like being tickled; she wanted it to stop, never wanted it to stop. She tried a different one, a buzzer.

'What d'ya want?' said Ed, sharply.

'Ed, for Christ's sake act your age,' said Doug, striding up the aisle towards them.

'He's doing a show!' said Grace.

Ed did his long gorilla arms and barreled towards her: 'Ooh! Ooh! Ooh! Ooh!'

'Get in the car,' said Doug, gripping Ed's jacket at the neck.

Amy appeared, carrying taps.

'We were only playing,' said Grace, panic rising.

'Let go of him.' Amy's face was stone.

'This is B&Q!' said Doug, shoving Ed forwards so that he almost fell.

Ed pulled hard at the hem of his jacket and looked at the ground as he touched his mouth as though there might be blood. The wrongness hit Grace like a smack. She felt it as a compulsion to run so she ran at Doug, aiming her whole body at him, winding him. He took a step back, laughed and wrapped his arms round her.

'Feel like a man now?' Amy said.

'That the best you can do?' Doug said to Grace, smiling at her proudly as though there was no one else there.

It was not the effect Grace was after, and she pulled herself free from Doug's grip and looked for Ed, who'd disappeared.

'Hello?' said Amy.

Doug raised his middle finger and pushed up imaginary glasses with it.

A B&Q assistant hurried by, carrying tester pots, and it felt like he was in their house by mistake.

'Come here, you,' said Doug, grabbing Grace. She fought him, but half-heartedly because it was hard not to enjoy it.

Amy watched Doug and Grace as though she couldn't quite place them. 'I'll wait in the car,' she said.

1.15: GRACE. DAMAGE. LOSS.

Grace watched Amy and Doug pretend they were not arguing. The adults stamped their feet and blew into their gloves.

'Come on!' Grace said to Polina, beckoning her towards the trees.

They slipped away to where the air was more dangerous and Polina inhaled deeply, cinnamon and bonfire. Grace was already climbing the biggest tree in the garden, the one they had climbed a thousand times. She was wearing a new hat and new gloves. They matched.

'I don't want to. It's too dark,' said Polina. Grace wasn't sure if Polina sounded sad because she was jealous of her hat and gloves or because she still thought there might be a tortoise stuck in the bonfire.

'Scaredy cat!'

Amy and Doug were really going for it now, their voices razor blades. Grace climbed faster, pulling herself up one branch higher than she had ever been before.

'Be careful!' Polina called.

Doug said: '… her mother, for fuck's sake.'

40

'You don't give him a chance,' said Amy.

They thought she didn't know anything but Grace swallowed the meaning down in the dark.

'… like somebody is jealous?' said Doug.

Grace pictured his face, appealing to spectators.

Suddenly Doug called, 'Stand back!' and *whoooosh*, a firework shot upwards in a perfectly straight line.

Grace gasped and looked down at Polina who was hugging the tree as if holding her friend steady. The adults made that oooh sound and clapped. It was cold up here.

'Polina? Polina?' Maggie called into the night, like an owl.

What if your mum doesn't love you? *Bang!* The firework exploded, shockingly big in their little garden, its tentacles illuminating everything. What if your dad loves you too tight? The light cleared Grace's mind like menthol and she knew exactly what to do. Caught in the brightness, the adults looked guilty. Maggie had one hand on her hat, and Grace's parents, their faces glowing pumpkins, caught sight of her at the very moment she jumped.

'Look at me!'

The ground got very big too quickly and, before she had time to blink, her ribs smacked down, hard. She saw only black, but buried in the black were dots and flickers, neon dancing worms. She imagined the ground was one end of a seesaw and that as she hit it, the other end pinged all the grown-ups way up into the sky until they were just specks of white, cartwheeling away from the Earth. She smiled at them as they slowed and spun before picking up speed, their parachutes puffed open like popcorn, now so close she thought she could see the zigzag patterns on the soles of their shoes. There was a sharp smell of burning as someone ripped a plaster off the screams and her pain erupted. She heard noises and tried to shut them out.

'What a … '

'Don't move her head.'

'… stupid thing to do!'

'Is she breathing?'

'How could you let this happen, Doug?'

'Called … on its way … '

'Can you hear me?'

'How could I let it happen?'

Polina knew what Grace was going to do; the air curdled a second before she did it, but there was no space to think between Grace falling and Grace on the ground. The sound a bag full of bones makes when it's dropped onto rock-hard ground is something Polina will never forget. She should have climbed the tree as well. She should have shouted, *don't do it!* Grace hit the ground and all the breath got sucked from them both.

DUTY

They were late. It was all Doug kept saying as he threw things into the boot of the car as though discarding them: two picnic blankets, one red, one tartan and scratchy like a terrier's fur, a sports bag that smelt of feet, a blow-up mattress, a pump, a cardboard box full of clinking bottles, which he didn't throw, some wellies, Connect 4 in its battered box.

'I don't feel very well,' said Grace, again, watching Doug.

Her face was burning and the air was too thick to breathe. Connect 4 didn't have all its pieces. Once, she had made extra ones, drawing uneven red circles on paper and cutting them out. Ed said they looked like boils and stuck them to his face with spit.

'Grace, have you been to the toilet?' said Amy. 'Where's the map?'

'Wherever you left it,' said Doug.

Ed was scowling at them through the lounge window and Grace wanted to go inside with him to press her face against the cool glass.

'Where do you think you're going, madam?' Amy called.

'I don't feel very well.'

'She's fine,' Doug said to Amy. He was pushing down on the boot but it wouldn't close. 'Fucking boot of this stupid car is fucked.'

'Doug, keep your voice down, for goodness sake.'

'I'm not fine!' Grace shouted, and then she fell over on the path as if to prove it.

The wailing brought one of the neighbours out.

'She fell over,' Amy called out, as the neighbour waved in sympathy.

'Kids!' Doug yelled, grinning.

So now they were all in the lounge except Doug. Grace lay on the sofa with a flannel over her eyes and a plaster on her knee. She felt wobbly as though she might fall again.

'Look at him,' said Ed, pointing through the window at Doug who was still outside, swearing at a fishing rod protruding from the car.

Amy stroked Grace's hair.

'He needs a holiday,' Amy said.

'Can't he go by himself?' said Ed.

'I need a holiday!' said Amy.

'I'll look after her,' said Ed, suddenly. Grace held her breath.

'What if she gets worse?'

'I'm fifteen, I'll take her to the doctors.' He sounded surprised by his own maturity.

Amy looked at the wall, chewing her bottom lip. Grace turned her head very slowly to look out of the window, the flannel sticking to one eye. Doug was pointing to his watch and turning an imaginary steering wheel.

Amy stood up as if she had no more energy, the movement making the sofa shudder, and Grace watched her write something on a piece of paper from her jacket pocket and give it to Ed.

'It's only the Lake District. Janet will come round.'

'I don't like Janet,' Grace muttered.

'We'll be back before you know it.'

Grace closed her eyes tightly and kept them shut when Amy kissed her quickly on the forehead. She heard her say to Ed: 'Make sure she actually moves things when she dusts.' She didn't open her eyes until she heard the car pull away. She had a temperature and Ed's face loomed over her so it wasn't surprising she was sick, a soupy pulsing all down herself, in and out of her cupped hands, onto the sofa, the cushions, the floor.

—◊—

NOW. A wine bar in the Lake District.
It's pouring. There is live music. It is
jazz.

                    AMY
    What was the name of that place you
    took me to that time? It was like
    this.

                    DOUG
    (Watching the jazz trio. Grimac-
    ing.) This music is heavy boots
    walking on my face.

—◊—

THEN. Tudor Rose restaurant 15 years
ago.

                    AMY
    (Excitedly.) Older men have so much
    more to say.

                    DOUG
    (Studying menu intently like a map.
    Silently.)

45

                    AMY

I've never been anywhere like this.
The Tudor Rose. Do you feel like
you're in a film?

                    DOUG

(Grabbing AMY's menu.) You can have
anything at all from this side. Except these.

                    AMY

Lovely, thank …

                    DOUG

Or these. Either of these. Can we
see the wine list?

                    AMY

(Flustered.) Oh well, we could …
could we share? Something?

                    DOUG

Good idea. You don't want to
bloat.

                    AMY

(Thinking about this.) No.

                    —◊—

NOW.

                    AMY

The Tudor Rose. It was called The
Tudor Rose.

                    DOUG
     (Downing large glass of red wine.)
     I don't remember.

                JAZZ FRONTMAN MIKE
     (Feedback from mic followed by two
     pops and a bang. There is a burning
     smell.) Testing one two one two,
     two two. (Muffled.) Is a fug me a
     darlin so fug me: ah one, two, ah
     one two three four –

                    AMY
     (Over the din.) I wanted the duck.

                    DOUG
     (Shaking his head and tapping on
     table slightly out of time with the
     music. A habit AMY can't stand.)

                    AMY
     (Ignoring him.) We shared the
     chicken supreme. You said it was a
     lean and sophisticated dish. It was
     tiny, do you remember? We got chips
     on the way home. Doug, they do have
     a phone here.

                    —◊—

THEN.

                    DOUG
     I rang the hospital again.

AMY

(Thrilled he's revealing his emo-
tional side this early in their relationship.) She'll be ok.

DOUG

Fuck. Excuse my French.

AMY

(Thinking about it then resting a
hand on his. Partly to stop him
tapping on the table. Although perhaps it's quite endearing.) I've
been watching the news.

DOUG

Did they show a picture or anything?

AMY

Nothing. That poor mother. You're a
hero for waiting with her all that
time.

DOUG

(Nothing.)

AMY

They'll probably never find the person who did it. He'll get off scot-
free. Or she. Isn't that awful? That
there are people like that who …

DOUG

Life goes on though, Amy. You can't

dwell. Even though it's terrible.
(Reaching his hand towards her. She
holds her breath.) What's this?
(Producing a coin from behind AMY'S
ear.) Oh? (And another one. Doing
it six more times while Amy looks
at him.)

—◇—

2.3: BACK AT HOME, ED AND GRACE. DUTY.

Ed made sure Grace was definitely asleep by prodding her. He held his clenched fist up to his mouth like a microphone and tapped it. 'Ladies and gentlemen, in a break from his sell-out world tour with his band, Sharks of Pain, for one night only, he's here to read from his latest best-selling novel, *Swallowing the Heartache*. Give it up for Mr … Ed … Mullin!'

Chapter 2: The Journey
There was a rift between them. I could feel it although the girls were speaking a different language which I think was Spanish. Or a Scandinavian language such as Norwegian.

Three sisters, all versions of the other. The eldest sat next to the father, brushing his arm, whispering to him about something one of the others had said or hadn't said.

I tried to read my book which was a biography about the drummer, Buddy Rich, but this was better. The book was good though. I would give it a nine out of ten for drummer biographies.

She – the accused – fiddled with her personal stereo, her chipped nails pressing at buttons. I think she liked me. But I am past all that because I have seen too much heartache. It was written all over my face. In permanent marker.

Guess what, you and me, it ain't never gonna happen. I expect she was listening to Dire Straits. Girls that age from Spain or

Norway listen to Dire Straits a lot. She looked up at the older girl – pitched her smile slap bang in the middle between sheepish and taunting. Boys can't do this. I know because I've tried and it comes out spiteful or devious like in afternoon break when Terry Bowman gets angry and spits, etc, but he never gets told off and you have to leave him be.

I watched as they stepped off the train. The father held coffee in a corrugated paper cup.

After they had gone, I went to the buffet car, and pulled some coins from my jeans. I don't know why, but I wanted the coffee he had. I figured if I could have the coffee he had, I might one day be the father he was, or at least have the father he was. I wasn't thinking straight. I'd swallowed too much heartache. It was like the time I saw the man with the massive beard and I stroked my face like he stroked his because it looked like it felt good and I hoped it might encourage my face to grow dark whiskers like he had, but obviously that doesn't tend to happen until you hit puberty and I was seven.

The girls colluded in the game which was that their father was in control. They let him gesture for them to hurry up. You could tell he kind of knew they had him. They pulled him like elastic stretched three ways from his heart. The feud between the girls hummed but they turned it down so the father couldn't hear. I heard. You can only hear if you don't care too much. I used to care too much. The eldest loped behind the others. Twice she glanced back as if she'd forgotten something. But she hadn't. She was sending out a message and I decoded it right away with my Enigma machine of experience and loss that I carried around in my heart all the time.

It was a movement that said look at the S of my body. S for Somewhere. Who knows? Maybe she and I were headed to the same place. If that place was down.

'And the crowd roars!' said Ed. 'Grace? Are you asleep?'

NOW.

                    AMY
It went straight to the answerphone.
Do you think they're alright?

                    DOUG
Both dead.

                    AMY
(Looking at him.) Hilarious, Doug.

                    DOUG
For Christ's sake. You couldn't
wait to leave, now you can't wait
to get back. Are you eating those?

                    AMY
I don't like walnuts.

            JAZZ FRONTMAN MIKE
Andy on the drums, ladies an gen-
namen.

                    AMY
(Decisively.) I look back and I
think I should have seen the signs.
Was it romantic, Doug? I really
don't know anymore. What did I have
then that I don't have now?

                    DOUG
An off-button?

There was no other sound, no scream, nothing to tell him he had just hit a little girl. But he saw her in his mirror as he drove away, lying on the ground with her white skirt ballooning up around her.

She sat up, rubbing her head with stick arms as if trying to remember where she'd put her glasses. Doug drove on but the car got slower until it ground to a halt although he was flooring the accelerator pedal. That was when he suspected.

'Come back here!' she commanded, pointing at the car.

She looked so cross it nearly made him laugh. Grace will sound like this one day, he thought, picturing her as she was now, six weeks' worth of the world packed inside her tiny body.

Of its own accord, the car creaked into reverse and rolled slowly back towards the girl who was wiping blood off her legs with the hem of her dress.

'Look at this mess,' she said. In Amy's voice.

That was when he knew it was this dream.

'Do I look like a dog to you? Why can't we have a dog? How do you know you're still allergic?'

He stepped out of the car. The ground was sticky. He slammed the car door but it wouldn't shut, although he tried over and over, rubber on rubber.

'This fucking door,' said Doug, looking hard at the door because he didn't want to turn around.

This is when he remembered there was nothing he could do. What did he do last time?

'Look at me,' said Amy, standing where the girl had been, arms folded, wearing the girl's dress.

'I can't.'

'Try.'

He couldn't not look. Blood was dripping bright red from a gash in her face and a bone was sticking out at a stupid angle from her elbow, the bright white of a spring onion. She looked put out. There was dried blood caked in her hair. The dress was too short. Embarrassing.

'When are you going to tell me the truth?' she said.

'Pull your dress down.'

'Lies grow to more than six feet inside you and doctors have to pull them out with hooks.'

He was so angry. That was tapeworm. They'd been through this.

'I told ... you know what hap ... so ... if been ... done same ... daughter ...'

'Breaking up.'

—◊—

THEN.

>   DOUG
> (Drunk.) I have a plan. (He is draw-
> ing or writing something on a ser-
> viette with a pencil.) Driving is
> just a temporary thing for me. In
> ten years? (He shoots his arm to-
> wards the stars, narrowly missing
> AMY'S face.)

>   AMY
> (Trying a joke.) You're going to be
> a Nazi?

>   DOUG
> (Looking at her.) I'm going to run
> my own multi-national business. See
> this? This is a ten-year business
> plan. It starts with cars. Cars are

my thing. I know cars. Not the me-
chanics, the … See this car in the
centre? That's me. (Looks at her as
if considering something.) Do you
want in?

                    AMY
I can't drive. (Realising what
she's said. They laugh.) Can I tell
you something?

                    DOUG
I know what you're going to say.
(Puts his serviette to one side and
takes another from the little dis-
penser.) Watch.

                    AMY
(Uncomfortable.)

(Draws something. Pencil tears the
serviette. He passes the serviette
across to AMY.) I felt it when I
first saw you.

                    AMY
(Peering at it.) Is it - balloons?

                    DOUG
It's a Venn diagram. (Pointing in
a patient way.) Me. You. Us. Look
how much us there is. (Watching
her.) You know what we should do?
We should get married.

                    AMY
    (Overwhelmed.) Oh my God, Doug.

                    DOUG
    We need champagne over here. Wait-
    er! Bring us your finest champagne!

                    AMY
    (Trying to pretend she can't hear
    Doug insisting there certainly are
    fine champagnes available within
    the low to low-medium price range.)
    Well, I'm not really drinking. At
    the moment.

                    —◊—

NOW.

                    DOUG
    (Glaring at the band.) I'm going to
    fucking murder them in a minute.
    They can shove their A Trains up
    their A Holes. (Looking quite
    pleased with himself.)

                    AMY
    "Do you want in?" How long did that
    last? Your business plan? Ten min-
    utes?

                    DOUG
    You had a nine-month business plan.
    It changed things.

                    AMY
I hate it when you drink.

                   DOUG
(Calling out to jazz trio who have
taken a break.) Do you know Chinese
Water Torture? You must know it?

                    AMY
Don't take it out on them.

                   DOUG
It was a joke.

                    AMY
Doug. Please.

                   DOUG
Don't "Doug. Please". Is it so terrible? To have ambition? We'll never know, will we?

                    AMY
You lied.

                   DOUG
You trapped me.

                    AMY
I didn't trap you.

                   DOUG
I don't want to talk about this.

                    AMY
It's all we ever talk about!

                    DOUG
We talk about lots of things.

                    AMY
I thought you were a hero.

                    DOUG
(Noise that could be laughing.) You
think everyone's a hero or a vil-
lain.

                    AMY
 I don't know who you are.

                    DOUG
Amy, sit down for fuck's sake.

                    AMY
How can you run someone over and
pretend you didn't? For eight
years. Eight years! I believed you.
I really did. You let me call you a
hero. (Laughs.)

                    DOUG
I never said hero. You made that up
all by yourself.

                    AMY
You're a conman.

DOUG

I'm a mug. I gave up everything for
a beautiful … for a slut.

AMY

(Quietly.) That is vile.

DOUG

(To jazz trio.) What are you looking at? Play something.

AMY

I made one mistake.

JAZZ FRONTMAN MIKE

(Looking at other band members and
back to Doug.) Say please.

DOUG

(To Mike.) What was that?

AMY

What are you going to do this time?
Saw me in half? Pull the ace of
spades out my arse?

(DOUG stands. Chair falls over. He
looks for a moment as though he's
been beamed in from space. He walks
over to JAZZ FRONTMAN MIKE. Picks
him up by the neck of his jumper
and, for a second, they both look
surprised, then shoves him backwards into the drum kit. Commotion.
DOUG walks straight out.)

—◇—

There were even more of them and they were faster. Grace counted them as they marched in straight lines up the wall, across the ceiling and down the other side, one hundred and sixty-one, one hundred and sixty-two. If she stopped, the ants would win; they must not win. They flowed like water but upwards which was all wrong and you could hear their feet tip-tapping on the woodchip. One hundred and sixty-three, one hundred and sixty-four.

Grace called, 'Dad!' and then, 'Mum? Ed?'

The bed was pressing down on the soggy floor, which was really the underside of the cardboard box and when it gave way – which would be any minute now – the bed with her in it would fall down into black and keep falling and no one would hear. She tried to keep still without breathing, one hundred and sixty-five.

Some of the ants crawled across her forehead and it was like being drawn on with a biro. They ran in and out of her belly button, so she searched for something real to pin down the ants with, a game, Who I Would Be If I Could Be Anyone. Last time they'd played it, she'd chosen Leroy from *Fame* and Polina had said, 'You'.

She heard Ed go shhh. The flannel he held to her forehead felt icy cold and wonderful, but then she couldn't bear it, so she slept and sometimes everything was black. He wasn't there when she woke up but then he appeared with a boiled egg and soldiers that she couldn't eat, so he did. The light when it came was too light and her parents were never coming back.

Ed: 'Course they are, silly. Let's dress up some of these ants, shall we? Bikinis?'

Ed: 'No crying, OK?'

Ed: '… read to us from your bestselling novel Mr Ed Mullin!'

59

THEN.

> DOUG
> (Grimly. Arm in arm with AMY, out-side, eating chips.) We'll say it's mine.

> AMY
> (Squeezing his arm. Crying.) You don't have to do this.

—◊—

NOW. Outside. DOUG is trying to start the car. AMY is knocking on the window.

> AMY
> You can't drive in this state. You'll kill someone. (Banging on window.) Come on.

> DOUG
> (Rolling down window.) She didn't die!

> AMY
> I'm not talking about her. Just get out of the car. You're scaring me. Give me the keys.

> DOUG
> (Trying car again, uselessly. Gets out, slams door, storms off in a random direction.)

                    DOUG and AMY huddled together side
                    by side, her arm around him. Dark.
                    A wooden bus shelter that looks
                    disused.

                                  AMY
                    (Silence. Complicated.) What are
                    we doing?

                                  DOUG
                    I don't know.

                                  AMY
                    (Without looking at him.) At least
                    you said 'beautiful' before you
                    said …

                                  DOUG
                    (Looks at her. Moves to kiss her.
                    They kiss. Briefly. She moves
                    away.)

                                  AMY
                    (Reaches for his hand without look-
                    ing at him.)

                              —◊—

Grace looked for him in the bathroom and the kitchen, her
slippers shooshing on the wooden floors. She wanted toast but
she wasn't supposed to make it by herself, although usually she
did anyway. She felt a bit better than yesterday, when there had
been several versions of her body, like echoes, each one following and colliding with the next; at least today she was real.
Looking up made her dizzy and she'd lost Ed so she went back

upstairs towards his bedroom to look for him. Half way up she stopped for a rest.

Standing outside his room, she heard him talking to himself. She mimed knocking and pushed open the door. He was sitting on the corner of the bed, his jeans and pants around his ankles, tugging at himself with the ferocity of a cartoon character thumbing a lift on fast-forward. A magazine lay open on the floor by his feet. His face was screwed up.

'Get out!' He was furious, hands everywhere, layers of clothing flying about. He looked as though he could explode.

'Can I have some toast?' Grace said, through the door that was slammed in her face. 'Or Shreddies?'

He wouldn't look at her for the rest of the morning, but she didn't know what to do with the power. She felt slow with the last of the illness, gloop bubbles swimming silently up and down her neck. She was angry with Ed for doing the thing that made the air between them bend, and angry with everyone who was outside when she was inside.

'I'm going out,' he told her.

'Where?'

'Café.' He looked at her without smiling. He sighed. 'Go and get dressed.' She scowled but it was relief.

The café was brilliant, Grace would tell Polina later, it was where the big boys went to play Space Invaders. Grace sat on a table with a red and white checked paper tablecloth, until the owner smacked her leg to make her get off. She wore her favourite skirt with a dragonfly pattern, which didn't go with her jumper, and watched Ed and the others staring at the Space Invaders screen. He was different when he was with them, the boyness of them solid enough that you could push against it like jelly. They were always shoving each other and they knew everything there was to know; she wanted them to shove her but they ignored her. Worse: they blanked her. She sipped the Fanta she had bought with her own money, nodding along as if to music only she could hear.

The café owner seemed to veer between wanting them gone and wanting to be mates with them. One of the boys – Mack? – shouted 'Yes!' after a new high score and the others opened a space to spew him out then closed ranks around the machine so it would not escape. It was Ed's go. Mack went to the counter for a celebratory Coke and on the way stopped to pull an imaginary lever in the air. Grace watched, wondering whether to laugh. He pointed at her then made his pointing finger into a pretend comb for his hair. Combed it.

Grace was so bored it felt like the next day.

The café owner sat at one of the tables with a customer, a fat man who bit down hard on a greasy bacon sandwich in thin white bread. Grace had to look away from the margarine inside the sandwich; the man licked each finger afterwards. The boys didn't turn around once and, when the bleep sped up for the zillionth time, it made her heart go funny. After the customer left, the café owner screeched up a chair at Grace's table and sat, one chunky leg crossed over the other. He slammed down his mug of tea and blew smoke in a line that just missed her face, then tapped the ash into a saucer, his fingers delicate compared to the rest of him.

'Which one's your boyfriend?'

She turned towards the boys, her heart fluttering like it was trying to get out. His hair kept escaping in jagged black grey blades and he wore an off-white apron over his off-white T-shirt, with trousers that weren't really jeans and weren't really anything. The apron had blobs on it, low down, as if a child had dipped their hands in a puddle and pushed against him.

'That one's my brother. He's called Ed.'

She pointed. The café owner didn't bother looking. He rubbed the cartilage at the end of his nose, making it wobble. Under the cigarette smell, Grace caught cooking oil, meat.

'Nice,' he said, his voice all raspy.

Grace didn't want to show herself up. It was bad enough that she was eight.

'But you must have a fella?'

The café owner's lips went thin when he smiled. His voice was loud even when it was quiet. She wanted him to clear his throat; he was always about to. The way he spoke to her felt like being up when other children were in bed, a satisfying, sick feeling.

'I do but he's in the army.'

'Is that right?' He coughed and laughed at the same time, and it made a piece of his hair jut forwards.

'He's in a regiment. He's called Steve.'

'In a regiment. Well I never.'

She hoped he wouldn't laugh again, she'd seen yellow teeth. Where were all the customers anyway? This café must be rubbish. Ed looked over, briefly, and when she felt his eyes on her back it made the air go glittery. Or perhaps she was feeling light-headed. She'd only had the toast.

She waited for the man to say something else but there was a lull, as though he was losing interest in her, or possibly dropping off. She tapped his hand with hers.

'How much is a sandwich; no margarine?'

'Well, let's see. How much have you got?'

'19p.'

'For 19p I can do you a knuckle sandwich.'

'OK, but no margarine?'

Now he really laughed, hard, and the sound hurt. He put his cigarette flat in the saucer and covered her hand in both of his.

'You're priceless,' he said. 'Give us a kiss and I'll put a bit of ham in that sandwich.'

He pointed to his cheek which looked like leather pulled over rock. He had his eyes closed. His eyelids were moths.

'I can't reach,' she said.

She hoped he'd go and make the sandwich soon.

His eyes moved round the café in a quick sweep. 'Come on, I'll help you.'

In one movement, he was up and across to her, his hands lifting her at the waist to stand her on the chair. Grace thought, this won't work because now I'm too tall. His hands, rough as cat's tongues, rubbed the outside of her thighs on their way to and from her waist. She leaned down towards him to get the kiss over with, puckering her lips.

'Hey! What are you doing with my sister?'

Ed was there, in between them, smelling of shampoo, and she wanted to reach out and ruffle his hair because it looked so soft.

'She's my sister,' he said, pulling Grace off the chair and dropping her with a bump onto the floor.

'He was going to make me a sandwich,' Grace said, wondering why Ed had to keep telling the man she was his sister.

'Yeah, in exchange for what?'

'19p.'

'All done, son?' said the café owner, his arms folded.

'We're going,' said Ed.

'You can say that again. You and your mates can all clear off with your can of Coke and ten straws. What am I, a charity?'

He was doing a show for the customer who'd just walked in with a whippet on a lead, both of them startled.

'Fucking hell, Grace.'

Ed didn't even say goodbye to the others. He dragged Grace out the door by her arm as the café owner shouted: 'And wash your bloody mouth out!' Mack exchanged a look with one of the other boys.

Someone had stolen Ed's bike, so after he stopped swearing they had to walk. It was almost dark but there was still some blue and pink at the top of the sky.

'This is the worst day ever,' said Ed. 'Don't puke.'

Having a piggyback was all right but her jaw kept bumping Ed's back and waking her up.

'Take smaller steps,' she said.

'Shut up.'

Eventually she found a part of Ed's back where the rope of his spine made a ledge for her cheek. She pressed into it.

'When did you get so heavy?' he said.

After for ever, she recognised the gap between the trees that meant they were close to their road; she matched her breathing with Ed's and tried to cry without moving a muscle. When he shunted her upwards, she had to find the ledge again. Her runny nose was leaving a trail on the back of Ed's jumper.

'OK,' he said, swinging her down to the pavement.

Ed rolled his shoulders, windmilling his arms. She was rubbing her nose on her sleeve, so it took her a moment to realise he was holding his arms out for her. She ran into him, like a wall, hard as she could. He smelt a bit of the café, a bit of himself as he rested his chin on top of her head. They went in.

Doug and Amy were sitting close together on the sofa in silence. Amy had her hands together as though in prayer.

'I thought it was tomorrow,' said Ed, stunned.

'We came back early,' said Amy, looking at her watch.

'Place looks like a pigsty,' said Doug.

'Didn't Janet come?' said Amy.

'I was going to –'

'Her colour's not good. Did you take her to the doctors?'

'We went to the café,' said Grace. 'I had Fanta.'

'I'm so disappointed, Ed,' said Amy, really quietly.

'We thought we could trust you,' said Doug, his hand on Amy's thigh.

'Up to bed,' said Amy to Grace. 'You look terrible.'

'I know. I've only had toast. All day.'

Doug and Amy looked at Ed. He was rubbing his face with his palm as if wiping his chin off.

—◊—

'What's wrong with that?' Maggie pointed at Polina's plate.

'Nothing.' It was difficult to concentrate with her mum staring at her. 'I might be in a play,' Polina said, trying to chew.

You could hear the clock ticking in the hall. The pile of dirty washing on the kitchen floor was still there from yesterday.

'You used to love macaroni cheese,' said Maggie.

'I've got PE tomorrow.'

'What's that got to do with anything?'

'I just saw my PE kit on the floor and it reminded me.'

Maggie had a list that Polina couldn't read upside down. She was ticking it.

'How does food make you feel?' said Maggie.

Polina shrugged her shoulders. 'Shall I wash it myself? It's not that dirty.'

'Are you trying to make me feel worse?' Maggie slammed the pen down. Polina jumped. She shouldn't have shrugged her shoulders. 'Because it's working. I haven't had time to wash your PE kit, Polina.'

'OK.'

'I'm a terrible mother. Just say it.'

'I don't want to say it.'

'I'm doing this by myself. You think it's easy, do you? You're off to school and in a play.'

Polina tried to focus her eyes somewhere else. Not on the washing.

Maggie bit down tentatively on her own fist like an apple. 'Well, good for you. The car needs a service and there's a gas bill but, by all means, point to your PE kit and rub my nose in it.'

'Is your hand all right?'

'What the hell is wrong with that meal?'

'It's bleeding.'

Maggie shook her head while examining the ceiling. The vein in her forehead was thick as a strawberry shoelace. Polina held her breath and counted to 24.

'Can I get down, please?'

'You've disappointed me.'

2.7: DUTY – BREACHED? AMY AND ED (AGED 16).

Even when he wasn't asking questions, Ed's whole body was a question he wouldn't stop asking. Amy watched him peel an orange and there it was in the urgent, irritated way he moved his hands, as though he was signing in the gaps between speaking. Ed glanced at her as he laid a larger piece of peel down like a cup to hold the smaller pieces.

'Want some?' he said.

She shook her head, trying to shake off the suspicion that he already knew who his father was, that this was all just a ruse to make her feel guilty.

'How was school?'

At this, he slouched back in his chair, deflated by her outrageous invasion of his privacy. She smiled because that was pure Doug. She waited.

'There's a boy in my class who eats science books,' he said, eventually.

Just back from school, he was humming with that energy teenage boys have, rage or sexual frustration, as if they were two different things. It unnerved her, which was her springboard into laughter, and you weren't supposed to laugh.

'He rips the pages under his desk and you think he's putting his hand up but he doesn't, he goes like this and then he has to chew it without making any noise.'

'Why does he eat science books?'

Ed shrugged. The way he did it told her he thought she was

68

missing the point. She sensed another question forming itself in the quiet, and to deflect from it, she said, 'Why don't you go and check that Grace has fed the rabbit?'

'Was he a nomad?'

'Who?'

'Because I feel like I want to roam. Could it be genetic?'

'I don't know what you're talking about.'

His answer was to get up fast, move to the fridge in two big strides and put his head inside it, leaning his arm along the top of the door. The silence stretched.

Sometimes she imagined telling him how it was, just to clock his reaction: you were conceived in the middle toilet of three. Repeated enough, nothing became in some way the truth for her, with a shape and a form. When she thought about him, which was hardly ever at all, it was as a series of flashcards, one after the other: mint, aftershave, brie, comfy chair. And the things he said, like: a man is a man.

She'd been very young and malleable; she'd thought she was moulding him, the poor man with the wife who didn't care about him. What a thrill it had been to be so important to him, her father's best friend. You don't understand what you mean to me, he told her, crying while still on top of her. Sometimes he touched her face with a kind of slow motion bewilderment, as though he'd never touched skin before.

I'm greedy, he liked to say, while she half closed her eyes and smiled and ignored the wobbling flap of skin that connected his chin to his neck.

Ed's head was still in the fridge. The open door was leaking electricity.

'We're having dinner soon; don't spoil it,' she said, feeling suddenly irritated.

As Ed turned to face her, his expression was impossible to read. He slammed the door shut without taking his eyes off her. If this was some kind of test, she was up to it. Don't laugh. She made herself not blink.

Madame Roberts. Last week, when she'd asked if he enjoyed playing the bass guitar – he didn't know she knew – she had looked impressed and also moved (he imagined her afterwards in the staffroom, smiling to herself, perhaps with tears close to the surface) when he'd said, 'Oui, Madame Roberts, mais j'aime aussi l'actualité'. Today, on his 17th birthday, he spent all lesson imagining making love to her in a pristine Parisian hotel room while she moaned in French.

Mack had given him a homemade card and written in blue crayon on the front, 'Happy Birthday you Fucker'. A condom fell out as Ed opened it, which he'd picked up casually like he picked up condoms all the time. He woke that morning in a rush, feeling alternately slack and tight, and a lot older, though you couldn't tell anyone that. Something gnawed at him like it always did, but it was worse today because he knew he should have been deeper into music by now. Real musicians were out there making it, not wasting time at school. The window was closing. He cried when he jerked off in the shower because his ageing spunk was talent down the plughole.

For breakfast, he cut himself a big slice of the carrot cake that was sitting on the kitchen table, still in its packaging. No one baked cakes in his family. Amy had tried to make a sponge for someone's birthday once, maybe Grace's, but it had a sink-hole, and Ed remembered Grace asking, 'Is it funnel cake?', and Doug's helpful observation: 'You opened the oven door too soon.'

All day, he escaped the bumps he'd been waiting for (hoping for?). Carrying the feeling of anticipation around had made him feel so sick that by the final bell he was wired, and there was a pressure in his head.

'Café,' Mack said. 'You coming?'

Ed saw cans of lager glinting in the black of Mack's rucksack.

'Edward!'

It was Doug. In the school bus lane. Doing a woman's voice and waving.

'Ed, isn't that your … '

Ed jogged over to the car all long-armed, as if he'd known this would happen. Best to try and head Doug off before he did something really embarrassing.

'Stick your bag on the back seat, son. You're driving.'

'Ed? You coming or what?'

Ed waved away Mack and the others then got in the driver's side. His belly rolled upside down then righted itself as he caught the distinct car smell of electrical equipment when you pull the bubble-wrap off, serious like an office, but undercut with chips.

'Happy birthday, son.'

Doug finished his cheeseburger, crumpling the packaging into a ball and throwing it in the glove compartment.

All the alien spaceship controls leered at Ed.

'Start her up.'

Ed looked at Doug, who yawned and stretched, challenging him like a cartoon bear, a cat's cradle of sinewy cheese on show in his open mouth.

'Here?'

'No. Let's push her into the sea and start her up there. Of course here. Hurry up, we've got a school bus up our arse.'

'I don't remember what to do.'

'Start her up, check your mirrors, ease her into first.'

Ed started the engine. It growled nastily. Madame Roberts chose that moment to glide by on her bike (of course she did), dinking her little bell and smiling with all those lovely French teeth. He tried to wave. He stalled. Doug laughed, mouthing a sorry to the queue of buses behind.

'Why did you have to park in the bus lane?'

Ed's knees were shaking. This was not going to work.

'Don't be a baby,' said Doug. 'Look, you've got a fan club.'

Two girls waiting for the bus were pointing at him. The one from his English class whose complicated bra he'd once felt (but never her complicated tits) had her hand over her mouth as though she'd never seen anything so funny. He pulled out, revving too hard. This was up there with the worst days of his life. All of them involved Doug.

'Easy does it,' said Doug, doing his professional smile, eyes front. 'You'll find I'm very patient when we – watch the fucking cars! You trying to kill us?'

'Sorry.' Ed's throat stopped working.

'Just watch the road.'

Ed watched the road and started to hum.

'Which is the most dangerous traffic light?' said Doug, scratching his armpit.

'Is this a joke?'

'Am I laughing? Watch the road. Stop humming.'

'I give up.'

'Don't give up.'

'Red.'

'Why red?'

'All right, green,' said Ed. He remembered there was a roundabout soon. After a hill. He felt nauseous.

'No, Ed, I'm asking, why red? Don't just cave in. Answer the question.'

'I'm not caving in.'

'The closer we go, the slower we go.'

'Red because people jump red lights?'

'It's not red.'

'Amber?'

'It's actually green,' said Doug. 'We drive on the left. Stay on the left.'

'I said green.'

'You said green without thinking. I wanted you to think.'

Ed thought.

'You're perfectly safe with me, Ed.'

'Can you stop talking like that?'

'Now, why is green the most dangerous traffic light?'

'Like that.'

'What?'

'That voice.'

'Up into fourth.'

It was just levers and pulleys. And an engine. It must be easy if Doug could do it. Ed imagined his real dad parked outside school, keys to a Porsche chucked at Ed and one of those chiselled faces everyone loves. Homemade cake.

'Ed, for fuck's sake!'

'Shit …'

'A car is a weapon.'

'All right!'

'Left.'

Ed's heart banged like a maniac.

'I told your mother you weren't ready.'

It was difficult to hear what Doug was saying.

'She said, "Is this because he stole some cake?".'

'It's my cake,' said Ed.

'That would work if you were five.'

'Fuck this.'

Ed swerved towards the kerb without signalling and braked so hard their heads tipped backwards in unison then forwards like a synchronised headbutt. Ed snatched at the seat belt, yanking it free from its clasp. They were miles from anywhere.

'Your real dad was Nigel Mansell,' said Doug. He folded his arms. 'Why don't you ask him to give you a lesson?'

Ed reached round to retrieve his school bag from the back seat. 'I'm walking.' He opened the door and climbed out, clumsy with shock.

'You got that right.'

Ed slammed the door so hard it jarred his arm. His legs were stiff with lactic acid, like he was walking on stilts.

'Other way.' Doug had already shuffled across to the driver's seat and rolled down the window.

He was right, the bastard. Ed turned and started walking back towards the car.

'Ed, get something out the boot for me, will you?'

'Get it yourself.'

'Just open the boot.'

Something in Doug's voice made Ed do it. A bass guitar flashed him, aching with its own newness. It was the one he'd told Doug about, metallic blue. It was incredible, but he forced himself not to touch it. Instead, he closed the boot. It was hard to step back from the car.

'You getting in?'

How could he say yes? How could he not say yes? The thick strings had that smell, a new tube of tennis balls.

'Suit yourself.'

Doug pulled away, fast. Ed watched the car get smaller.

BREACH

3.1: EXAMINE WHETHER THE DEFENDANT HAS FALLEN BELOW THE
STANDARD OF CARE WE EXPECT FROM HIM/HER.
3.1.2: ALSO KNOWN AS LETTING OTHER PEOPLE DOWN.

'Where's the bacon?' said Amy.

'Why, were you going to burn us a sandwich?' said Doug,
sneaking a glance at Grace across the kitchen table.

Doug's fountain pen was difficult to control but Grace had
no choice now her felt-tip had dried up.

'I'm sure there was bacon in here yesterday,' said Amy.

Grace wrote: I want to join the Dennis the Mennis fan club because Dennis is funny EG when he made a cake with Walter's face
on and made Walter have some for his birthday but it was mud!

'And all the eggs?' said Amy. 'Janet?'

'Yes, dear?' said Doug in a falsetto voice.

Grace giggled. 'This pen is actually rubbish,' she said.

'Or was it Ed?' said Amy. 'We'll just have to have toast. If he
hasn't eaten all the bread.'

Doug snapped the newspaper. 'We're not having toast,' he
said. 'We're having Ed go to the shops for bacon and eggs out
of his own money.'

Grace sighed. 'It was Carl,' she said.

'Where is he anyway?' said Doug, looking round for Ed.

There was nothing you could do once Doug went this red.

'I don't want bacon and eggs,' said Grace. 'Can I have Coco
Nut Sacks?'

'Can you have what?' said Doug.

'Ed says it's a new cereal.'

'Right, where is he?' said Doug.

Grace moved the Shreddies box to cover the spot on the table where the fountain pen had just leaked dark blue ink. She said: 'It was Carl but no one ever listens to me.'

Amy now looked thoughtful like a teacher. 'Well, maybe it was Carl, right, Doug?' she said.

'Who the fuck is Carl?'

'Doug! Carl is obviously Grace's friend.'

'Not my friend. Ed's.'

Her parents were very stupid.

'Ed's friend then,' said Amy, winking at Grace.

'He looks like Father Christmas,' Grace said, warming up. 'He's a bit like Daddy but nicer.'

Doug sprang up and threw the paper at the table, but it stuck to his hands and he had to pull at it to get it off.

'When I get back there had better be bacon. Understood?'

He pointed at the space between Amy and Grace. They looked at one another.

'Understood!' Grace said, saluting with the fountain pen and accidentally gouging a bit from her forehead.

'Is that my pen?'

3.2: CHRISTMAS DAY – POLINA AND MAGGIE AT GRACE'S HOUSE.

The fairy lights were on too early in the day and the giant snowflake, Grace's favourite decoration, was lying dead in the middle of the carpet. It was something Doug had brought home from work one night, metallic blue like a shout, in a box marked 'CHUCK?' full of dusty, spiky things and now it had fallen from its drawing pin on the ceiling.

Christmas morning. She dreamt that all her presents got sucked up the chimney and they wouldn't let her climb up to get them. When she hadn't been able to wait any longer to see if the dream was true, she crept downstairs and found Ed sitting cross-legged on the floor in his dressing gown, listening to a new yellow Walkman he'd already unwrapped. He put his finger on his lips. In the armchair, Carl was asleep, his head off to one side. A tin of Quality Street lay open on his lap.

'It's five in the morning, Grace, go back to bed.'

Carl's bottom lip wobbled every time he breathed in. He smelt of warm crisps and wee and it was mixing with the smell of carpet.

'Daddy's going to kill you,' Grace whispered. She unwrapped a purple chocolate from the tin.

'Well, don't tell him.'

She tried to suck the caramel from the inside before the chocolate shell caved in.

'Can I have your Milky Bar Buttons if you get any?' she said, thickly.

'Yes.'

'Can I have your Walkman?' Its yellow was a perfect yellow like the yolk of a fried egg sweet.

'If you want Carl to be homeless on Christmas day then why don't you go and wake mum and dad up right now? Go on.'

'Are you going to keep him secret? You can't.'

'Watch me.'

He put the earphones back in his ears. She waited for him to open his eyes. On the way out of the lounge she accidentally kicked Carl's foot on purpose.

'Let's get you two out of this rain.'

Doug opened the front door with a flourish, as though he'd been hiding behind it, and yanked Polina's mum's arm so hard that her thank you sounded nothing like it had when Polina heard her saying it to the mirror in the hall.

Then they were in, blinking against the bright light, and it felt to Polina like being in the airport of a louder country. She liked it so much she almost forgot the dizziness that wafted around her when she was with her mum.

'That rain!' said Doug.

It wasn't even raining that hard. Maggie handed him the bottle of wine she'd been holding and he ignored them while he examined the label.

Amy called from the kitchen, 'Be with you in a jiffy.'

There was a tangy smell of burning rubber.

'Something smells nice,' said Maggie.

'Where's Grace?' said Polina, and Maggie flashed her a warning look for being rude, but that's because she didn't know it wasn't rude to speak like that at Grace's house.

Grace ran in from the garden with a towel on her head. She stopped dead in front of Polina and mouthed: 'I've got a secret.'

'Here she is,' said Doug.

'Mum? I can't find the hairdryer,' said Grace.

'I'm using it,' Amy called.

'In the kitchen?'

'Yes.'

'Merry Christmas!' said Doug, as he put a glass of champagne into Maggie's hand and downed his own in two swallows.

'You've all certainly got some lungs on you in this house,' said Maggie.

'Not me,' said Doug, seriously. 'They think I have impaired lung function after a childhood infection.'

Ed slammed the back door behind him as he came in. He was wet through.

'I just need to do a thing,' he said, picking up the bowl of nuts from the table and leaving.

'We're expecting Amy's father any time now,' said Doug to Maggie. In an undertone, he said, 'We're also expecting a Gloucester Old Spot to do a fly-by,' and pointed to the ceiling, moving his finger in an arc for their eyes to follow.

Grace pressed play on the stereo at the same time as she asked: 'Can I put some music on?' Straight into crazy dancing, she lunged towards Polina while Slade shouted, gripping her arms and holding them in the air. Over the din, Grace said something to Polina that sounded like 'girls in the garden'.

'Bloody hell, Grace, turn that down. Sorry, excuse my French, Maggie.'

Maggie was perched on the edge of the sofa, holding her empty glass, blinking. Champagne is not for people like us, she'd told Polina once.

'I've gone with instinct,' said Amy, carrying a silver tray gingerly from the kitchen, as though transporting something precious. 'I don't think the label always gets it right about turkey defrosting times, do you, Maggie?'

She put the tray on the table.

'Soak up the booze.' She looked at Doug.

On the tray was a cereal bowl that Amy had filled with roughly chopped pieces of carrot and celery, about the size of children's thumbs.

'Did you slice these with a spoon?' said Doug, holding up a carrot chunk.

'There should be some salted peanuts at the bottom,' said Amy.

'Mmmmm,' said Grace, pretending to adore the aroma. She and Polina looked at one another.

'Shall we have a drink?' said Doug.

—◊—

'At home we have turkey crown, don't we, Mum,' said Polina to Maggie.

Grace prodded the meat on her plate. 'Does it have frozen bits?'

'We have the same turkey everyone else has,' said Maggie, her paper hat somehow stiffer on her head than everyone else's.

The telephone rang and Amy's body jerked as though she'd been asleep. 'Maybe that's dad?' she said.

Doug's hat was slipping down his forehead. He could drink red wine really fast.

Over the ringing, Maggie said: 'I'd never have thought to put avocado pear with Twiglets to make a starter, Amy.'

Amy looked at Doug. 'Phone?' she said.

'I'll get it,' said Ed.

Polina saw him ball up some turkey and a roast potato in his napkin, which he carried with him to the phone. A stray pea rolled quite a way from his plate.

'I must get the recipe from you,' said Maggie.

'It's Sunny View,' Ed called, holding the phone in the air. 'Gran's waiting for Dad.'

'She's having Christmas there,' said Doug.

'Oh Christ,' said Amy.

'She says she isn't,' said Ed.

Maggie refilled her glass slowly. Grace kicked Polina under the table to make her notice the new Speak & Spell on her lap.

'She is,' said Doug.

Polina wasn't allowed Speak & Spell because it did American spellings.

'I can't go and get her now anyway, can I?' said Doug, holding up his glass and trying to drink from it at the same time.

'Put her in a taxi,' said Ed, down the phone.

'You paying?' said Doug. 'Cost a fucking fortune from there.'

'Spell "beautiful".'

'Who said that?' said Doug.

Polina focused on the pea and on things that weren't funny like dead people and famine. The pea looked like skin that's been too long in the bath. Grace was blowing her cheeks out to hold the laughter in.

'Girls, stop mucking about,' said Maggie, sharply. 'If you could be bothered to learn some spellings, Grace, you wouldn't need that rubbish.'

In the quiet that followed, Polina heard the washing machine go into its spin cycle.

Amy coughed. 'Hopefully Dad should be here any minute,' she said, starting to clear the plates. 'I'll save him some dinner.'

'Good idea,' said Doug, as he filled Maggie's glass again.

Grace put her Speak & Spell on the table and dusted the screen with her finger. 'Spell "color"'.

'I think I'll get a glass of water,' said Maggie. Her chair scraped the floor as she pushed it back.

—◊—

They had to have *It's a Wonderful Life* at full volume for Gran, who talked over it while sinking deep into the sofa. She'd eaten the first layer of biscuits before the film even started, all the Jammie Dodgers and the shortbread.

'We won't hear the phone if it goes, Doug,' said Amy, reaching for the remote which Gran did not seem keen to release from her bony grip. Polina knew that grip; sometimes Gran grabbed you for a dance.

'Isn't this lovely, Doug? Who's this one?' She pointed at the screen. 'Is it Jimmy Dean.'

'Jimmy Stewart.'

She patted Doug's knee. He was right next to her and trying to stay upright, which was like trying to sit still on a bouncy castle, both hands cupped around his goldfish bowl of a brandy glass. Polina imagined a little bronze fish in there, gasping for air.

'Here she is,' Gran said, tugging at Maggie's sleeve. She had to pull at you or touch you to check you were real. Polina's mum looked seasick. 'How's Maggie? Hubby still doing the rounds?'

'It's lucky she's not diabetic,' said Maggie, brushing biscuit crumbs briskly from Gran's lap.

'I am,' said Gran, happily.

Cross-legged on the floor, Polina got a flash of Gran's enormous knickers from under the dogtooth skirt she was wearing, held together with a giant safety pin. There was a petticoat as well, possibly two of them. Couldn't she have worn tights? Her knickers were shiny like the inside of a shell. Polina had seen them before, when she and Grace had tried to spy on the neighbours through heavy binoculars from Gran's shed. They couldn't get the lenses to do distance and what they got instead was a close-up of the grimy shed window, then an even closer-up of Gran's knickers flapping on the washing line, three pairs, cloned and angry. She'd seen Gran's bra too, its cups deadly serious like clay bowls.

Gran fell asleep and started snoring. The farting followed, silently at first.

'What are they feeding her in that place?' Doug said, turning the volume up even louder.

'Is Ed still out there?' Maggie said. 'I'll go and have a look.'

'That's it, bit of fresh air,' said Doug.

She was almost out the door when Grace said, 'No, you can't!' and stopped the fart noises she was making under her armpit to keep Gran's farting company. 'He's doing a … project.'

Maggie looked at her.

'Don't be silly, Grace,' said Amy, wistfully. She was looking out the window watching the cars.

As soon as Maggie was gone, Grace dragged Polina up to her bedroom.

'Look,' Grace said, pointing down from her window.

Maggie was standing with Ed in the back garden, her arms folded.

'Who's that man with them?'

'Carl. He's my friend.'

'Has he been there all day?'

'Yep.'

'Does he live in your garden?'

Grace shrugged. 'Do you want a Milky Bar Button?'

'Can't he come in?' His white hair looked kind.

'He smells,' said Grace.

Polina looked again. Carl was playing air guitar and her mum laughed, which was a shock, then he rested his hand for a moment on Ed's shoulder.

—◊—

'What a charming man your father is. You look very much like him,' said Maggie, flushed from the garden. She had an empty glass in her hand.

Amy looked stunned. 'He's out there?' she said, and her hand went to her mouth.

In the quiet that followed, Polina thought she heard Gran singing.

'He said he likes being outdoors.'

'This I've got to see,' said Doug.

'He's my father!'

They both ran for the back door just as Ed opened it. As they shoved him aside, he stared accusingly at Grace. 'Hey!' he said.

'I couldn't stop them.'

From outside, Doug shouted, 'Call the police.'

'Let's put the kettle on,' said Maggie. The force of the cold tap spilled water in and out of the kettle and splashed down the front of her jumper. She didn't seem to mind.

There was a noise like a dustbin lid being dropped and then Doug stumbled through the door holding his throat with both hands.

'You hit him,' said Amy, coming in behind Doug and closing the door. To no one in particular she said: 'It wasn't Dad.'

'What was I supposed to do? He came at me.'

'You hit him?' said Ed.

'He missed,' said Amy. 'Your father punched a dustbin lid, which then hit him in the face.'

'Don't go out there, Grace, there's a tramp in our garden,' said Doug.

'He's gone,' said Amy and she sat on a stool.

'Am I bleeding?' Doug bunched up a tea towel and held it to his chin, then his eye. He reached blindly towards the freezer.

Ed said: 'He's got nowhere to go.'

'How long have you been letting a stranger steal food from us?' said Doug, a packet of frozen peas on his head.

'It's not stealing if you give it to them,' said Grace.

'It was just some turkey. It's Christmas day,' said Ed.

Polina noticed Maggie let herself out of the back door.

'He didn't eat the bits that weren't cooked, Mum,' said Grace.

'Well, he won't be back,' said Doug. 'Do I look concussed?'

They could hear Gran singing different words to the tune of 'Jingle Bells': 'I am stuck, I am stuck, stu-uck in the loo …'

'Is anyone going to help her?' Ed said.

Polina slipped outside and there was her mum, standing in the middle of the lawn holding two mugs. Polina watched her, the droop in her shoulders, and started to walk towards her but stopped. It felt rude, as though she might be interrupting something. Carl had gone.

She waited for her mum to turn. She made a bet with herself: if she turns right now and isn't cross, it could still be the best Christmas on record. Right now. Or in the next ten seconds. The next twelve seconds. It was raining again, fat cold blobs. I'll start singing something, Polina thought, and was about to, her lips in the right place for the S of 'Silent Night' when her mum turned.

'We'll make a move, shall we?' said Maggie.

When Polina saw her mum's face, she felt the hope in her chest go flat, like giving back a Christmas present.

—◊—

3.3: A FEW MONTHS LATER. A SCRAP (ALMOST).

Grace pulled the bra strap on one of the dummies. The shop assistant noticed, the one with glasses on a cord around her neck.

'Do you have any other colours or just this … ?'

'Hue,' said Polina, face to breasts with a dummy.

'Hugh?' said Grace.

'All right, you're bothering my real customers. Out!' The shop assistant's voice was brave and wobbly.

Polina turned. There was no one else in the shop. They all realised this at the same time.

'We shall leave,' said Grace, her voice cracking on the last word, tugging at Polina's arm.

They walked, picked up speed, and Polina nearly tripped as they ran for the exit.

'I know your mothers!'

'I'm going to wee myself,' said Grace.

'We're very sorry,' Polina called.

—◊—

3.4: LISA ARRIVES AT SCHOOL – GRACE AND POLINA APPROX 14.

3.4.1: QUESTION: IS LETTING YOURSELF DOWN THE SAME AS LETTING YOURSELF GO?

'You have the time it takes for me to write the name of the play on the board, Grace.'

The aeroplane landed on her desk with a little whoosh like an exhalation. Grace quickly unfolded its paper wings and smoothed it out, reading the single word it revealed. Ambition. She looked across at Polina who was gazing too nonchalantly out of the window. Mr Davies wrote *Macbeth* and underlined it with a flourish.

'It's about ambition,' Grace said.

'All right. Anything else?'

'Is this the one with the pretty chickens in it?'

'I'm glad you've memorised one part of one line, Grace. Can we expect further insight of this calibre?'

The classroom door opened and a girl walked in without

looking up. She moved to an empty desk and slumped into its seat. She had no bag and her jumper wasn't the school colour. She looked like she'd been up all night.

'You must be Lisa? Lisa everyone,' said Mr Davies.

Grace used the moment to turn towards Polina again. 'Thanks,' she mouthed. Polina had folded her arms high up on her chest, a habit of hers. It reminded Grace of a PE lesson, years ago, Polina's arms folded across a horrible pink vest.

Except Polina wasn't looking at Grace. She was looking at Lisa. So, Grace looked at Lisa, who was rubbing one eye with the heel of her hand, her skin so thin it was almost see-through. Something about Lisa made Grace feel afraid. Just like that, like cold air.

To break the spell, Grace laughed and picked up a rubber from her desk. She turned to hurl it in Polina's direction. Except Polina was already engrossed in the play again, eyes down, frowning and serious.

3.5: FLASHBACK/PRIMARY SCHOOL PE – GRACE RESCUES POLINA.

Nicola raised her eyebrows as Polina passed her. 'Nice pants.'

'I forgot my kit.'

'Girls!' said Mrs Webster.

Polina closed her eyes and folded her arms across her chest. She tried to listen to the music but she hated the vest she was wearing. It wasn't even pink anymore. Someone pinched the back of her thigh. The pain throbbed. She said nothing. It happened again, much harder. She tried to get the teacher's attention, but Mrs Webster was wandering around the room.

'Have you got boobs?' Nicola said.

'No,' said Polina, her skin hot.

'Why are you doing this then?' Nicola mimicked Polina's arms, still folded tightly.

Polina turned her head to look at Nicola, who poked her tongue out.

'All right, find a partner please, girls,' said Mrs Webster.

Nicola took a giant step away from Polina, looking her up and down with exaggerated revulsion. 'No one's going to want to be your partner,' she said, wrinkling her nose. Really quietly she said, 'Can't you afford a proper PE kit?'

'Get out of the way,' said Grace, sighing as she elbowed Nicola hard in the side. 'I'm with Poli.'

'Miss!' said Nicola.

'I wish I had boobs like you,' said Grace to Polina. 'I'd hate to look' (she half turned to Nicola) 'like a really ugly boy.'

3.6: BACK TO SCHOOL – POLINA. FALLING.

Polina unwrapped her corned beef sandwiches from the tinfoil packaging. Grace had forgotten her lunch again but she was on another diet so it didn't matter, and Lisa had already smoked two cigarettes in front of the prefects. The sun had scorched the school field in uneven corn-coloured patches.

'How long have you smoked?' said Polina, watching Lisa's bony fingers hold the cigarette to her lips.

'Years.' Her mouth made a suck sound as she pulled the cigarette out.

'Your mum and dad cool with it?' said Grace. Polina looked at her. Cool?

'I don't give a shit about my dad.'

'What's that?' Grace was pointing to the underside of Lisa's left forearm, facing upwards, a picket fence of off-white scratches.

'Nothing.'

'My parents are separated,' said Polina.

'Great,' said Lisa, pulling the sleeve of her jumper down over her arm.

'I've met her dad, like never,' said Grace.

'I really like your hair,' said Polina to Lisa.

Grace rolled her eyes.

'Shit.' Lisa stubbed the last of her cigarette out on the lid of Polina's lunchbox and cupped a hand over her right eye as if to stop it escaping. 'Something in my eye.'

'Shall I get a teacher?' said Polina, standing, her legs numb with pins and needles.

'Don't be stupid,' said Grace, and to Lisa, 'Just rub it.'

'I think you're supposed to pull the top eyelid over the lower one,' said Polina.

'Stings like fuck,' said Lisa, tugging at her eyelid as though it were rubber. Her mascara made a messy black rivulet down her cheek.

'Maybe it was a fly?' said Polina, wanting very much to stop the mascara's track with her finger.

Under her breath, Grace said: 'Or a drama queen.'

Lisa pulled a dirty green T-shirt out of her bag and balled it up against her eye.

They both watched her for a few seconds in silence then Grace yawned exaggeratedly and raised her eyebrows at Polina. 'Right. Coming?'

'In a minute.'

'Suit yourself.'

She snatched up her bag from the grass and walked away.

Lisa looked in a different direction, watching the horizon. After a while, she got to her feet and brushed herself down. Polina stood too, her heart hammering. She searched for the right thing to say.

'If you want, I could get my mum to wash your T-shirt? She wouldn't mind.'

'No.' Lisa stuffed it roughly back into her bag.

'I wasn't …'

'Why? Because my mum's dead?'

'Is she?'

They looked at each other. Polina didn't want to hear any more now that this was going in the wrong direction. Lisa took a quick step towards Polina, who took one back, but Lisa moved in again and kissed her on the lips for three, four seconds. Polina waited, frozen, to see if it was a joke. Lisa stepped back, her face serious, then she laughed. She never laughed. 'Happy now?'

Afterwards, Polina tried to work out what Lisa meant. In bed, she screwed up her eyes and held her breath to get back to the field. It made her dizzy. Sometimes she almost caught it, the buzz of heat from Lisa's skin, the way the light made them older. Most of all, the earthy smell of wanting: cigarettes, grass, perfume.

—◊—

Grace walked into the changing rooms, hockey boots clacking on the wooden floor.

'Polina? Hurry up! Miss Morgan's really pissed off with you.'

'I'll be there in a minute.'

'Where are you?'

Grace moved towards the toilet cubicles, forcing herself not to hurry. Polina was standing over one of the sinks, next to Lisa, the tap on full and the water splashing over Lisa's bare forearm. Lisa looked ill, as though she had a fever. She and Polina looked up at exactly the same time.

'What's going on?' said Grace.

'Nothing,' said Lisa.

'She's doing an "L",' said Polina, amazed.

Grace saw the razor blade next to the tap, washed clean. She felt the room tilt. She said: 'Miss Morgan's on the warpath.'

That evening, Grace told her dad that Lisa had waved a razor blade in the changing rooms. It's like she's out of control. Her dad called the headmistress at nine o'clock at night and Lisa left the school soon after that.

—◇—

'Can I join the literature club? They meet after school on Wednesdays and there's this form.' Polina dumped her school-bag on the kitchen table, heavy with a hardback book about Sylvia Plath.

Maggie read the form as though it were a death warrant. She sat down hard on a chair and the pine table rocked where it needed another bit of paper wedged under the leg.

'There's a fee.'

'I know. But Mr Davies said ...'

'Would you like me to get a third job to pay for this? Two not enough?'

'Sorry.' Polina went to snatch the form back.

'What is this literature club?' said Maggie. 'Is it absolutely necessary?'

'Not absolutely necessary if you mean do I need it like I need air.' Polina felt the thrill of having gone too far.

'You sound so much like your father,' Maggie said, quietly.

Polina poured boiling water into her mug, ripped open the soup packet, stirred and stirred.

'Do you still see that boy?'

Polina flushed. 'What's that go to do with anything?'

'Whose mother had the hysterectomy?'

'I know who you mean.'

'So you're not seeing him anymore?'

Maggie breathed out hard, sifting through post. She tossed the bills to one side, the rest to the other. There was a postcard.

'Is that from Dad?'

'He's sunning himself on a beach somewhere.'

Maggie forced a tinny laugh. Its pitch bothered Polina.

'Can I look?'

'He used to say money didn't matter. It didn't "motivate" him.'

'Can I see the postcard?'

'Easy to say from a beach in the Seychelles.'

'Is that where he is? Can I see it?'

'It doesn't say anything.'

'Can I –'

Maggie slapped her palm flat on the table, like a belly flop. Polina leaned backwards against the work surface, her hands gripping the edge so tightly she made her knuckles livid.

'He's getting married.'

'Let me see.' Polina made a grab for the postcard but missed. Maggie held it high. 'Mum?'

'You know nothing.' Maggie ripped the postcard in half. That did it.

'Oh yes, run up to your room!' Maggie called after Polina. 'Her name is Kerri-Ann!'

Polina slammed her bedroom door.

'This is real life, Poli. You can't hide.'

It sounded like her mother was torturing chairs down there. Polina got into bed in her clothes and wrapped the duvet around her but she couldn't get warm and she couldn't cry. Maybe Kerri-Ann would be the kind of person who would come and tuck you in, even if you were too old for it. It got dark.

—◊—

Kerri-Ann wasn't a real name, it was a plastic name with fake breasts. Maggie picked up the scissors and snipped through the postcard halves and the scissors made a sound, She put the pieces in the pockets of her cardigan, two each side, the sharp corners poking out.

The way that looked reminded her of a winter afternoon, years ago, when Polina was small, the knobbly, burnt biscuits poking out of her coat pockets because she wanted to take them to school the next day. Together, they'd steamed the kitchen up as they baked, flour clapped into puffs. Howard must have gone, or nearly gone, but on that afternoon it hadn't mattered so long as Maggie could watch Polina being Polina. The memory played itself out with such vitality it made Maggie reach for a chair to steady herself.

She opened the drawer and took out the packet of pills, popping two onto her hand. She closed her mouth around them like a horse taking sugar lumps, then popped out another two and did the same. When the pills stuck in her throat, she turned on the tap and filled a mug with water, tipping her head back as she drank. She tapped the postcard pieces to check they were still there. Later, she might put them in the box where all his letters went, or just throw them away.

Without warning, the scissors on the table looked so dangerous she had to put them in the bin. The air had gone gluey so she dropped the mug from head height, hoping the noise would smash her awake. It hit the ground and shattered pleasingly into large shards like a broken Easter egg. She rearranged the chairs around the table in a different order and, for a while, the physical exertion was satisfying, she forgot herself, but then she got side-tracked by the sound, the squeal-groan each chair made as she moved it. Where had he met Kerri-Ann? How had he found the energy?

She noticed Polina's soup swimming around its cup like vomit, but there wasn't time to think about that now. She stepped over the broken bits of mug, went to the hall and put her coat on, trying not to look in the mirror.

She locked the door and started to walk, then went back to check she'd locked the door. She might ask Bob at the warehouse for two extra hours. Literature club. She could say she was saving for a particular event, a holiday or Christmas, lots of people did that. She nipped back a second time to check the door then worried Polina might think someone was trying to break in. It probably wasn't safe to lock the door from the outside anyway, what if there was a fire? She unlocked the door and now she was definitely going to be late, plus a familiar low-level paranoia was starting to creep its way over her skin. Don't think about Kerri-Ann. These weren't the shoes for hurrying but they were the only good pair she owned; you couldn't go to work in your slippers or your gardening shoes. Kerri-Ann probably had a hundred pairs of shoes.

—◇—

'I'm fucked. I'm going to fail,' said Grace, rolling the waistband of her skirt tighter.

They were walking home from school. It was April pretending to be June.

'Shall we run away?' said Polina.

The first time they ran away was years ago, Polina carefully placing items from their list (her list) into a bag brought from home – baked beans and half a toilet roll – while Grace rammed Sherbet Dip Dabs into every pocket. They were at the bus stop when Polina's mum had driven by, stopped the car, nodded for them to get in.

'If I can't do GCSEs, I'm screwed,' said Grace.

She applied more cherry lip balm and offered it to Polina, who couldn't leave her spot alone. Right in the centre of her chin.

'You're good at art.'

'You're good at everything.' Grace mimed puking.

'I'm not.'

Grace was gazing over the road. The three boys on the other side were older than Grace and Polina but not by much. One of them had a skateboard. He was holding it up to examine its red wheels, pushing them round with his hand. He looked over at Grace from under his cap. Spun the wheels extra fast.

'Go on then,' said Polina to Grace, stinging with the certainty that the boy wasn't interested in her.

Grace was already crossing the road, blowing a bubble. Polina heard her say something that sounded like yeah yeah, and at that moment she would have traded anything to feel what it felt like to be Grace. Just to try it on.

After a few minutes waiting, Polina called out: 'Bye!'

Grace was transfixed or pretending to be transfixed by the boy's cap, which she touched as she spoke. He looked like an insect, all wiry, the legs too long. Polina turned and walked away, ignoring the hollowed-out feeling. Who could fancy an insect?

Grace caught up with her when Polina was nearly home. She was breathless from running, laughing as though she'd just won a race. She was carrying the skateboard.

'Are you going to give that back?' Polina was sharper than she meant to be.

'I think we need to find you a boyfriend,' said Grace.

'I think we don't.'

Grace sighed, tracing the graffiti of names and swirls on the front of the board with her finger. 'He'll come and get it if he wants it that badly.'

They both knew he would.

—◊—

'Bet your mum's never hit you.'

'You said it was just a slap,' said Polina, trying not to think about the look that Maggie gave her when she was really angry, how she worked herself up to it.

A few girls from their school strolled towards the bench in the park where Polina and Grace were sitting. Polina watched them back off when they saw Grace. It made her smile that Grace owned the things that belonged to no one, that was just the way it was, the bench and the space around it.

'Dad gave me this.' Grace held up a five pound note. 'Loser.'

Polina did not remember planning it and yet afterwards she felt responsible. Yesterday, in Boots, they held lipsticks to their mouths and pouted into the tiny mirror, Grace pushing Polina out of the way. All Polina had said was she wished she could afford one. Maybe there had been something extra jittery about Grace – she sometimes got that way when she smoked too much – but the next second she was trying on a pair of round sunglasses from the stand and tapping Polina on the arm. 'Give it here,' she said, taking the lipstick from Polina. Suddenly, she was running full pelt for the exit, so Polina ran too, there wasn't time to think about why, it felt freeing, life was looser with Grace; all you had to do was run.

The tag on the sunglasses made the machine go nuts and Grace got disorientated once they were outside, like she'd forgotten who she was. The bald security guard in the black shirt was heavier with Grace than he needed to be, gripping her shoulders, his B.O. stunning her, and before Polina could think about what she was doing, she had grabbed his fat arm and shouted: 'Get off her!'

Grace used the confusion to struggle free, but he grabbed her by the hair and she grabbed back (later Polina pictured that part over and over because it was so ugly and silly) and Polina thought, wouldn't it be funny if Grace had stolen a wig and it came off in his hands. But then he elbowed Polina in her chest and hefted her backwards so she lost her balance and fell hard onto the shiny, dirty floor of the mall.

Grace called, 'Run!' but Polina didn't run. Her body was a dead weight and, as the numbness wore off, she felt a sharp pain in her coccyx. Grace now had her arms pinioned behind her back by the security guard, who was swearing at her, shaking her for emphasis: 'You whore. What you think you doing? You both as fucking bad.' She laughed the security guard into swearing harder, the serrated edges of his shouting and her laughter making Polina want to stick her fingers in her ears. People had stopped to watch. Polina got to her feet, shakily.

Grace pretending to chew gum made Polina realise how scared she was, even as she said to the security guard: 'So what you going to do with me, sexy?'

'You shut your mouth,' he said, turning on his walkie-talkie.

Grace stopped chewing.

'Is it … Grace? Polina?'

Polina and Grace looked at one another. Grace was still wearing the sunglasses. They didn't suit her at all. Somehow, that was the most embarrassing part.

'What on earth is going on here?' said Caroline's mother.

'Oh, perfect,' said Grace.

—◊—

'Over-reaction or what? They were only sunglasses. And a lipstick. Mum?'

Amy sat with her back to Grace in the lounge. On TV, two bouncing women in matching red T-shirts ran around a muddy field shouting at bric-a-brac, the camera struggling to keep up.

'What's this crap? Mum?'

The only sign she wasn't dead was Amy's breathing.

'Thanks for having an opinion,' Grace said.

Amy was up and across to Grace in a second. 'Here's my opinion,' she said, slapping Grace hard across the face.

They both looked at Amy's hand, then Amy left, a look of panic on her face as though momentarily unsure where the door was. Grace was so surprised she cried, for real, but only for a few seconds until she couldn't sustain it anymore and what was left was mostly admiration for the slap. She felt for some remorse, but it wasn't there.

The front door slamming meant Doug was home and she heard the low buzz of them talking about her in the hall. Grace went to find him in case he tried to find her first. He was in his study, swivelling on a chair with his eyes closed. You had to call it his study or he sulked, but it was just a spare room that smelled of damp, stuffed with two desks, three chairs (one broken), a bookcase and a wonky filing cabinet that didn't shut and which he'd brought home from the tiny office space he shared at work with other driving instructors. She'd been there once, it was horrible. They had a curling old calendar on the wall and each month was a car with a woman sitting on the bonnet. He went deaf when she'd asked about the logistics of emergency stops in a Datsun Cherry when you had Miss July clinging to the front by her buttocks. Green box files sat on top of one another on the blue carpet, stickers on the side of each saying things she didn't ever want to understand like 'Admin II' and '1976-77 outstanding'.

Grace picked up a book from the floor she hadn't seen for years; one of those books for kids about the human body made extra boring to ward off difficult questions. She held it by the spine to see if it still fell open at the penis page, but it didn't. Maybe it had matured while she hadn't. She sighed and waited for Doug to speak but he seemed to have been struck dumb.

'Have you got something in your eyes?' she said.

'Do you need money?' he said, desperately. 'Is that it?'

Grace was so put off by his crying that she wondered for a second what he was talking about. He leaned back in the chair and pushed a hand into his pocket, pulled money out, a ten pound note, two fivers, slapped them on the desk.

'Take the lot.'

'I've got money.' She tried to sound disgusted as she picked up a note quickly. Now he was pulling out coins as well – how much did he have in there? There was something about the ten pences and coppers rolling around on the desk that turned Grace's stomach. There was tissue fluff.

'Stop it, Dad.'

Amy appeared at the door just as Doug started to sob, his head down on the desk.

'Oh God,' Amy said, sounding revolted.

'I love the greenness of it,' said Polina, holding up her ice cream.

In the park, a football team of under-fives in matching lumi-nous vests and too-big shorts ran in different directions away from the ball, and Grace stopped to look at their coach.

'He's older than your dad,' said Polina.

'Look at all that hair.'

'Is hair good?'

'Sehr good,' said Grace.

'That's what I just said.'

They high-fived their current top-three favourite joke.

The coach squatted down to talk to one of the kids, ruffling the boy's hair like dads in films. Grace liked that his hand was large enough, with the fingers splayed, to cover the boy's little head like Lego hair. He glanced across at Grace as he did it. She felt her gut lurch.

'Mine's quite grainy. Is yours?' said Polina.

Grace looked at her own ice cream, bubblegum blue with extra monkey blood.

'If it's ice crystals, we could get salmonella,' said Grace, loudly enough so the ice cream man could hear, but just in case he didn't, she looked back over her shoulder towards his van. 'We might die from these!'

'We live in hope,' he shouted back.

They had a free period. The sun was warm but not warm enough. They found a spot on the grass and lay back. In the clouds, Grace said she saw a goblin, a tampon, a goblin chewing a tampon, an active volcano. Polina, who couldn't just play the fucking game like a normal person, saw foreboding and malevolence. ('Stop trying to make me play it like you play it.' 'What about a cock? Look, there, the balls.' 'I don't see it, Grace.')

In the lull where no one spoke, Grace homed in on the sounds you only hear when you're lying on your back and the sun pools onto your face and you open your eyes a tiny bit, seagulls way off, the faint, reassuring neenaw of a siren. Time elongated itself like caramel in the warmth; she'd had this feeling before, you had to hold onto it for as long as you could, a moment of utter confidence stretching out in front of her. If nothing could go wrong, then just how far could you push your luck?

Polina was now propped up on one elbow, pretending to smoke a buttercup. 'Your freckles have all come out,' she said.

Grace undid the two top buttons on her school shirt to show Polina the freckles on her neck. 'You should get a refund if you're not going to eat the cone,' she said.

Polina held the pointy stump of it on Grace's nose. It smelt sickly sweet like babies. 'When shall we three meet again?' Grace said. She closed her eyes and there was Lisa and the razor blade. 'Did they ever meet again? I hated that play,' she said.

'No because they forgot to synchronise their witches.'

'Lame,' said Grace, smiling.

Polina bit the end from the cone and crunched it, the sound like footsteps on gravel. When Grace opened her eyes, Polina was coming in for another bite, very close. Grace's first thought was: I've won.

Polina's tongue was pointy, the tip of it, neat and warm compared to the blind crashing of a boy's tongue, and Grace wanted to go further, past the noises in the park, past their breathing and the rustling of their school shirts. Why not? Further in, until something changed, the tone of Polina's mouth maybe, if it was still Polina's – it felt like someone else's – metallic like a gun. Polina pulled away suddenly.

'What are you looking at?' she said, in a ragged voice to the two kids who had sneaked up on them.

The one on the bike was sniggering. Polina's hair had come loose and it really suited her. Grace sat up fast and started to tuck her shirt in, her face flushed.

'Are you lezzoids?'

'Bugger off,' said Polina, angrily. Grace looked at her, surprised at her reaction.

Arm in arm on their way home, she felt for words to fill the silence. It was hard to think of any because her mind kept drifting to the underwater feeling of the kiss, so she leaned into Polina more than usual to show her everything was totally, completely the same.

'Why don't we go and see a film soon?' she said, her arm round Polina's waist. It felt like begging. 'Anything. This Saturday, I'll pay.'

'OK.'

'We'll get popcorn.'

'Great.'

They stopped to watch a little dog down a side street straining for a shit. It shuffled in a circle while a man with a comb-over chased it round with a plastic bag. 'Lara!' His Welsh accent was comically strong. 'I'm warning you.' When they looked at each other it almost made things right.

They always hugged outside her front door, but this time they didn't, until they did. Grace felt a tugging sensation under the ribs as she ignored Polina who was ignoring a cobweb in the porch. Fuck this, Grace thought.

'See you tomorrow then?' said Grace. She pushed open the front door and disappeared inside.

—◊—

The new boyfriend was already there and Grace's bedroom smelt stale with smoke and hairspray when Polina arrived. He was wearing Grace's jumper as a scarf and the two of them sat on the bed, their backs against the wall. He was shorter than her. This used to irritate Grace. He kept leaning his head on her shoulder as if he was about to fall asleep.

'I thought we were going to the cinema?' Polina said, her arms folded.

'Yeah,' said Grace.

The new boyfriend smiled to himself without looking at Polina and she wondered how it might feel to smash his head against the wall. She tried an insouciant lean against a shelf, but it wasn't completely successful.

'Are we not going then? I don't care either way but ... .' Polina looked at her watch as if to suggest they might be late, although she had no idea when the film was due to start. If there was a film. She touched her neck, feeling a blush.

'Do you want to go?' Grace asked the new boyfriend, narrowing her eyes at him and smiling.

He offered her a cigarette, which she took, and then he lit it for her and she blew smoke in the air, straight, like a wand. She caught Polina's eye and looked away. It was a scene from the kind of film that Grace and Polina sometimes rented from the video shop just to ridicule.

'You go,' said Grace. And then, coughing, she said, 'Ring me later?'

'Enjoy,' said the new boyfriend, waving.

Grace was stretched out with some boy on the back seat of the car. Polina sat on Nick's lap in the passenger seat. Or Mick's lap. It had been so loud in the club and she couldn't ask his name again. When he smiled, N/Mick's teeth looked like milk-teeth, like the inside of his mouth had forgotten to grow up. When they kissed, she let him feel her breasts over the top of her jumper. Where does kissing end? It was a question she wanted to ask Grace, but she was doing a show with the boy on the back seat, and Polina and N/Mick turned to watch.

It was not so dark that Polina couldn't see N/Mick watching Grace, moving his gaze the full length of her legs from her socks to the tops of her thighs where the skin was the colour of the moon, to the appendix scar, the flash of bra (blue?), her neck, her lips that were right now biting the lips of this boy. Polina could read Grace's mind and it was fine; any minute, she'd stop and wipe her mouth with the back of her hand.

The boy grabbed at Grace and she wasn't fazed, she knew what to do, or didn't look like she didn't, which was practically the same thing. Polina was mesmerized, but there was something else, too, a nagging feeling that lagged just behind.

When the boy shifted his weight so he was almost on top of Grace, she glanced sideways at Polina, feigning something like surprise at being watched going to this new place. Except it wasn't new; Grace had been here before and now that she saw that, Polina knew she'd always known, that her knowing made her complicit in Grace's lie, if you could call it a lie when it wasn't exactly a lie.

Kneeling on the front seat, she felt her breath stop. She couldn't rip her eyes away. When was she supposed to step in?

Grace said something to the boy that Polina didn't hear, although she caught the husky, grown-up tone of it. It scared Polina because it wasn't meant for her and yet she wished it was. The boy faltered, fumbling for something in his pocket, and Polina thought, if that were me, I would have been ready. N/Mick was smoking a cigarette in quick puffs and Polina didn't want to see anymore. The sides were closing in but then, at the last second, Grace put her hands on the boy's shoulders and pushed him back, saying: 'We should have some toast.'

It was directed at Polina.

'What?'

'Toast.'

It was their code word and it was such a surprise, it split the dark sky clean open.

'What's so funny?' the boy said.

But it was too late for all that and when they laughed, she and Grace, it turned everyone back into themselves, so now there was just a car park, the painted spaces worn away, and two girls and two boys in a grubby Cortina with a fir tree lavender air-freshener swinging from its mirror.

—◊—

Ed heard them before he saw them. He stopped dead.

'I've seen this one before,' said Grace.

'Is that the same guy, in this one?' said Polina, her voice low.

'Course it's the same. Same arse.'

'Is that your mum?'

'No. Is it? I don't know, it's too grainy. That's definitely not Dad.' Grace pointed.

They'd found his Polaroid photographs. What had they been doing poking about in his wardrobe? They peered at the photo for a long time, tilting their heads. If they turned, they'd see him, but they were too engrossed. He knew exactly which one they were looking at and he couldn't breathe. If it had just been Grace, he'd have ripped it from her hand, but his head was throbbing as he backed away from the door, his body not his. It felt as though he was watching himself as he tiptoed exaggeratedly to a point halfway down the stairs, his rucksack still over his shoulder like a pantomime burglar with a swag bag. He could still remember the secret language of each creak and how he'd once jumped thirteen, a record, and the excruciating jarring pain that mashed you up like glass from your heels to the back of your neck, even when you bent your knees. If you survived that you were invincible.

At stair seven, he was back inside his body, so he stopped and reached back with one hand into the zipped side pocket of his rucksack. Make it all better, he willed the cheery little yellow pill that was nestling in there.

'But where are you from originally?'

In the lounge, Doug was still interrogating Ed's mate, Jonty.

'Like I said, London.'

'Brixton?'

'Doug, will you come in the kitchen and check on the beef for me,' Amy called.

'Fancy a beer?' said Ed to Jonty.

His face felt heavy as a mask. Maybe Grace wouldn't say anything? Course she would. His appetite had disappeared and a bass line of anxiety reverberated in his ears. He leaned towards Jonty. 'I took an E but there's one left for you,' he whispered.

Before he could get to the fridge, Grace appeared at the bottom of the stairs, followed by Polina.

'Hey, Ed, taken any photos recen … Hello. Hi.'

Grace stopped in mid-flow on her way to hug Ed. Her voice dropped into what Ed presumed was her sexy register.

'Who are you?' she said.

'This is Jonty, from the band,' said Ed, trying to sound relaxed. He couldn't look at them, so he looked at Jonty. 'Jonty came over on a banana boat originally.'

'Yeah?' said Grace, looking Jonty up and down.

Jonty held up his middle finger to Ed. Just as Ed was wondering whether the ecstasy tablet was a dud, its effects started to unfurl very gently so that Jonty's finger wasn't Jonty's finger but a beckoning in reverse, a tendril of hope and energy that alerted Ed to new possibilities. Like, he could encourage Grace's attraction to Jonty to distract her from the photos! Polina was looking at him, alertly, as if memorising him.

'Are you all right?' she said.

A remarkable phenomenon occurred. She became completely transparent. Literally see-through. This hadn't happened to Jonty or Grace – a good thing – nor (he looked down to his feet) to him. He could have passed a hand behind her and counted his fingers. He peeked inside her, fascinated and a little shy, his gaze moving through her beaming white ribs which caged her canary heart, chirruping, down to the lungs, the colour of clay, stretching and slackening, down further to a humming pipework of intestines. Braver, he stared at the hidden machinery of her, all the dripping, ticking parts, blood whizzing around arteries like bullet trains. Were you allowed to watch the internal workings of a woman? Was it prurience?

Was it anything like having sex with someone who was asleep? He made himself look away just in case and, when he glanced back, she was all sealed up again and he smiled his warmest smile as a thank you.

He remembered his plan. Clearing his throat, he almost forgot his plan again, thrilled by the memory of Polina's insides.

'Jonty's a great guy, Grace.'

He smacked Jonty very hard on the back a few times, raising his voice. 'You're going to love him. You'll really love him. He's really great.'

Jonty touched Ed's forehead with the flat of his palm as if checking his temperature. Ed laughed at this very funny thing that Jonty was doing and saw Polina stifle a smile. She'd better not fancy Jonty too.

'Hey!' he said, pointing at her in a mock telling off.

They were back in the lounge and Ed was on the sofa, stretched out with a beer in his hand. He wiggled his toes. Who took time out to look at their toes anymore? Ten perfect digits on the end of his feet. He didn't exactly remember how he had got there but that was how memories were supposed to be, all the mundane stuff cut away and just the good bits showing, the love and the friends you love and your sister and especially your sister's friend. There was a lot of noise coming from the kitchen, pots banging and doors slamming, the symphony of his home. Ed was about to comment on it but Polina was saying something to him. 'I said, what's your band called? For the third time.' She was wearing a pale green top over leggings. A toe-ring and painted toenails. Her clothes looked grateful to be wearing her.

'Can I get you another beer?' said Grace to Jonty.

Were Ed's parents even in the house anymore? They seemed to have been gone for days.

'Ladywell Fox,' said Ed, pushing himself up on the sofa.

He really wanted to touch Polina's cheek but stopped himself. He wanted to ask her to dance. He had a great little melody in his head right now, the kind of thing girls liked. 'We're jazz funk. We're doing gigs in London.'

His feelings were fogging the air and he couldn't see properly, so he closed his eyes for a few seconds. We're a jazz/funk outfit? Was that better? 'We're kind of a jazz slash fuck band. You should come to a gig.'

'OK,' said Polina, smiling.

'Yeah!'

'I think the oven's faulty,' said Amy, marching into the lounge, her cheeks red.

Ed was finding it difficult not to slide off the sofa.

'There she is! Mother!' He clapped.

He thought he might weep with the strength of the love he felt for his mum at that moment. He got up so that he could hug her but as he stumbled towards her, she took a step back, apparently horrified. Thinking she was only pretending, Ed played along, doing a zombie face and holding his arms outstretched, hands turned down at the wrist.

'He probably needs some food,' said Polina, looking almost as surprised as Amy. 'Right, Ed?'

He really tried but he couldn't keep a straight face. 'Ten marks to Brainy!'

'Where's his rucksack?' said Jonty. 'I need to get something from it.'

'Can I have one?' said Grace.

Ed didn't want Amy to feel as uptight as she looked. If she danced it might loosen some of that tension in her; the house should have a little shimmy.

'So, the meat looks a little tiny bit overdone to me,' Amy said, not looking at Ed. 'I might have to get the man back in to look at the thermostat. Is it hot in here?' She pointed to Ed. 'He looks very warm.'

'Let the meat go, Mum,' said Ed. 'Do you want to do a dance?' He waggled his shoulders to demonstrate the fun dance they might do together. 'I'm serious.'

'We might not be staying for dinner, actually,' said Grace.

'But your brother and his friend are here,' said Amy.

Ed moved from side to side to show them what a party looked like.

'My brother and his friend? Here?' said Grace, sarcastically.

'Maybe we can stay,' said Polina. 'I don't mind.'

She was gorgeous. And wise. And troubled. An implosion of good intentions, he thought, like a demolished tower block falling in on itself very politely, straight down through the earth. He wanted to show her he understood. His own family was all about the outside, explosions and big bangs. That meant they were both as lost as each other, and he should tell her. In words. He would say: 'You are the centre of my maze and I am the centre of yours.' But he'd got caught out that way before, saying things that turned out to be bollocks. What if she followed wool all the way to the centre of him and there was nothing there? She'd be left holding a big ball of disappointing wool. Or worse, what if a stranger lurked there at his core, sick, cynical, telling people what he already knew: He isn't worth it. He swallowed. His heartbeat was getting faster, biting chunks from his chest.

'It's cranking me up, Jonty,' he said, touching his chest with his right hand. 'I can feel it. I think I want it!'

'Yeah,' said Jonty.

'I really wish I understood what everyone was talking about,' said Amy.

Ed stopped dancing. He felt so sorry for Amy, standing underneath the force of their youth, getting drenched. What could you do in the face of all that rushing energy? You couldn't fight it. Was this what it was like to be a parent?

From nowhere and with perfect clarity, his hand still on his heart, he saw a version of himself in the future, sharp and crisp like a promise, a panoramic view through an arch. He was holding his hands up and laughing as if to say I give in, then he was bent over with his palms pressed to his legs, exhausted, his future children way ahead of him, running, knees high, not looking back. The sun was setting so orange and bright that he had to squint just to see their outlines through splintered shards of light. Or perhaps he was crying. The pride he felt in their lunatic courage spread like ink spilled on blotting paper and he wanted to sing to them, hard and loud, so they would hear how much he loved them. But with this came awful, exquisite pain because they didn't look back. Not once. Which was exactly as it should be, as he wanted it to be. Even so. He couldn't remember ever having had such a hit of the rightness of himself, existing somewhere ahead, his children waiting to tether him to life. The feeling was palpable like thirst. He realised he was incredibly thirsty. He really needed some water.

'Shall we all have a big glass of water?' he said.

'The beef's fucked!' shouted Doug from the kitchen.

'Do you like Chinese food, Jonty?' said Amy, quickly. 'Come on, our treat.'

Ed laughed, holding his arms wide to show Jonty his life.

'Do you boys, like, share a flat?' said Grace, directing the question at Jonty. She might as well have licked her lips.

'I am between accommodations,' Jonty said, enigmatically.

Grace and Polina stayed for dinner after all. It seemed like hours before they finally ate. They sat in the lounge, silver cartons of Chinese food spread over the carpet. Doug insisted on having the television on, the sound turned down. He wasn't watching but shushed if anyone talked above a whisper. Ed wasn't certain, but he thought the programme they weren't watching was a documentary about testing on animals because masked men were running about in silence throwing bricks at the windows of 1950s' buildings. Curling barbed wire adorned the tops of walls like doodles as the scene cut to a rabbit in a tiny cage, its eyes bubblegum pink, and then to a scientist in a white coat was doing an interview straight to camera. Ed found it intensely disturbing. He told himself the rabbit was not doing the interview to camera. But it was.

'Bastard,' said Doug, struggling with the cork on the bottle of wine he was holding between his legs.

'This rib is incredible,' said Jonty, his eyes closed, leaning back in an armchair.

Ed was sure Jonty must have taken the other E. Who loves a spare rib that much? Plus, they couldn't all be spares. Ed looked at the rib as Jonty gnawed its edges. It looked all ragged and sorry for itself, like Jesus.

'How's the music shop going?' Polina asked.

Ed did an expansive thumbs-up sign at Polina and held it for quite a while, aware that this was deeply unattractive but unable to stop. His head felt very heavy. He was still feeling a strong compulsion to dance, but very slowly, and he imagined himself at a school disco, doing a slow dance at the end with Polina to 'China In Your Hand', the two of them entirely complicit in the irony of the scene. You had to be careful because it was one of those cheeky songs that you thought had finished when it hadn't. They would know, though, and he would hold still as other boys, relieved it was over, pulled away, only to be grabbed again when the music came back.

'He'd be earning decent money by now,' said Doug, still tugging at the corkscrew. 'If he wasn't a dropout.'

Amy held a hand up as if to say stop. 'He's an artist.'

'He's a piss artist.'

'I'm here. I can hear you,' said Ed.

Grace turned to Jonty. 'Try some of the noodles, they're really good too.'

'We gloss over failure in this family, do we? Yes! You fucker!' The cork made a pop sound as it finally came free.

'You should know, darling,' said Amy.

Doug wobbled a little as he raised his glass to the air, drank from it and then became transfixed by the television screen. However high you got, Ed thought, it was never high enough to get away from him.

Then Polina said: 'I think it's nice you and Jonty are a couple.'

Ed coughed, which turned into choking and, next thing, he was pointing to his back, struggling for breath, eyes streaming. Grace tutted and thumped him half-heartedly, while Polina was over to him quickly with a glass of water.

Doug put his wine glass down and the base made a deep red incomplete O on the carpet. 'He's black,' he said to Amy in an urgent whisper.

'So?'

'God,' said Ed, wheezing.

'You're bi though, right?' said Grace to Jonty.

'I'm so sorry,' said Polina, looking to Ed as though she were about to cry.

'I'm not gay,' said Ed, weakly.

'I got it all wrong about the photos.'

'What photos?' said Doug, pressing the off button on the television.

'Nothing,' Ed and Polina blurted at the same time. They looked at each other.

'Ed – are you gay?' said Amy.

She pronounced each word with the urgency and volume of a paramedic trying to pull a victim back from the brink of unconsciousness.

'Ed – are you deaf?' said Grace.

Jonty laughed, a boom that made the ground shake.

'What photos?' said Doug, standing, unsteady on his feet. 'If there's gay porn in this house, I want to see it.'

Jonty laughed again, boom. Doug turned on him and you could tell he was grateful to have something to be furious with him about.

'If you and him are – bumming,' he said.

'Calm down, Dad,' said Grace.

'I ain't no bender,' said Jonty, holding up his hands.

'Where are the fucking photos?'

—◊—

Chinese burns hurt for a whole day. The second time Grace waits until Ed is out.

He's hidden it on page twenty-seven of *Space Station Seventh Grade* which smells of jumble sales. She reads it three times and then again, slower. It still makes no sense and the photograph that was there has disappeared: a tree, two people underneath it, a man and a woman.

Similarities of Facial Features To Mine Out Of Ten
(Plus Observations)
Feb – man one: 3/10 (suave but wispy hair)
March – man two: no score (inconclusive)
Late April – man three: no score (can't tell if man)
May & June – man four: 9/10 (numerous sightings. Old? Sometimes punches air when laughs. So do I!! Mum v close. Shows chemistry)

—◊—

3.9: PHOTOS OF MEN.

Doug was already upstairs, swearing and knocking things over. He ran down with the shoebox in his hand.

'Photos of men!' he said, sounding triumphant. 'So, who's this then? Huh?' He held out one of the photos towards Ed. 'Look at it. You took it. You must know who these people are.'

Everyone looked at Ed. It was a very bad dream. His brain was working hard. Even Jonty looked miffed.

'Well?' said Doug. 'What about this? These are disgusting.'

He let them fall to the floor, one by one.

'They're not disgusting, Dad,' said Grace.

'Homosexuality is absolutely disgusting,' said Doug.

'Well, that's helpful,' said Amy. 'Can I see?' She grabbed at the one Doug was holding in his hand. 'This is me.' She stopped.

'I thought one of them might be my real dad,' said Ed, looking at the carpet. 'I was a kid.'

'You followed me?' said Amy.

'I thought you might be going to meet him. It was a long time ago.' His voice cracked. It didn't feel like a long time ago.

'So, you're not gay?' said Doug, rolling his eyes at Jonty as if expecting to find solidarity with him.

Jonty leaned back in his chair and fixed his gaze on Doug. Serve you right, Ed thought. He didn't want to think about why Doug's reaction mattered so much.

'Let's put these away, shall we,' said Amy, already on her knees trying to stuff the photos back into the shoebox.

'I'm going back to London,' Ed said.

'I'm sorry,' said Polina, reaching an arm towards him. They weren't close enough to touch.

'Fuck off,' Ed said.

'It's not her fault,' said Grace.

Ed watched his mother jamming down the lid on the box as though she were wrestling an animal. She glanced up at him and he thought he saw from her expression that he'd been right about one of the men. It was years ago, just before he stopped the investigations because they made things worse. For weeks, she met the same man at the same time. Sometimes they sat under a tree in the field where all the kids from the bad school went to smoke. They never kissed, or not that Ed saw. They didn't have to. Watching them talk was like watching them kiss. He didn't say anything in case the man was his father and they were planning to get back together, and for a long time he felt sure this would happen.

'Are you never going to tell me, Mum?' he said, so quietly he wondered whether he'd actually said it out loud.

All the warmth of the ecstasy was gone. He was shivering.

Doug said: 'Nothing to tell. He's dead.'

Amy looked sharply at Doug. 'We don't know that.'

'Dead to me.'

Ed closed his eyes. He saw secrets spilling like scree and Amy trying to pile them back.

—◊—

3.10: POLINA – UNIVERSITY.

The boat race was a drinking game in which two teams stood in rows and drank bright blue alcohol from two vats as quickly as possible. The men were sweaty, their hair standing up in damp clumps, and everyone was shouting, the acoustics making the noise echo like a swimming-pool. Polina drank as much of the blue liquid as she could stomach despite its harsh, sugary burn, and every day of fresher's week she woke wondering when it was going to get fun.

After the drinking game, she went to the college bar and talked to anyone and smoked cigarettes sold individually by the barman, who lit matches for you on a brick.

'The first pint you neck, the second you savour,' Simon said. They were on their third. He smiled a big open smile at her and in that moment it made things better. 'To Us!'

Cigarette smoke hung about the room like dirty sheets and condensation dripped from the wood-panelled ceiling. Someone shouted what sounded like his A level results at Polina, ('So I'm like history and maths, A! A! Also a *something she couldn't hear properly* and I'm saying "what?" A fucking A!') and he patted her arse as you might pat a nervous horse.

A girl was on her knees, laughing into the crotch of a startled looking second year called Bob or Rob, while Polina stood still, looking around her and holding a drink in the air so no one crashed into it. Grace would be fluent in all this if she were here. The jukebox played 'Love Shack' and a girl Polina recognised from her tutorial group danced slowly on the pool table with her eyes closed while two boys tried to pot balls.

When the bar closed, Simon said: 'Let's get out of here.'

'I turn into a bumkin at minnight,' Polina said.

'I'd like to see that.'

They went back to Polina's room and she showed him the view from her bedroom window. Alleyway. Dustbins. Dog shit. She showed everyone this view, it was so depressing it was funny. A week ago, on her first day, while her mum was still with her, making and remaking her bed, a shiny-haired young woman in a huge primary-coloured stripy jumper had bounced in to introduce herself. Polina remembered the moment as like being hit very hard with a rainbow.

'I'm Jackie,' the woman had said, too keen, smelling of goodness and soap.

'Look at this,' Polina said, irritated immediately by Jackie's exuberance, but mainly by her jumper, and wanting to silence them both. Jackie had looked at the view without speaking.

'I don't have coffee,' she said to Simon, feeling suddenly queasy and tired, all the excitement she'd faked catching up with her. She filled the kettle from the tiny sink in the corner of her room.

'That's some view,' Simon said.

'You do maths, don't you?'

'No.'

After the small talk, they kissed. She felt nothing very much. She still held the kettle in one hand and had an image she couldn't shift of her mouth as a plug socket that Simon was trying to fill with his tongue to make the kettle boil. He opened his mouth too wide and every time they stopped, Polina wanted to gulp air. She felt him struggling behind her back with her bra strap, so she leaned down to put the kettle on the carpet, stood and undid the strap. They fell onto the bed with him on top of her, grabbing at the belt of his jeans, the shiny silver buckle with its cowboy motif digging into her belly. She noticed that his plum coloured Y-fronts were almost the same colour as the mystery stain she had recently discovered on the wall behind her bed. Blood? Wine? Would it ever come off?

'I've got to sleep,' she said.

Simon stopped moving as though someone just turned the music off and got up without looking at her, trying to rebuckle his jeans, roughly, the exertion making his face go red until he gave up and gripped the jeans at the front to hold them up. With the other hand, he scooped up his trainers from the floor and slammed the door behind him.

3.11: MAGGIE IS COPING WELL WITH POLINA BEING AWAY AND DEFINITELY NO LONGER MAKES ENDLESS TO DO LISTS …
3.11.1: NB NOR DOES SHE WONDER WHO IS GOING TO LOOK AFTER HER NOW.

To do
1. *Go for brisk walk and swing arms.*
2. *Might be gland. Nine times out of ten.*
3. *Call P? Casual.*
4. *Do not agree to more coffee mornings even if Gloria says not churchy.*

—◊—

3.12: POLINA/JEN.

Polina's boot made a dirty leaf print on the invitation she picked up from the floor: JEN WESTON. YOU ARE CODIALLY INVITED TO THE LES-BI-GAY BALL. DRESS CODE OUTRAGEOUS!

Polina's pigeonhole was empty. She put the invitation in it and took a step back to look. A couple of students ran down the stairs towards her, shouting at one another, 'Yeah, which is nothing compared to Matt!'

'Er – Matt who?!'

She quickly took the invitation out and put it in the right pigeonhole next to hers.

—◊—

'How was the ball?'

'Amazing,' said Jen, looking up. 'Were you there?'

'I couldn't make it,' said Polina, picking up a leaflet without looking at it from the table Jen was manning. 'This looks good, I might join this.' She shook it.

Jen looked at the leaflet and at Polina. 'You sure?'

'Yes,' said Polina, decisively.

Jen was taller than Polina had imagined her to be, but she'd got the hair just about right, dark red and seemingly manufacturing its own wiry curls like a Slinky going down stairs.

Polina looked properly at the leaflet. It was on vivisection.

'Hey!'

Jen's lopsided smile was directed at the woman standing behind Polina, a come-on and a back-off. Polina let herself think for a moment how it might feel to have that complicated smile directed at her. They were talking now, Jen and this girl; how would it be if she cut them off with a joke? Something about vivisection? Where were all the vivisection jokes when you needed them? A few minutes later, the little crowd dispersed, leaving just her and Jen. From nowhere, she remembered Lisa from school who died on a skiing trip in Val d'Isere. It was in the *County Press*. How that news had hurt so much because Polina had no idea that Lisa could even ski.

'You OK?' said Jen, counting names on the petition.

'Can you ski?'

—◊—

The lecture theatre was freezing. Polina couldn't take her eyes off Dr Manniford who kept himself warm with numerous tics that contorted his face as he spoke. Did he know he was doing it?

Her notes said: *Predetermined or is sex just boring with boys?*

'In law, as in life, it is human nature to be interested in causation,' said Dr Manniford, raising and lowering his brow.

Polina looked up. This was supposed to be on breach. Causation was next week. Did it matter? No one else seemed to think so. While she thought about that, she wrote Jen's name on her notes and looked at it, made the J bigger then scribbled it out.

'A man walked into a hospital complaining of stomach pains.'

Dr Manniford winced, his face haunted by its exertions like a hollow-eyed Russian gymnast. Along the row, Neil blew Polina a kiss and she blew one back, noticing that today he wore pyjamas under his duffel coat – it must have been a late night – and a black feather boa wrapped once around his neck and tossed over a shoulder.

'He was not examined by the casualty doctor. He was sent home by a nurse and advised to see his GP in the morning if his condition had not improved, but he did not see his GP in the morning or at all. Why? Because he died that night from arsenic poisoning.'

Polina blew warm breath into her hands. This revelation seemed to affect Dr Manniford as though he himself had just been poisoned, possibly by treacherous students. Something about him reminded her of her mother. Call mum, she wrote.

'Medical evidence revealed that the condition was so advanced that even the most thorough examination would have come too late to save this man. Was the doctor in breach of his duty to this patient? Undoubtedly. But did that breach cause the man's loss?'

Polina unfolded Neil's note when it reached her. COFFEE? COPPER POT? They escaped just as Dr Manniford was beginning an ill-advised joke in a terrible cockney accent about teenagers complaining they hadn't asked to be born.

She wanted to have changed at some chemical level, for the change to be as obvious and as startling as liquid to solid. But after a term away she was still sliding about inside herself, unsure of her footing. Polina felt nauseous with a kind of lust for home, but sickened by the thought of three weeks stuck here. What was wrong with her? Couldn't you ever just leave?

Polina drove past the line of shops, exactly the same as they'd always been. It was like driving past a photograph of a memory, an unreliable, irretrievable proof of who you were. It was a sensation so heavy she had to put the radio on.

The shop that got her was the one with tinted yellow cellophane stretched across the inside of its window like a huge sweet wrapper, the one selling flesh-coloured underwear to women whose flesh was not that colour. No one's flesh was that colour. The dummy was still there. There was the dusty shop with the fake gold jewellery and trinket boxes and incense sticks (WALK IN PLEASE, WALK OUT PLEASED!), the chemist with its odd-tasting lollipops, the only sweets in the shop, apart from those packets of powdery dextrose tablets that Grace once shotgunned between cigarettes when she was on a health kick.

She looked in the window of the café where she used to write love letters to Sting and drove past two bars to see who was drinking at noon.

She pulled up at Grace's house. They hadn't seen each other since Polina left and Grace didn't. It had only been eight weeks. Nothing could go wrong in eight weeks.

The shops were nothing compared to the tremor when Polina arrived home and there was her mother, standing like she always did, slightly thinner perhaps, hands on her hips, trying not to smile. Until she blinked, Polina's mother's mouth looked wrong, slightly off-kilter as though she was an impostor doing a convincing impersonation.

They looked at each other and Polina tried to hide the long-ing and dread that chose that moment to bloom like a lie all the way up her neck and over her face. To cover her confu-sion, Maggie stepped forward and opened her arms and Polina breathed in the scent of her mother's neck, a palimpsest so familiar it was as difficult to describe as your own smell – soap, peanuts, lime, disappointment, vanilla – layer on layer of it. Home. At first the hug made them inarticulate. Shy.

'I don't take milk in tea anymore.'

'I'm losing you,' said Maggie.

'Can I borrow the car?'

They hadn't exactly arranged to meet up, Polina and Grace. The car seemed to make the decision all by itself. Polina smiled at the cobweb that had been swinging in Grace's porch for twenty years.

'Ed! Hello.'

'Gran's ill. They're all at the hospital.'

'But not you?'

'I left when they arrived.'

He held up a bottle of wine.

'I like the beard,' Polina said.

'Thanks,' Ed said, blushing under it, pouring. 'I like yours.'

Another bottle after the first one was just joining the dots. Food would have been a good idea. When had it got dark?

'She's ninety-six, I'm twenty-six,' Ed said, although Polina didn't remember asking. He shook his head. 'All those years.'

At some point, Polina must have said: 'University's so lonely.' And she laughed to fill the silence and couldn't stop.

'You still haven't come to a gig,' Ed said.

'"All those years"!'

'Sorry. Aysha says I should stop at the point where poetry butts bollocks.' Ed steepled his hands to demonstrate. 'Bollockry.'

'Who's Aysha?'

She knew, and she was sure he did too, that the line they crossed wasn't later when they fucked standing up in the beach hut – no room to swing a cat, they said at the same time, to cover their surprise, or else neither of them said it at all – but here, much earlier, when all options were still on the table, before the table was even laid, when he said I'm sorry you're lonely and she forgot to say something back.

She and Grace discovered the unlocked beach hut years ago. Down near the old pier where the tramps and their dogs hung out. You could be there in half an hour if you ran some of the way. Teenagers rediscovered it every year, which would explain the salty spunk smell of the woodwork, the empty beer cans and the single-ring gas stove broken on the floor. Ed tried the door and it gave. It was like sitting in a doll's house and Polina remembered her doll's house, the musty smell of it, how sad it always made her, one of the reasons she'd loved it. She may have tried to tell Ed but, if she did, it was only nerves. He asked if he could kiss her – who asks? So sweet – and she thought, have we done it or are we about to?

'I had an Action Man,' he said. 'I loved every limb of him.'

'I wasn't allowed one.'

'Did you want one?'

'Doesn't everyone?'

He kissed her again and she tried, she really tried but it was nothing like being kissed by a girl. The third bottle tipped over. She heard it go and imagined it spinning, pointing first at her and then at Ed. Maybe not Ed. He did everything right with his hands and they barely shook at all. Polina couldn't look at him and he didn't ask her to. She felt him try to laugh with her at the absurdity of it all but she'd left it too late for laughing and he was already sunk, you could tell, so she stopped in case he thought she was laughing at him. She concentrated instead on the business of being fucked in a beach hut and managed it so well that when he pulled back to ask if she was OK, she meant it when she said: 'I'm so close.'

—◊—

'You look very pale.'

'Grace's gran died in the night,' said Polina.

She curled and released her toes, feeling the grains of sand irritating the skin between them.

'I thought it must have been something like that. When you didn't ring,' said Maggie, putting one of Polina's jumpers on a hanger.

The smell of ironing slowed everything down and Polina tried not to think about Ed.

'She was ninety-six,' said Polina.

Maggie shrugged.

'I'm sorry I didn't ring.'

The thing with my mother, Polina had told Ed, she waits and waits for the sun to come out and when it does she says she can taste rain. Ed hadn't laughed. Polina thought: he thinks I'm describing myself.

The iron went *sssssss*.

—◊—

DOUG and AMY's bedroom. DOUG is sitting on the end of the bed wearing only pants and socks, staring into space.

                    AMY
    She was old, Doug.

                    GRACE
    (Opening door.) Mum, there are –
    Jesus, Dad.

                    AMY
    Your father's upset.

                    GRACE
      (Still staring.)

                    AMY
      Go and take the lids off the Tup-
      perware.

                    GRACE
      There are people in the lounge.

                    DOUG
      (In "Godfather" scraped voice.)
      This is very difficult for me.

                    —◊—

In hearse.

                    DOUG
      It's disrespectful.

                    ED
      I don't have another suit.

                    AMY
      His tie's black.

                    DOUG
      Look at these. (Hold up hands.
      Shaking.)

                    ED
      I expect you need a drink.

                    DOUG
Stop the car! (Holding throat and
trying to get up.)

                    AMY
He's hyperventilating. Does anyone
have a paper bag?

                    GRACE
I have a plastic one?

                    AMY
Can we just drop the sarcasm,
Grace?

                    GRACE
Take his side like you always do.

                    AMY
I'm not taking anyone's side.

                    GRACE
(Quietly.) Your other speciality.

                    DOUG
(Viciously.) How would any of you
know how this feels?

                    ED
(Very quietly.) Fuck. You.

                    GRACE
Can't we go any faster?

                    —◊—

At the crematorium.

A MALE RELATIVE
(Shaking DOUG's hand.) I lost my
own mother when I was a boy. As you
know. I was nine.

DOUG
Right but in some ways this is
tougher.

AMY
Let's go in, Doug.

DOUG
I can't be rushed.

AMY
They want to start.

DOUG
They won't start without me.

—◇—

Funeral service has started.

VICAR
I'd now like to invite Rose's son,
Doug, to read a tribute he's com-
posed himself.

DOUG
(Moving into place. Opening his
piece of paper which is folded

many times. Smoothing it. Looking at the audience. Taking a deep
breath.) When. (Pausing.) When I
was. (Shakes his head.)

                    AMY
Do you want Grace to do it?

                    GRACE
(Reacting.)

                    DOUG
When I was a boy. No. (Breaking
down.)

                    ED
(Moving to DOUG's side and taking
the piece of paper. Scanning it,
then reading without looking up.)
When I was a boy, it was mum who
was there for me, she loved me, and
I can be difficult to love. (A little laughter.) Having been blessed
with a family of my own – my wife,
Amy, our children, Ed and Grace – I
know mum was as proud a mother-in-
law and grandmother as she was a
mother. This is a sad day for us
all but it's also a day to celebrate
the long, happy life of Rose Mullin, my spunky and spirited mother.
We will miss you so much.

                    AMY
Doug, that was quite moving.

> GRACE
> (Grabbing paper from ED's hand be-
> fore he can stop her.) Spunky?

'"Vol-au-vent" means windy vole. I bet they don't teach you that at Cambridge.'

Grace held a tray out to Polina. The air in their house was looser now the funeral was done, old people's perfume hovering in invisible puffs.

'Your mum didn't make them, did she?'

'Course not.'

They still hadn't seen each other properly since Polina came home for the holidays and Gran messed up their plans by dying.

Polina took another one. 'Mm, vole,' she said.

A white wine belch burned its way up her neck as Grace tried to decide what it was that was getting to her about Polina. Maybe it was the smug way she was sipping sherry from a tiny glass, which made Grace want to knock it from her hand, or maybe it was nothing, just the awkwardness you get when you haven't seen someone for a while, even your best friend.

'So?' said Polina.

'You can fuck off if you think we're doing small talk, Pols.'

'What did I do?' Polina took a small step back.

'Do you have to drink sherry like that?'

'Like what?'

They both looked at the glass in Polina's hand. She stuck her little finger out. 'Is this better?'

Grace's laugh came out as a single cough. 'Much better.'

Ed was piling his plate too high and not looking over at them so hard it was like a poke.

'Look at him, still love-struck after all these years.'

'Is he?' said Polina, looking at her fingers.

'Oh, come off it. He still thinks he's got a chance with you.

126

Isn't that sweet? Isn't he just like a peach you have to squash a bit but now it's all bruised? Like a puppy?'

Polina took yet another vol-au-vent. 'I think he's just upset about your gran.'

Grace put the tray down, moved it out of Polina's reach and took a piece of paper from the waistband of her skirt. Maybe she's got an eating disorder, she thought.

'What's this?' said Polina, smoothing out the paper.

'Dad's speech.'

'"When I was a boy – give an example." Is that it?'

'Ed made it all up on the spot,' said Grace. 'What a hero.'

Grace saw Polina's expression change. Something dropping and being reeled back in super-fast.

'What's up with you?' said Grace. 'Is it bulimia? I won't tell.'

'Nothing's wrong.'

Grace looked at her.

'I miss you,' said Polina.

'So why did you leave me here to rot?'

We should have had more children, Maggie thought as she pulled a book, *The Secret History*, from the library shelf and examined its front cover. It might have soldered things together or soured them more quickly. It might have given me more time before they left home. It was a thought she taunted herself with, now and then.

One child was difficult enough and two or three would have been two or three times more difficult. What if she'd had three like Polina; secretive, clever, scared? When you breathed life into your children didn't you condemn them to inhale your life too? She had heard somewhere that you were only as happy as your unhappiest child and she had one unhappy child. They should have had more.

Maggie looked along the row for another book to go with

the first, something more upbeat. Granted, most parents didn't have spare children in case the tyre burst on the first. Howard would have been happier with more. She used to imagine him hanging them about himself like accessories, showing them off and pretending to complain, 'My brood!' And then handing them back when something shinier caught his eye, a glint of the romance his own marriage lacked reflected in the window of some other woman's life. What do you want me to say? You pushed me away and she pulled.

'Just these two Maggie?'

'Please.'

'How's Polina doing? You must be so proud.'

'Yes.'

'We missed you at the coffee morning. You should come to another one.'

Maggie fixed her face into a smile aimed at the desk.

'It's church but we're not churchy,' said Gloria. 'We discuss all sorts.'

Maggie nodded as she put the books into her string bag.

'Geoff asked after you,' said Gloria, lowering her numerous chins conspiratorially.

'I'll come along.'

'I'll drop a card in, shall I?'

Outside, it was one of those misty days that confuses things. Sparrows bickered on top of the balding privet hedge that ran alongside the path from the library to the road. A car beeped its horn and when Maggie looked up, there was Doug waving at her from the passenger seat of a car being driven by one of his learners. He wasn't ageing well.

She read that if you smiled a fake smile, it tricked the body into producing the same hormones as if the smile was real. And yet she felt terrible.

'Maggie!'

Maggie was still beaming as she turned to see Gloria wobbling along the path.

'I found one of our cards. The next one's a week on Wednesday. Here we are.'

'Super.'

Maggie took the card and gave it all her attention.

'Are you all right, Maggie? You don't look very well.'

'I'm fine.'

'Says I,' said Gloria, still wheezing a little from the exertion. 'My husband says I have the body of a twenty year old. "Give it back," he says. "You're making it all wrinkly." He got that line from a greetings card, he thinks I don't know.'

'Oh. Yes.'

Maggie sat on a bench in the park. The plaque said: *For Joan, who never made it to the moon.* It was where she and Howard had sat on the day he told her she was brittle. Does that mean frigid? She looked at the string bag on the seat beside her and considered pulling out a book, but it was too cold for reading. He'd said she was less fun these days, and he phrased it like a question, upturned at the end like the nose of the woman he left her for. Whom Maggie followed once or twice. (Upturned noses had more fun.) All she and Howard could do by then was ask each other questions. They piled up.

'Less fun?'

'Can't you see it?' he'd said.

'See what?'

'Is this what you want?'

Maggie felt a pain, sharp as a stitch. Not a heart attack, although it stabbed her in the chest, more like a needle, a knitting needle, pushing through her skin from the inside out. She put her hand to her heart, half expecting to feel the needle's tip. This wasn't the first time. The sensation was always so shocking and so excruciating it made the world shrink, so that she was a giant in terrible pain and it was all she could do not to call for help.

She straitjacketed her arms around herself as she stared at the grass which was unspeakably green. Crying was a provocation so here came the tears; praying was beneath her. Through the thick air, she tried to compel a message to Polina to be brave. What if it didn't reach her?

When the pain subsided, Maggie opened her eyes. She had no recollection of closing them. She was sweating, or it may have been this mist, the tiny water droplets clinging to her coat and her hair. She got to her feet and waited for the buzz to quiet itself. It always did.

Except this time it didn't. As Maggie stood, light-headed, she experienced the strangest sensation as though everything peripheral had dropped away and all she saw was her life shearing off in two directions, forwards and backwards. Without pausing to think, she ran. Hers wasn't a body made for running, everything flapped, her knees got in each other's way, the metal tines on her belt clinked against the buckle over and over like a blacksmith far away knocking a horseshoe into shape. It all hurt but not nearly enough. She grappled with her thoughts although really there was only one thought: do I keep going or do I stop? She kept going to elongate the argument and to end it. Where on earth did she think she was going?

She arrived. The church. Dripping with cold sweat down her back and between her breasts, she tried not to feel disappointed that she had brought herself here. Her feet ached. She smiled at her own audacity, but the huge arched wooden doorway spattered with pigeon droppings bleached the good feeling and turned it into dread: she had brought herself to the headmaster's office. She noticed a crack snaking up through the bricks and followed it with her eyes as high as she could.

The interior of the church was smaller than she needed it to be. The rusted latch had snapped upwards like a bite and, after she'd stepped inside and her eyes got used to the light, she remembered she'd left her bag on the bench. The aroma in there was strong, soup and damp, and whatever had propelled her inside was already receding, leaving her alone, so that panic butterflied the backs of her knees. She sat in a pew.

It was difficult trying to think about God when distracted by a vacuum cleaner's long yellow lead. She was wary; waiting for the vacuum to start up again was like being a child waiting for her father to get home, willing it because the waiting was worse. Upstairs in bed, she knew when he was back, not because of any sound but because of the tension that hummed in the silence.

Someone switched the vacuum on and the roar was terrible; it rode up the walls and careened off the ceilings. The lead had looped itself around a little octagonal table with one leg differently coloured from the rest. An accident waiting to happen. Maggie closed her eyes.

When a man sat down next to her, she realised the noise had stopped. He wore a tie under a round-neck jumper. He must have been there a while.

'I'm quite all right,' Maggie said, quickly wiping her eyes with her sleeves.

The paper of the hymn books was see-through and most of the front covers were missing.

'I'm not the vicar. Were you hoping to see him?'

'No.'

'I just do the cleaning, you see. My mother did it until she passed away.'

The delicacy of the hymn books' paper reminded Maggie of Howard's letters to Polina.

'Shall I leave you in peace?' the man said.

'Was it sudden? Your mother?' said Maggie, reaching for a hymn book.

She had burnt the letters to cauterize the pain. Some of the pages had curled and resisted. *Boyfriends and all that kind of thing? … So now I have two daughters! … Busy with school but if you ever get the chance … Worried because our new address …*

'Sudden-ish,' the man said. 'She contracted one of these infections in the hospital. They said congenital heart failure was lurking in the wings? Apparently it's always lurking in the wings? She was lucky in a way, because a friend of hers got hit on the head with a coconut? On the holiday of a lifetime?'

If there was a hell she was going straight there for the letters. The burning smell was the smell of her burning and it was horrifying like an erotic charge.

She said: 'Is transubstantiation you or is that the other lot?'

When he said nothing, she looked at him and saw that his face was blotchy and raw with distress and that she was supposed to do something. She patted his shoulder.

'I'd better get on,' he said. But he was hesitating. 'Have you lost someone too?'

He looked at her with a hopefulness that made her want to be unkind.

'We've all lost someone,' she said, and stopped patting him.

It wasn't until he was about to start up the vacuum again that she remembered her bag on the bench, if it hadn't been stolen by now. The thought of it there made her taut, she would have to go back for it, and at the same time, she felt gripped by the need to share something important with this man. She racked her brain for the other lost thing she needed to find. What was it?

The table was about to go. Maggie said, 'Polina!', louder than she meant to, as though she couldn't help it. As he started the vacuum, the man glanced across at her and she called out: 'My daughter's a lesbian.'

Over it went with slow motion inevitability, a thud-bounce, taking the vase with it, water everywhere.

They both moved at the same time. He ran, she wasn't sure why, and reached for the vase, cradling it like a baby, stricken, while she picked up a daffodil by the petal.

'Did you say something?' he said, wincing without looking at her, barely maintaining his composure.

'I said, I knew that was going to happen.'

'Right, well, I can take it from here.'

—◊—

Polina looked for somewhere to put her bike. The partially-covered college car park was sepia-tinged like an old photograph, smelling of the gym when the rowers had used it, a pear drop scented fug hanging over the cars. Hers was a skinny racing bike she'd bought at home from Caroline for a tenner. She couldn't ride it, it wouldn't let her, with its curling horns for handlebars and a pointy seat that had nipped and humiliated her all the way back from the swimming pool. Right now, its pedal was biting her ankle with each revolution and she swore as she shoved it hard into one of the rusting iron grooves that always shaved a bit from the tyre.

Jen stood up from where she'd been crouching.

'How did you know I was here?' she said.

'Hiya!' said Polina, paralysed.

'Come and hold this, will you? I've got a puncture.'

Jen had one of those beautiful, old-fashioned bikes hand-crafted from air. It had a basket. Wearing tracksuit bottoms and the college hoodie, because everyone – except Polina – wore the college hoodie when they weren't in black-tie, Jen squatted down to examine the tyre while Polina held the bike and studied the top of Jen's head, her curling red hair pulled into a ponytail by an elastic band, a few narrow paths of pale scalp, thin as veins.

'What do I do with this?' Jen said, holding up a small piece of rubber.

'What is it – a condom?' Grace would crucify her for that.

'I'll get Lou to look at it later.'

Jen stood and took the bike back from Polina. Lou?

'You coming tonight?' Jen said.

Maybe Polina imagined that Jen looked at her for longer than necessary.

'The party?' said Jen. 'Come along to mine before if you want.'

'I don't know … ' said Polina.

'What you going as?'

'I don't know.'

'Me neither.'

Later, Polina stood motionless in her room, still wearing the rucksack with a heavy wet towel inside. Fancy dress parties had always been awful unless Grace was there. Polina shrugged off the rucksack and tipped herself backwards onto her bed, searching the ceiling for reasons not to go. There were plenty. The essay due the next morning wouldn't get finished if she went. *What is tort?* She got up and looked at the view from her window: alleyway, dustbin, dog shit.

Jen's room, identical to Polina's but back-to front, had a lived-in, easy feel as though she'd been doing it up for years. A map of the world filled one wall, creased and old, the creases like extra mountains she probably scaled during her gap year, alongside a collage of photographs showing her and a thousand friends having dazzling adventures miles away. It wasn't as though Polina hadn't been to the poster fair during freshers' week like everyone else; she'd bought the usuals, the blue Matisse man with no hands, the magical 3D image hidden in the picture (she hated it already) but she couldn't make her college room feel anything other than a tired, stale space loaned to her by grown-ups like a mouldy library book.

Another student arrived at the same time as Polina. 'You're Basil Brush!' Polina said to her. 'I love Basil Brush.'

'I'm supposed to be a fox.'

'He is a fox, isn't he?'

Polina was dressed as a Mexican but that was just an excuse to drink tequila while she tried to think of a better costume. She'd drunk most of the bottle before she knocked on Jen's door, which was open already. Jen had commandeered the whole corridor including the tiny kitchen at one end, where three women in matching hula skirts were singing while they heated dozens of tins of soup in a huge pot. Tequila inspired, she'd picked up the rag rug from the floor in her room and held the scissors next to it, nearly cutting until finally she cut it. A poncho. Grace wouldn't have hesitated. She'd have looked good in whatever she'd made. Now that Polina was in Jen's room, her nerves and the alcohol were kicking in, and the music skittered and juddered and put her off.

Basil Brush handed her the plastic cup from the top of a medicine bottle and waited for Polina to work out that she was supposed to share the tequila she was clutching. They sat on the carpet, cross-legged, and after some slammers, half-heartedly done – warm, no lime, no salt – Polina allowed herself to scan the room for a face she recognised, but there was no one (and no men at all; was this a lesbian party? What a dizzying thought). Basil had disappeared and the bottle was empty, so Polina got to her feet and meandered around the room looking for someone to talk to, smiling benignly like a pope.

Someone's aggressive heel punched down through the top of Polina's flip-flop. She watched it happen in slow motion, thinking this will hurt in the morning, but smiling all the same. It didn't hurt now and that was miraculous, as was the face of the woman who turned to apologise because, was it a man's face? It was a face slick with foundation and Polina found that she was studying it up close for signs of gender, a lantern jaw or a five o'clock shadow. What did it matter? She almost said what are you? But Basil Brush was back and so Polina boomed: 'Boom, boom!'

'Got any more tequila?'

'All gone.' Polina held the bottle upside down and shook it.

'Who are you meant to be?' said Jen. Where had Jen come from? This room had hidden rooms.

'A Mehican.'

Polina's throat was suddenly so dry it hurt to swallow. Jen looked at her and then took her hand and held it high and danced a circle underneath it.

'So, are you a fish? A sardine?' Polina said, loosening herself from Jen's grip because she wanted it so badly.

'I'm a mermaid.'

'A fish out of water!' said Polina, wishing she could reel that one back.

Then Jen wandered away, just like that and Polina didn't catch what she said but it might have been, *you have beautiful eyes.*

How did other people know how to do this? Polina queued in the corridor for the loo just for some thinking time and also to check out her beautiful eyes in the mirror. Get a fucking grip, she told herself. They weren't beautiful, they were red. The toilet didn't flush anymore and there was loo roll overflowing from the bowl like ectoplasm. Someone banged on the door. 'Get a move on!'

When she came out, the wo/man with the heels was leaning her forehead against a wall. The heels were now missing.

There was a fire exit propped open near the kitchen, leading to a balcony you weren't allowed to use. Out there, Polina watched two topless women share a joint in the dark. She wanted to drink them down, the slow coolness of their dancing bodies, back to back, quiet. The one in the blonde wig threw her head back to laugh, and if they were talking it sounded like buzzing. Polina stepped back inside and closed her eyes. You weren't supposed to cry. She envied them their certainty, that they didn't have to turn around to check the other one was still there.

Back inside, Jen was playing cards.

'Where's your girlfriend?' Polina said, sitting down heavily next to her and touching her lightly on the knee just to test the water.

'You're sitting next to her,' said Jen, laughing. 'This is Lou.' The cavewoman with the folded arms was suddenly unnaturally interested in her own left elbow.

Later, Polina danced because they were all dancing, or the room was dancing round them. The women from the balcony had gone. She couldn't even find the balcony; no one seemed to know about any balcony. She was hungry but all the crisps had been eaten or stamped into the rug, so she downed the drink in her hand and held her glass in the air: 'To liquid food!' It wasn't tequila, she didn't know what it was, although it had that tequila afterburn. Bang, the room tipped on its side and took her with it, rolling down its walls to a trick floor. In its new state, her body rejoined Jen, picking its way daintily as though stepping over broken glass.

'Would you like to dance?' Polina couldn't stop the words smearing into one another.

Jen took a while to answer. Maybe she wasn't a dancer.

'You know I would if I could,' Jen said.

Like that explained anything. They stood for a while, looking at each other, not dancing.

Then it was suddenly later and she couldn't find her Mexican moustache. At first it was funny, people humoured her, stepping aside to let her look under their feet, but it got serious because without the moustache, her outfit was just a rag rug poncho that didn't look like a poncho, it looked like a rag rug; worse, like the piece of carpet that old ladies put around toilets, with Polina's head where the toilet would go. People were moving on (where to?) but this was not a joke and she was sweaty. She unzipped a cushion cover to look inside. It looked roomy. She pulled books from a shelf and started shaking them. A thought formed: if she couldn't leave without the moustache, she couldn't leave. She put the book she was holding carefully back on the shelf to think about that.

Things got even better because now Jen helped her look, or pretended to, Polina didn't care which, while the cavewoman looked pointedly at the ceiling and under her breath said: 'She should try her own face.'

Jen's hand held Polina's for a few seconds as they felt under the armchair from different sides. Polina stood, light-headed, and then Jen touched the small of her back as though guiding her. Maybe that was nothing to people like Jen but Polina felt so euphoric she wanted to fly.

Nearly everyone had gone when a woman, whose face Polina was sure she knew from somewhere, turned up by herself. Sashaying over in what she hoped was the direction of the visitor, Polina's flip-flopped foot was really starting to throb.

'I thought you were the porter come to shut us down,' Jen said. Polina noticed Jen take a while to appraise the newcomer, like she was weighing her, approvingly. Then Lou's arm clamped itself around Jen's waist to drag her away, and the combination of the appraisal and the arm were pins that burst Polina's bubble (*pop!*). Now she had no protection from her intoxication nor from the doom that threatened to steamroller her flat, right there in Jen's room. Everything was too bright. The visitor looked at Polina and laughed. It was Grace, who else?

'You two know each other?' said Jen.

'You need a rug in here,' Grace said. She sat on the floor of Polina's room and rubbed her hand across the rough beige carpet. 'The décor's very – brave.'

Polina hung over the side of the bed, gazing into the wastepaper basket she held under her chin.

'Have you got anything to drink?'

'Drank it,' said Polina.

'You have a moustache on your forehead.'

'Have I?'

Sheets of A4 paper were stuck with Blu Tack to the wall next to Polina's bed. Grace read one: MRS DONOGHUE – GINGER BEER – SNAIL.

'So, she's your girlfriend?' she said.

'Who?'

'You could've told me. I mean, I knew.' Grace tried to turn it into a joke. 'I leave you for two minutes and you're a lesbian.'

Polina hesitated, then threw up decisively into the bin.

Maybe it had been a mistake to come. On the train, Grace at first felt cowed – clever fens, clever trees, clever us, clever us – then angry with the landscape for trying to intimidate her. By the time she arrived at the station she was bolshy, swearing at the bikes lined up like swots. She argued with the cab driver because he wouldn't take her to the university, he kept asking, which college, which college? So, she got out without paying. 'I'm going to report you,' she told him, slamming the door and running before he could stop her (she had £4 left and the meter was already on £6.06).

'Did she say anything to you?' said Polina, wiping her mouth with her hand.

'Who?'

'Jen. She obviously fancied you.'

'Have you got anything to eat?' said Grace.

'I think there's a banana.'

In the fruit bowl, a dark brown banana scowled. Grace filled the kettle.

'So, I'm doing this catering thing. Fuck the resits. You get experience with real chefs. Pols, are you listening?'

'Catering,' said Polina. She looked green.

Grace found a carton of milk on the window sill.

'Wow, what an inspiring view. No wonder you're always off your tits.'

Polina breathed carefully, in and out.

'Ed says hi, by the way. Like this.' Grace put her head to one side, batted her eyelids like a fawn. 'Hi!'

Polina looked up. 'Oh God, the beach hut,' she said.

'Our beach hut?'

'He told you, right?'

Grace felt wrong-footed.

Polina said: 'For some of it I was thinking, what if this was Jen? Or even you. Isn't that stupid?'

Grace blinked. She didn't trust herself to speak.

Then Polina puked again. Grace watched her. The woodchip on the walls looked like porridge oats, separated and trapped, and those bits of paper stuck everywhere were as embarrassing as hand-written poems on a teenager's wall. Grace thought of Polina's bedroom at home with its single poster of Sting and his dream of the blue fucking somethings. Whales?

Ed had come home last weekend – he rarely came home anymore, except for funerals – and he'd looked terrible, pink-eyed, his face bloated. Even Doug had left him alone. He'd been living on a houseboat with this woman, he told Grace; she had a baby boy he was mad about but he'd had to break it off and now he had nowhere to live. She'd wanted to shout at him, *stop getting bruised!* Could you admire people so much it made you want to punch them?

They went to the nearest pub that did food, The Smugglers' Inn; sticky carpet, terrible watercolours and kids from her school drinking pints of cider and black because the barman never asked for ID. Ed ordered them scampi and chips without asking what she wanted and when it came, he didn't touch his. She didn't blame him, the pungent smell of old cooking oil coming from the kitchen was pretty off-putting. He's high, she thought, let him talk. And he did talk, but only to his chips. He wouldn't tell her what he'd done that was so bad. He rambled, and though she tried to stay with him her mind kept wandering away to other things (what is scampi?)

Polina was now swirling the vomit around in the bottom of the bin.

'That is disgusting,' Grace said.

Ed had gone to the bar and she'd heard him ask for a freshly squeezed orange juice so that was that, he had to be high or terminally ill. He came back with the juice, which the barman had put a little cocktail umbrella in. Ed took out and fiddled with it, up and down, and said: 'Do you miss Polina?'

'Do I miss her? I'm the rocket up her arse. She's the one who must be missing me.'

Yes, I miss her, she thought.

Ed looked at her for a long time, as though he was struggling to translate a difficult foreign phrase.

'You should go and see her,' he said.

'I might.'

He placed the umbrella down flat on the table.

'I'll drive you up if you want.'

'I'll probably get the train.'

Somewhere in the next hour they fell into the same game they always played, if you could call it a game, the one that started as ironic nostalgia for some sour memory from childhood and went downhill from there. With Ed in a state it was a bad idea, but the game was an itch you had to scratch.

'Why did Mum tell me at all? That's what I'd like to know. Why give me just enough information so I knew I wasn't wanted?' Ed said.

He always got onto this.

'You don't want to hear Dad's version,' said Grace.

'Well actually I'd love to hear it.'

She changed the subject. 'Ed, I've decided I'm not going to resit my A levels.'

'One day he might explain to me why he thought it was alright to give you everything and me nothing?'

They couldn't find the right pitch after that. Ed said: 'I think I need retuning. Ignore me. I'm sorry.'

She tried to get her arm around his waist as they walked home but his body was stiff. He must have been so close to telling her.

'Where are you going?' said Polina, pushing the hair out of her eyes.

The room was too warm.

'Get us some food,' said Grace.

'Wait. I think there's a banana.'

Two glasses of water and an empty mug lay on the floor next to her bed.

'Grace?'

Polina closed her eyes but that only made it worse. She pictured herself sitting in her mum's rotting deckchair in winter, her body about to fall through. It jolted her awake from somewhere that wasn't sleep and, in the lull after the jolt, it happened again, the deckchair, the almost falling, like an earworm in your body, a semi-dream loop that wouldn't stop. It was so vivid she could feel the stiff, striped material between her finger. When she closed her eyes, it was worse. A sharp pain travelled fast across her skull like a hairline crack. She couldn't sleep. She felt wretched and deeply hungover, her breath too warm, something sickening like dread or regret rearing up and forcing her to shunt herself to the edge of the bed to stop any memories in their tracks. She paused to get her breath and to listen but now her balance was wrong and she found herself lolling headfirst towards the floor.

In her dressing gown and a baseball cap, Polina walked unsteadily across the lawn that separated her block from the porter's lodge. Grace had to be here somewhere. It was difficult to see properly with her heartbeat throbbing too loudly in her temple, and she nearly bumped into Neil as he scanned the noticeboard, his feather boa wrapped tightly round his neck and trailing down his spine like a feathered snake. The smell of his bacon roll nearly toppled her.

'Get that thing away from me.'

'You look very sexy this morning, my darling. Do the nurses know you're out?'

'Stop talking,' said Polina, and she got the cold creeps as he held a piece of bacon rind in the air and dropped it into his open mouth. They tiptoed up the staircase towards Jen's room, Polina's bare feet already numb with cold. It was a bad idea but Polina didn't know where else to start; she wasn't even sure now whether Grace had come back with her after the party.

'I met someone last night,' said Neil. 'He rows. Think Lycra. Think giant cock.'

Another wave of nausea rose and fell. 'Do I have to?'

Jen's door was ajar.

'This is a waste of time,' said Polina.

She didn't want to go any further, but Neil was already knocking, quietly. He pushed open the door a little and she could tell he was enjoying this far too much. She should have come by herself.

'Yoo-hoo!'

'Neil, let's go.' The throbbing pain in her head was clamping her eyes shut.

The room was a classic crime scene, missing only the chalk outline of a body, the black and yellow tape. There were odd shoes everywhere, an inflatable pink chair lying upside down, lots of empty bottles, tequila, vodka, beer, squashed cans of Red Bull, cigarette butts like lugworms poking their heads up from the carpet. There was even a gas mask. The bed was buried under a pile of laundry and coats.

Neil whispered: 'Someone got lucky'. He winked at Polina, his expression so gleeful it threw her, so she looked and now she was implicated too because she would have to see Jen in bed with the cavewoman. When she looked – glanced, it was a glance – she couldn't see anything of the cavewoman, but she saw Jen's unmistakable hair, jagged wire you could cut your hands on. Then she saw a bare arm, a hand, and written on the hand in blue biro was Polina's room number in a blue box, a reminder for Grace in case she got lost.

Neil's answer to everything was to go out for tea. He forced Polina to get dressed, actually stood over her while she clumsily stepped into her pants, and dragged her by the arm to The Copper Pot where she stirred and stirred a cup of tea until he pressed his hand on hers to make her stop. An elderly couple with crepe paper skin ordered Welsh rarebit and she found it much easier to keep a handle on their conversation than the one she was supposed to be having. Neil asked: 'So, who are you more jealous of, Grace or Jen?' And it was such an ugly, gaping question.

When Polina got back to her room, she knew Grace was gone. There was no note, no sign she'd ever been there, except for the fruit bowl, full of bananas.

—◊—

The knocking woke her up.

'I know you're in there.' It was Neil.

There were kids in the alley. She heard the thwack of skipping ropes and feet.

'I'm not.'

—◊—

3.14: POLINA FLASHBACK – SKIPPING. BREECH.

Grace stopped skipping.

'I know where babies come from,' She pointed to her bottom.

Polina looked at her, expressionless.

'And I was a breech which made everything complicated.'

'Did it?' said Polina.

'If you're a breech you die.'

'They had to use four steps on Caroline,' said Polina.

'But I didn't die because I am exceptionally strong.'

Polina had no answer to that.

—◊—

3.15: LIBRARY.

It felt like hide and seek, a game she detested, that light-headed anticipation of being caught soon turning to utter dread as you began to feel hunted. There wasn't time to tuck away the form she was filling in.

'Hi,' said Jen.

Polina forced herself to look surprised. 'Hi.'

She was in a corner of the college library, the desk lamp pulled towards her. Now this place is spoilt too.

'Breakfast?' Jen nodded at the empty Twix wrapper.

Polina couldn't think of anything to say.

'What are you up to?' Jen tilted her head towards the form, headed, in unnecessarily bold font, APPLICATION FOR COLLEGE HARDSHIP FUND. Polina rested her arm over it casually.

'Just an essay,' she said.

Jen nodded. 'I'll leave you to it.'

Polina missed her mother momentarily; a new and confusing pain in a category all of its own. She reached down into her bag and coughed to cover the sound of a can being opened, then poured the ready mixed (very expensive) vodka and tonic into her travel mug.

CAUSATION

4.1: DID THE BREACH CAUSE THE LOSS OR WOULD THE LOSS HAVE
HAPPENED ANYWAY?
4.1.2: BARNETT V CHELSEA & KENSINGTON HOSPITAL (1969) 1 QB
428.
4.1.3: POLINA – PUPILLAGE.

When Polina got back to chambers, the party had started, if you could call it a party. Her headache was also in full swing, but she was ignoring that. As a pupil barrister, she had to attend every party going because you never knew if a solicitor might be there who might decide they'd like to instruct you, based on your expertise at topping up their glass with fake champagne and being a little less erudite than them.

The other pupil, Stefan, laughed ostentatiously at something one of the solicitors was saying then scanned the room to see who had noticed. He saw Polina wave at him and had the grace to flush. When she next looked over, he held up his glass towards her and smiled an oily smile as though nothing had happened.

The room she shared with her pupil master was empty, so she dumped her bag on the floor and sat behind his desk, opening the appointments diary on his computer. There was nothing booked in for her. He had a paperweight like a big glass tumour, which she touched as she swung in his leather chair that smelt a bit like him, the way your hand smells when you hold pennies. She checked Stefan's diary and saw he had two appointments tomorrow. Two? And they were easy winding-up orders, which just meant putting your wig on and reciting some words you didn't fully understand. Couldn't they have had one each?

'Poli?' Leon, the head clerk, put his head round the door. 'Busy?' He shut it behind him.

'I was just going to come down.'

'Word in your shell-like.'

'Right?'

'We talk about pupillage being about profile, don't we?' He moved to the window and stood with his back to her, as though the room – the whole building – belonged to him. He turned. 'Yours could be higher, we feel.'

'I was just about to come down, Leon. I've only just got back. The hearing was adjourned.'

He held up a hand to stop her. She noticed the gold ring on his little finger.

'Long and short of it, we're a business, Polina. End of the day, we need to see some more investment from you into the business. Yes?'

'Do we?'

Leon glanced quickly at the door and moved to the desk. He sat heavily on the corner, his knee pointing towards her. He touched his tie, like a teacher who wants you to see how much he is controlling his tested patience. She could smell his fruity aftershave. Cigars.

'Stefan is down there now. Call it schmoozing. Keeping them happy. Call it whatever you like. Every morning he's early. Leaves later than you. It gets noticed.'

He picked a fleck of dust from his knee.

'What more do you want me to do?'

Polina thought about the times she had found Stefan in the print room with a panicky face photocopying cases back to front, big stacks of them, the idiot, the staples in the bottom right corner so you couldn't even turn the pages.

'Between you and me?' Leon shook his head. 'He wouldn't be our first choice, Poli. I don't know if I can make it any clearer.'

He put his hand on hers and held it there. She could have moved her hand if she'd really tried.

'Ask yourself, "Do I fit? And if I do, am I a tight fit?".'

The questions made the air around her hum, repeating themselves in the silence. Polina looked at his hand on hers.

He stood up, abruptly. 'Get yourself downstairs and start mingling.'

He was already at the door. 'Oh.' He fished a hand into his pocket. 'For the contact order you did last week. Solicitors have paid up already.' He threw the cheque at her. 'A miracle. I won't tell Michael you're using his desk.' He winked without smiling. 'See you downstairs.'

She picked up the cheque. Forty-two pounds.

Most of the old wooden windows in chambers had absorbed so many coats of paint they wouldn't open any more, making the place feel like a greenhouse. His finger followed the words Polina had written, twice; she felt herself sweating, a perpetual state these days, and she imagined her make-up sliding, along with her face, to reveal a completely different person underneath. He didn't even ask her to sit. She thought about the word obsequiousness with all its syllables, how you couldn't rush the ousness bit because it wouldn't let you.

'How's Polina?' he said. 'How's pupillage?' Both of these he said with his head cocked to one side. 'Sit down.'

The thing about Isaac was he looked fifteen, smooth skinned, yet here he was, established, a Windsor knot in his tie, Territorial Army at the weekends. The joke in chambers was that he had done pupillage when still a foetus. It was plausible. *The Legal 500* called his progression 'meteoric' and sometimes she wondered what you had to give up in return for being meteoric. She waited for his BIG WORD.

'Did I get the formula wrong?' She pointed to the section she was worried about, reading it upside down. 'Is that wrong?'

'Never apologise. First rule of being a barrister.'

'I didn't. Did I?'

'Bullshit and control is what the punters pay us for. Second rule: cope. No room at the inn for the pusillanimous.'

And there it was. Definitely no room on the sign at the inn prohibiting the pusillanimous.

'No vacancies,' she agreed.

He looked at her, picking up his pen and ticking something on the page. The expression on his face was always a mixture of fear and glee, as though he was just about to drive his father's car without permission.

'Everyone has coping mechanisms, Polina.'

He quickly put the pen down and reached a hand into the pocket of the jacket hanging on his chair. He took out a key, unlocked the desk drawer and pulled out a lime-green water pistol, which he pointed at her. 'Bang!' She held up her hands half-heartedly.

He dropped it back in the drawer. 'So we have the obvious.' He held up an almost empty bottle of vodka, shook it, replaced it and then carefully relocked the drawer. She got the feeling he thought his fastidiousness would fascinate her. He looked at her and then pressed his nostril, sniffing hard. 'And the not so obvious.'

Even though the not so obvious seemed fairly obvious, she still felt a frisson, exactly as she suspected he wanted her to. Did all pupils get this show?

'So, can you use that?' She nodded her head at the page on his desk.

'Probably. You're right that this bit's a balls-up though. I suggest you rock on up to Paul's room and check out the latest formula on his computer. I don't have it on this piece of crap.'

His telephone rang just at that moment as if he'd planned it that way. He picked it up.

'Isaac speaking.'

It looked too big for him.

—◊—

'Help yourself,' Paul said, waving towards his desk.

He was sitting at the conference table in the centre of the room, flicking through case reports, swearing. The air smelt of wood, fresh from a lathe.

He'd been the only friendly one during Polina's pupillage interview. Her voice shook with all the stupid things it couldn't stop saying and he had asked: 'But what about this client? Put yourself in his shoes.' In a conspiratorial whisper, he'd added: 'Forget what you think you're supposed to say or I can't see who you are.'

'I'm not even sure there's any intention to create legal relations here,' Polina had said.

'Thank you!'

She remembered his hands in particular, how clean they were. His blue shirt, bluer after her answer, and she'd glimpsed in that moment how things could be. These were other people's lives and they were easy! Paul had peeled back the sky to release a deluge of good fortune; all she had to do was cup her hands.

She clicked his computer. On his desk was a photograph in a chunky frame of a woman with dyed blonde hair, beaming at the camera, the sun in her eyes. In another, two babies in a bath looked delighted with their mohican shampooed hair. The other picture was a much younger Paul leaning on a bright orange motorbike.

'You're not married, Polina?'

'No.'

'No. Well, don't. You'll only end up here, paying us to divvy up the bloody teaspoons.'

What she found, without meaning to, was not the formula but a calendar, filling the screen whichever key she pressed. The dates of forthcoming hearings with the initials of one particular judge, MK, in red, the others in black. Under each mention of MK was a number: 750k, 400k to her plus house, 600k and half his income. She clicked delete. Escape. Return. It was all very odd.

'Sorry, Paul, I can't seem to – '

'Problem? Hang on.'

—◊—

4.2: GRACE MEETS NATHAN (WAS THE MEETING CAUSED BY A FAULTY ALARM?)

'It's done it again,' said Grace.

'I can't hear you.'

'The alarm!' Grace shouted into the phone, pressed buttons at random on the alarm keypad. Something was burning in one of the ovens. A customer walked in and straight out of the café.

'You need to key in the code,' said Graham.

'No shit! It's not working. You'll have to come in.'

'924 or 934. It might be 934.'

'You can't leave me here on my own.'

'934. Definitely. Or – wait – is this the security alarm or the smoke alarm because if it's the smoke alarm it's … Hey, honey. It's fine. Go back to bed. Grace, my wife just had a baby. I've got to – '

'I may kill someone.'

'It worked when it did it before.'

'I tried 934,' Grace said.

The sticker on the keypad gave a number to call in case of emergency. All but one of the digits had worn away.

'Look, Grace? After twenty minutes it stops. OK? Grace?'

Her brain splintered. She hung up.

A man walked purposefully in wearing paint-spattered jeans and rubbing his nose as though trying to make up his mind. He might have had paint in his hair, Grace thought, or else little patches were going grey. She nodded when he pointed at the keypad. For all she knew he was an armed robber; she really hoped so. He pressed some of the keys and smacked his head with his hand, laughing. She didn't see what was funny, but he pressed more buttons and everything stopped and then she wanted to laugh as well.

The silence after all that noise was so loud it was blinding and it made her want to cover her eyes. She did.

'OVERRIDE,' he said.

He had a cigarette behind his ear (she didn't think people did that for real) and the kind of mouth you wanted to watch blowing on a hot roast potato. She was so dazed she almost said 'roast potato'.

'I USED TO WORK WITH THEM,' he said.

'THANKS. YOU CAN STOP SHOUTING NOW. UN-LESS YOU ALWAYS TALK LIKE THIS?'

'Sorry. What's burning?'

'Shit.'

Grace pulled open the oven door. The smoke was thick like an acrid punch in the face, and she flapped a tea towel over the black lemon drizzle cake as she laid it down on the counter. It reeked of ash and acid. He'd moved again and she took the opportunity to look at his knees. Mostly his knees.

'No battery. Tut tut,' he said, standing on a chair to unscrew the smoke alarm attached to the ceiling.

You could tell a lot from the knees.

Two women came in and sniffed the air.

'We had a small inferno,' Grace said.

'I'm Nathan,' the man said, deciding to introduce himself to the ladies.

'Hello, Nathan,' said one of the women, pronouncing her words very carefully so that the simple person could lip-read. 'We'll have two coffees, please.'

'I'll make three,' said Grace, grinning at Nathan.

'We should do this more often,' said Stefan, sipping from his wine glass.

'Definitely,' said Polina.

The double vodka (after the last one) was sanding the edges smooth. In that moment, she meant it. She may have been wrong about him.

'So,' he said. 'A week to go. I've noticed you're drinking more?'

She hadn't been wrong about him.

He added: 'You're all over Leon like a rash.'

'He's a sleaze.'

'Oh, OK. It's him. OK.'

'How are you doing, Stefan? Have you solved the riddle of the photocopier yet? Here's a clue: it doesn't do hot beverages.'

He pulled open his dry roasted peanuts and smiled as he threw them into the middle of the table as if raising the stakes.

'I wouldn't say no,' said Polina, tipping a small pile of nuts into her hand.

'So I hear.'

'Oh, come off it. I don't want to do this. Help me out. Who is MK? A judge called MK?'

'Marcus Kellen. He and Paul are like this.' He wrapped one finger around another. 'Why?'

She hadn't meant to say anything but now he looked expectant like a hawk, all sharp angles.

'Why would Paul highlight all the trials he's got coming up with MK? Why would he have settlement figures in little boxes under the dates? Why does that seem weird?'

'Have you mentioned this to anyone?' Stefan leaned forward.

'No. Just you.'

'You don't want to be making allegations about the head of chambers, Polina. Especially not now. Unless you have proof that they're in cahoots? That is what you're alleging?'

Cahoots. It nearly derailed her. She swallowed a mouthful of vodka.

'What's funny?' he said.

'Nothing. Forget it.'

He was peeved. Indignant rosy blobs appeared on his cheeks and suddenly she was tired and wanted to be far away from him. He crossed his legs too flamboyantly and his humourlessness and the pantomime quality of the move made her miss Grace, who would have made mincemeat of him. She sat looking at nothing much until the complicated longing dissipated and she trusted herself to get up.

Back at chambers, Polina went to her desk to find the papers she'd forgotten to take with her. Her vision was a hall of mirrors and it was wonderful; even Leon leaning against the open door couldn't spoil her mood all that much.

'It's late, Polina.'

'I've been out with Stefan.'

'Oh, right.'

'We had some drinks together. In the pub.'

'Good to see you letting your hair down. Even if it is with Stefan.'

Polina giggled. 'I forgot these.' She held up the box files.

'So, it's not true, then?'

'What?'

'Little bird told me you – you bat for the other side? I said, "I doubt that".'

She needed him to keep still so she could tell the right one to mind his own fucking business.

'I'm not seeing Stefan.'

'Right, but you're not … ?' He stepped into the room, laughing. 'Usually I can tell. But you're wearing make-up; I mean there's no facial hair to speak of.'

She rattled the box files unnecessarily; they were heavier than she'd bargained for. 'Night, Leon.'

Leon took the files from her in a way that made it impossible to refuse his help without seeming churlish, and he nodded for her to go ahead of him.

'Not sure it would be de rigueur here,' he said, pushing into her from behind as though he himself had been shunted. She took the files back.

'You'll be all right getting home?' He held his concerned face.

'I'm fine,' Polina said.

He winked. 'Good girl.'

—◊—

'I'll be mother,' Leon said.

Polina tried to be somewhere else without leaving the room. This was tea, the daily four o'clock humiliation and Leon poured delicately through a little strainer one of the barristers had brought back from Paris. She imagined him at home in an apron. Scalloped.

There were lots of them in today and you could sense the scale of their victories and defeats in court from the way they poured their tea: milk in first meant they'd won; tea in first meant the judge was an imbecile. Stefan waved away the offer of tea, smugly holding up his own mug with its herbal infusion. The writing on the side said: BARRI-STAR!

Chambers tea made Polina nervous, waiting to say the thing she shouldn't say. She bit into a coconut macaroon. Who likes coconut macaroons? She hadn't meant to take one, they're stale before they're out of the oven and now she was feeling every stage of its journey down her throat.

'Polina, get me up to speed on Wilson, will you?'

That was Andrew, who reminded Polina every time of a walrus tusk. A deaf walrus tusk (he was deaf in one ear and a shouter.) She quite liked the long, pale, whiskery curve of him, it was the stuff of children's stories, although he was so tall, and so uncomfortable with being so tall, that when he spoke he tipped himself forwards and you feared for the top of your head.

'Nothing's changed,' said Stefan. 'They appealed and lost.

Sorry, Polina, is that what you were going to say? I didn't mean to steal your thunder.' Sip.

'Ah. Thank you, Steven,' Andrew said, gravely.

'Stefan.'

Then Ruth started to talk to Andrew about decorators and his expression said I wish I were deaf in both ears. Polina tried to block it out. Ruth could imbue her swearing with such gravitas it made you want to thank her at the end of every sentence.

'Because I'm a single woman with a child, Andrew, is that it? Well, you recommended them! Ergo ... fucking imbecile! ... Tell them from me ... sucking uber-pricks ... or tiny chihuahua bollocks.'

'Perhaps,' Andrew conceded. 'In hindsight.'

Paul pushed into the room and poured his own tea without looking at anyone. Something was wrong. Polina wished she could put the rest of the macaroon in the bin but she had to hold it in the air like a badge she'd just made. Meanwhile, Paul took a slug of tea like it was whiskey and winced, and Stefan had got very interested in his shoes.

'You all right, Paul?' Leon said.

'That depends.' He leant on the hostess trolley, which moved a little.

'Remind me, Polina, about the meeting we had the other day.'

'When I – came to see you to get – '

'What was that?' said Andrew.

'After that. Two days after that,' said Paul, gesturing with his hand for her to hurry up.

'I came to see you because I'd seen some figures on your computer and I didn't understand them.'

'And?'

'Fucks to all this, soy Himalayan busy,' said Ruth, waving a queenly adios as she left the room. Some of them waved back.

'You thought I was match-fixing,' said Paul.

'They were from last year. It's obvious now.'

'Look, I'm glad you came to see me. But I wish you'd come to see me before you spoke to him.' Paul nodded at Stefan.

Only Paul and Stefan seemed to understand what was going on. You could feel a crackling in the room like a poor connection to somewhere miles away. Isaac bounded in, pushing open the door with such force it banged on its hinges. 'I hope it's hot and wet, Leon!'

Polina tried to put the macaroon in the pocket of her suit jacket but it wasn't really a pocket and her hand was shaking. Stefan said: 'Surely it's best to get these things out in the open?'

'I'm glad we agree,' said Paul. 'You have ten minutes to clear your desk. Polina, congratulations, the tenancy's yours. And for the avoidance of doubt, it was yours anyway.'

'Come on! That's it?' said Stefan, his voice high.

'Which one are we ditching?' Andrew shouted.

'What chance did I have?' Stefan pointed at Leon and then at Polina as if joining them together with invisible string.

4.3: GRACE CALLS POLINA (FINALLY)

(BEEP)
'I think me and Nathan got into it too quickly. We got a cat on the third date; isn't that what lesbians do? Joke! Not lesbianism, Pols, that's no joke is it. Joke.'
(CLICK)

(BEEP)
'Anyway I'm allergic to cat hair. We didn't get a cat.'
(CLICK)

(BEEP)
'Me again, I'm a brilliant chef now so invite me up and I'll make us dinner. Bye.'
(CLICK)

Grace's voice sounded rough, as though she'd stayed up late or smoked too much. The thrill of hearing it forced Polina to stand still.

(BEEP)
'So I came home early and he was having a wank in front of Carol Vorderman!'
(CLICK)

Something in Polina got turned loose after Grace slept with Jen, a running argument with herself, garbled and shocking; it was a rant that she could not bear and could not bear to stop. In response, the silence from Grace, until now, had been deafening.

(BEEP)
…
(CLICK)

(BEEP)
'Your answer machine keeps cutting me…'
(CLICK)

(BEEP)
'I said, "Don't you mean two from the top and three from anywhere else?"'
(CLICK)

There was no point telling anyone how it felt. Grace was the only person she could have told, so Polina carried on and turned the volume up and did all the things you're supposed to do at university; she went to lectures and slept with people, sometimes the wrong people, she drank and suffered and did it again, and some of it hurt so much she couldn't feel a thing. One afternoon she overheard a woman in the street talk about the eviscerating pain of losing her husband and she thought: that's what I've got. It was the same day she'd somehow bent the key to her room out of shape and locked herself in. It had been three hours before someone heard her banging. She'd had to piss in the cafetiere.

(BEEP)
'Give me a call? Please? If you want?'
(CLICK)

(BEEP)
'Nathan smells of bricks. Is that normal? Hang on, why am I asking you?'
(CLICK)

—◊—

The stick man wore a harness. Polina's client pointed at it then sat back, satisfied. She looked at his drawing for some time, and then across the client – they were sitting side by side on uncomfortable chairs; the plastic, sweating kind – to her instructing solicitor, a man older than her and at that difficult age where, if you weren't careful, you got stuck doing whatever you were doing for the rest of your legal career. His sheened face matched the lapels of his suit, which was sprinkled here and there with specks of dandruff that twinkled like far away galaxies.

'And you say your employer gave you no training on using the harness?' said Polina to her client. 'Because before, if you remember, you said he'd given you some training but you didn't understand it. It's important to be very clear about this.'

'Very clear,' the man agreed, swallowing. 'Yes.'

'I've asked him this already,' the solicitor said.

'You've been doing this work for some time now. Six years?'

'Six year. Seven year.'

'The judge might find it odd that after six or seven years you didn't appreciate you had to wear the harness.'

'Yes. It was not fit me,' he said, carefully.

The solicitor wrote something down and ticked it. Even the way he held his pen was irritating.

She wasn't sleeping. There wasn't time, with work, and the lack of sleep was playing games with her, chasing her while she chased something she couldn't catch.

'Was a "D" harness,' said the client. 'He tell me "D" harness. Like this.'

The man pointed again at the stick figure on the page. Polina had no idea what he was talking about, but he was looking at her as though waiting for reassurance.

'Yes, I see,' she said.

'Because I could not because of my back.'

'We're on,' said the solicitor, as he checked text messages on his phone. A clerk had appeared and summoned them in, her arms folded. The only reason Polina supposed this solicitor instructed her was because she was still relatively junior and therefore cheap. 'Give me one minute,' she said.

In the cubicle, she closed the lid of the toilet to sit on while she drank from her travel mug. It wasn't the quantity of vodka that was important so much as having access to it at exactly the right moment. Getting that spot on was a small thrill in itself, then the trick was to hold on without tipping over into too much. She took another small gulp. Most of her colleagues worked hard on their coke habits but that wasn't for her, the paranoia that followed the high being even darker than the paranoia that made you want to take it in the first place. Which was one of those neat equations that made her feel as virtuous and clean as it's possible to feel when you know deep down you're screwed.

What she wanted to do was rest her forehead on the porcelain cistern and sleep. She touched it with the flat of her hand just to feel its coolness and recited to herself the technical this and that words, the jargony poetry of this particular case, its flow and narrative, the part she always enjoyed the most. All you had to do was persuade the client and your instructing solicitor that you were in control and then do a little show for them in court. The show had to appeal to both of them at the same time and that was the tricky bit when they came at you from different places wanting different things. It helped if you really were in control but that was a luxury Polina rarely experienced. No one so far had ever pulled her up on it or even seemed to notice. In chambers, they tried to tell you it was all a game, but for Polina it was two games played at the same time: one where you pretended you didn't care and another where you pretended you did.

Her bowels were suddenly screaming at her, just as someone else came in. She heard clicking heels and a cubicle door being bolted, but she had to go, so she flushed while in full flow to distract from the sound and the smell. Then there was the wait for the cistern to refill, during which she coughed, trying to make the cough sound professional and resigned, as if the problem she was dealing with here had not been caused by her but by the previous administration. She flushed a second time.

It wasn't good to keep a judge waiting, but who was it who said if you were five minutes late, be ten? She was fifteen.

4.4: PAUL'S HOUSE. ISAAC IN TROUBLE.

The spiralling stairs said climb me, but Paul hadn't said anything about stairs. The toilet wasn't where Paul said it was but, then again, nothing is where anyone says it is after three glasses of punch on an empty stomach. A pair of marble lions guarded the hall, a dark and vast space after the dazzle of the garden. From somewhere close by, Polina heard vomiting, a hoarse, panicked sound.

She waited close to the toilet door. Should she pretend she'd heard nothing when whoever it was came out? She was peering at a tiny portrait of a judge, 19th century – Lord Justice Lindley? – her back to Isaac when he appeared. His teeth were chattering and he was so pale it was hard to look at him. He leaned against the doorframe, breathing hard, holding a nearly empty bottle protectively against his stomach. The stench of vomit from the toilet was the kind your throat registers before your nose.

'Isaac?'

The white gleam of the tiled room behind him flashed her. A childish homemade sign on a hook said, 'NOW WASH YOUR HANDS'.

He looked bemused. 'You gonna have a help me, OK?'

His head had developed a shake. He handed her the bottle of vodka, which she took, then he slumped to the floor in stages, giggling or about to cry, it was hard to tell. He was shouting at the shiny floor, really laying into it, and when he looked up, it was as though he'd spotted her for the first time.

'Polina!' He tried to touch her face. 'Pretty.'

'What happened?'

He snatched the bottle back like a spoilt child, twisted the lid (there was no lid) and sat, knees pulled up. She sat near him, keeping half an eye on the garden. He took a long pull from the bottle, his little Adam's apple jerking up and down like a sprout in a lift.

'So?' she said, as he pulled the bottle away from his mouth with a kind of flourish.

He said: 'She ain't gonna budge.'

She wondered how long it would be before someone came in and found them.

'We should get you – '

'She aingonnabudge. I was in a hospital.' He looked at her, as if to say, get it now? 'Even when I was in a hospital.'

'Why were you in a hospital?'

He tried to get up. 'All those eyes! I saw them!' He pointed at his head. She let that image develop. A wave of laughter rolled in, second-hand, from the garden.

'They've gone now,' he said.

She got him to his feet, but Isaac's weight was thick liquid pitching side to side, rolling into whichever part of his body was closest to the ground. He accidentally elbowed her hard in the eye and then started a shuffling kind of dance on the spot while she pressed a hand over her eye to stop it watering.

'You could help me here,' she said.

'I have a tassi waiting.'

He had the shakes now, worse than before. He slapped himself on the chest as he tried to tell a joke and there was a stain down his pink shirt, but still she let him drape his arm heavily round her neck as they lurched through the front door and somehow reached the road. From a distance, they were mates, paralytic, or one of those too-tactile couples, always splitting up and having sex.

The taxi's engine was running. Had he ordered it between rounds of puking? The taxi driver looked at Polina as thought this was her fault. He extinguished his cigarette so that he and she could bundle Isaac into the back seat. Isaac tried to grip the driver's hair.

'It's 50 quid if he pukes.'

Isaac tipped sideways onto the back seat so that his arse was the last she saw of him as the driver smacked the door shut and drove off. She realised she hadn't given an address, not that she had one to give. She felt bereft, standing there, frightened in some unclassifiable way. Her eye was swelling.

'What happened to you?' said Leon.

'I walked into a pillar.'

'Anita's got some powder. In her bag of tricks. You've met my wife?'

Leon pushed Anita forwards, his hand pressing into the small of her back.

'I'm fine, thanks' said Polina, hoping she didn't smell of vomit.

Anita gently touched the skin around Polina's eye. 'Is sore?'

'Top-up, ladies?'

Leon filled their glasses from a jug, Polina's so full that she had to drink down into it to stop it spilling. She felt him watch her do it. Anita looked straight into the sun, squinting.

Ruth arrived through the back gate, pram first.

'Fuck … it!'

'Punch, darling?' Polina watched Paul smooth over.

'Why is it completely fucking impossible to get a babysitter in this country?'

'It is Sunday,' said Andrew, his voice audible everywhere. He leaned his head inside the pram's hood.

'You have see Isaac?' Anita pronounced it *I-Zak*.

'Not for a while,' said Polina.

'He is here but he go?'

Ruth was suddenly on top of them, air-kissing, the pram ditched.

'I know it's Sunday but we're not in the fucking Third World! No offence, Anita,' said Ruth.

'How old is he now?' Polina asked.

'Fuck knows! I'm joking,' said Ruth, stabbing a text message on her mobile.

Anita was watching Leon, who was off to one side demonstrating an expansive golf swing to Andrew. Repeatedly. They fixed their gaze on an imaginary ball flying into space.

'I go.' Anita pointed to the house.

'Pols, look at these. I'm fucking leaking.' Ruth pushed her boobs in Polina's face. She blinked at them.

Leon was agitated, it was obvious, coming loose already. 'Where's she going?' he said, as Anita disappeared into the house.

'Did you let your wife off the leash again, darling?' said Ruth, massaging her nipples with her palms.

Leon frowned at Polina. 'I expect you to keep an eye on her.'

'You are fucking joking?' said Ruth.

The baby wailed.

—◇—

4.5: DID THE POLICE CAUSE ISAAC'S LOSS?

'What's going on?' said Polina. She put her shaking down to the coffee.

'It was a fucking water pistol,' said Ruth.

Leon and the others had the volume up loud on the portable TV in the clerks' room. Paul hadn't taken his coat off.

'Can we lock down our website?' he said. 'We're getting bombarded.'

There were mugs everywhere. It was only 8.30am and all the telephones were going mad.

'I only saw him last night, after your party,' said Leon. 'He must have gone from ours to …'

A reporter on the TV said: 'Police issued a statement early this morning saying Isaac Daniels, aged 28, was apprehended last night at this petrol station while allegedly attempting to rob the cashier at gun-point. A witness described Mr Daniels as "intoxicated and confused". Police say he failed to give up his weapon when asked repeatedly to do so after which a police marksman shot and seriously wounded him. The police have so far declined to comment on the suggestion that the weapon was a child's water pistol similar to this one. CCTV footage is currently being examined. Meanwhile, Mr Daniels remains in a serious but stable condition in hospital. His family have already stated they intend to push for a full investigation into what they say were operational failings by the police.'

'He'd had a couple of drinks,' said Leon.

'Everyone knew he had a problem,' said Ruth.

'He said he needed to speak to my wife. Why did he need to speak to my wife?'

Polina felt as though she'd stepped down but missed the step. 'I told him she was out,' said Leon.

4.6: EVIDENCE?

The CCTV gives you barely enough. Pumps on the forecourt of a petrol station. He, the doomed one – except you don't know he's doomed yet, or maybe you do because it emanates from him like inevitability; even his coat looks tired – walks towards the forecourt shop. He stumbles once. He is either not that drunk or so used to being drunk he has finely honed the art of drunk walking, elevating it to performance level, a master-class. There are two cameras. It's late and the petrol station shop is closed but you can still pay through a tiny window at the side. A woman sits behind the glass. The time in the corner of the screen flickers, 22:22.

The action is jerky, comedic, like a snippet from a silent film, black and white and grainy. Polina has watched this clip so many times and still it makes her heart stop, the moment when the policeman's hand pops white like a firecracker.

She drank wine while she watched. When it was over (it lasted the length of time it took to drain a glass, four minutes, thirty-nine seconds), she rewound it and played it again. If you asked her why she watched the same footage over and over again, she might have said she was desensitizing herself or waiting for a different ending. She pressed pause to refill her glass. She imagined the video playing without her, unburdening itself. She watched it because while she watched, it hadn't happened yet, and the more she drank, the more filmic and the more real it became.

She pressed play.

22:23. The second camera. This one is positioned above and behind the doomed man, who has made it to the window. You see a movement from inside, the arm of the woman who sits on the other side moves up and across as though she's swatting a fly. The man steps backwards and spreads his arms as though he wants to introduce a friend at this point (May I present?). You can't see his face so it is difficult to gauge the mood. There isn't time because the face of the woman behind the glass is now a mouth and the mouth is an O. She could be laughing or screaming or neither, maybe this is just the natural shape of her mouth, always surprised, fellatio-ready like a blow-up doll.

The camera malfunctions, the image razored grey. The other camera sputters to life. Have we missed something? The doomed man faces the camera now, startled white as though in the beam of an interrogation. He holds his arms in the air as if to attract attention or wave down a plane. The nose of a police car pushes into view. 22:26. Two policemen get out, drop to the ground. This time they won't do it. They will see, before it's too late, that the gun the man holds isn't real, that it's a water-pistol. The policeman points – are words exchanged? – and something in his hand explodes. The doomed man, Isaac, considers his options carefully before falling to his knees, a bit-part actor milking his moment.

The scrap of pink paper Polina was looking for contained the name of the instructing solicitor she was supposed to call before she got to court. This commuter train was too warm with the leathery, biscuit smell of other people's lives. Polina sipped from her travel mug and tried to remember the point she wanted to make to the judge about costs. Two text messages appeared on her mobile, both from Grace. She thought about deleting them.

Me n Nathan over. He prob won't notice. Prick.
Online now. Where best for hols? Greece/Spain? N still a prick.

The man sitting opposite made a point of lowering his newspaper from time to time to glare at Polina's pen as it slid along the table, as if by staring he could stop it in its tracks. Polina felt sweat drip down her back. Her suit was a little tight at the waist and she didn't want to take her jacket off in case there were visible patches under her arms. She wondered whether the piece of paper with the name she needed had fallen under the table but it was too difficult to manoeuvre out of her seat, so she leaned back a little and, with straight legs, tried to waft her feet around, as though the missing paper might decide obligingly to adhere itself to the sole of one of her shoes.

Her mobile rang. As she grabbed it, her arm knocked the travel mug which flew for a second in a perfect arc before landing in the lap of the man opposite. His mouth actually fell open like a cartoon character.

'Polina?' said a woman's voice on the telephone. 'Becca Hamilton. Are you – ?'

'Becca!' Now that she had the solicitor's name, Polina couldn't stop using it. 'Can I call you back, Becca? Cheers, Becca.'

'Oh,' said the man, flapping at his trousers. 'It's – '

He was probably about to say 'hot' but stopped because the liquid soaking his trousers wasn't hot at all. It was cool and clear like …

'Water,' said the man, as if delighted by his grasp of key words in the English language.

Polina didn't correct him. She fished the soggiest page from the pile on the table and held it up in the air to dry as her mobile rang again. She noticed the start time of the hearing at the top of the page.

'Bollocks,' she said, into the phone.

'It's Becca. You're late.'

'Becca, hi.' Never apologise.

The man opposite had stopped flapping his hands and was now shaking his head and pointing at the window. A peeling sticker on the glass said: 'This is a quiet carriage.'

—◊—

Grace pushed the card into its slot. She was standing inside a Greek telephone booth, a see-through, blue-grey box on a stick, open to the air. The man behind her coughed and smoked. Grace felt too hot as she pulled at her T-shirt with her free hand, hearing her own voice suggest smugly that she leave a message. She took a breath as if to speak but said nothing.

Sitting at a table by the harbour, she listened to the owner of the boat tell her and the others about the trip they would take today. She could smell diesel and fish and saw mopeds speeding up and down, ridden by kids with no helmets.

'We sail to Fiscardo,' the boat owner said, motioning towards the sea. 'We stop, have delicious lunch on the beach. Maybe swim a while. You like to swim?'

A few people nodded. Someone said, 'Yeah!' Don't let this be interactive, Grace thought, and wondered whether it was too late to change her mind.

'Anyone sat here?' asked a smiling woman.

'Go ahead,' Grace said, lifting her sunglasses.

'I'm Sasha.'

'I'm shit company.'

A large, red-faced woman at another table fiddled with a tiny battery-operated fan that she held very close to her face, blowing her cheeks out. The fan buzzed angrily then broke.

'Don't let me get too hot, Keith,' the woman said to the man sitting next to her, as she shook the fan in both hands.

Keith rummaged through a huge bag on his lap. As she took a photo, Sasha's camera made a neat, professional sound like a chef's knife slicing through an onion.

'Will there be shade on the boat or not?' the woman shouted.

'Do you want this, love?' said Keith, holding out a floppy pink sun hat he had pulled from the bag.

'There is plenty shade,' said the boat owner, laughing. 'Or you can …' He made a diving sign with outstretched arms.

'I'm a journalist,' said Sasha, holding up the camera in answer to Grace's look.

Grace immediately arranged her face, chin angled down. She thought of Polina, who said it was still vanity even when you gurned at the last second; it was worse than vanity, it was mock-ironic vanity. Polina said a lot of irritating things.

'You could call this one "Post break-up package holiday from hell".'

'Ah, I see,' said Sasha, smiling sympathetically.

Grace nodded, hoping the nod spoke of pain and break-ups and not the sudden disappointment she was feeling that Sasha hadn't taken her photo.

'I don't want another flare-up,' the fat woman said. 'Make sure there's shade, Keith.'

Sasha leaned towards Grace. 'I hope there's shade,' she said. 'For Keith's sake.'

'If I were Keith, I think I would …' Grace made the diving sign.

'Yeah, or …' Sasha mimed hanging herself.

No one else seemed to need to hang on to every chunky link in the iron chain of the walkway that connected the boat to the quay. Grace envied them all; even the fat woman was making the journey to shore look easy, the gangplank bouncing good-naturedly as she stepped along it with tiny feet (why did all fat people have tiny feet?) sending little shockwaves forwards and backwards.

Grace had lost Sasha a few times during the trip, first to a group of Japanese tourists and then to an old couple who instantly loved her and let her take dozens of pictures of them holding hands or eating fish that the captain – in his captain's hat and too-tight white shorts – had barbecued for everyone on the beach. You like to eat fish? Grace liked to throw up fish. And ouzo. And the mint some idiot had given her to stop her feeling sick.

She missed Nathan. He would have known what to do to keep her calm on the boat (distraction, ridicule, arm-wrestling) and she would have let him, which with anyone else would be shaming, a weakness when she prided herself on never yielding the way other women did. She'd looked for him on the boat, quickly scanning faces just in case, and when he wasn't there she let some poor bastard start to chat her up, torture for her and confusing for him, whatever his name was (Ian?) from somewhere. He didn't know what to do. 'I'm afraid I'm all at sea,' he said, repeating the line and pointing at the water when she didn't laugh.

Back on dry land, Grace felt instantly better. When she felt Sasha's hand on her back, she said: 'I think the antibiotics reacted with the booze.'

'That can happen,' said Sasha, not quite laughing, and something in that good-natured teasing reminded Grace so much of Nathan, she wanted to take the fucking camera and drop it over the side.

'Are you in a rush?' said Sasha. 'I've got a whole day off, which never happens, so I feel like I'm on holiday. Shall we get a drink?'

'Why not?'

'If you fancy a beer without an umbrella in it, I'm only five minutes' away.'

'Ladies! Is it Karen? And a friend?'

'It's Grace.'

The holiday rep in her sweating polyester uniform homed in on them as soon as they stepped off the boat. Grace could not take her eyes off the slow-motion journey of the woman's eyelashes as she blinked; thick blue mascara had clotted the lashes into such a mess that they threatened each time to glue themselves to one another. You had to really want to blink. The woman's name badge read, in an inexplicably sad font: *I'M ARABELLA!*

'How would you rate your trip this morning on a scale of one to ten with one being not what I had hoped for and ten being all that I had hoped for and more?'

'It was all that I had hoped for but no more, Arabella,' said Sasha.

Grace smiled. She watched Arabella click her pen twice.

'And yourself?'

'Two.'

'Two's quite low.'

'It's one for each of the captain's bollocks.'

'All right, ladies.' Arabella seemed to have given up looking at them. 'So, it's two for one drinks at the Kudos bar.' She pointed with her pen to the only bar open at this time of day, pumping out the Greek classic, 'Fantastic Day' by Haircut 100. Grace watched a barman in a cowboy hat pour a green cocktail from height into a triangular glass. The fat woman from the boat trip could barely wait; she leaned forwards eagerly on her stool, one of those metallic ones with a shiny round seat and a single leg coming down from its centre. It made her look like a cocktail cherry on the end of a stick.

'That looks great!' said Sasha, too keenly, which was when Grace decided they would be friends.

Arabella looked murderous. 'I've got you down as tentative for "Jason and the Argo Nuts", Grace. I need a yay or nay.'

Sasha stepped aside to take an urgent photo of the Kudos bar.

'I think nay,' Grace said. 'Thank yay.'

—◊—

Back home, the telephone jolted Nathan awake. He rolled onto his back and took a few experimental breaths, listening to the beep on the answerphone. No message. No Grace. As he moved, he caught a faint, reassuring, peat-like scent from the unchanged bedding, and something stronger from his body, a smell Grace loved like the tang of goat's cheese. A woman who wasn't Grace was singing in his kitchen. He closed his eyes.

He squinted at himself in the bathroom mirror, his skin dry and almost the same cigar-grey as his hair. He took off his watch and placed it next to the sink as he lathered his chin with shaving foam, his face all sharp angles, chin, jaw, nose. He felt soothed by the steam, by the gentle plopping sound as he dipped his razor and watched the blade push a path across his skin like a snow-plough. He tried to hum but no sound came.

'Nathan? Do you have any herbal tea?'

What was that accent? American? Canadian?

'Just a minute.'

A bead of blood wobbled on his chin and he reached for a flannel, which he pressed to the cut. The flannel felt greasy and retained its shape like putty as he squeezed it. He heard Grace's weary voice in his head: *Don't use your face flannel, Nathan. Why do you do that? It's horrible.*

He examined his streaked reflection. His face looked unconvinced, strained, and for a second he wanted to pull back his arm and smash his fist into the mirror. He dropped the flannel and clutched the rim of the sink with both hands, gazing down at the scummy water. The woman, whoever she was, opened the bathroom door and leaned against the doorframe, wearing one of his shirts.

'Hello,' he said.

'That was longer than a minute.'

They sat side by side on the only two stools at the cramped kitchen bench. Had she brought those flip-flops with her? He tried to fit the pieces together: a woman, this one, shouting, close to his face, in a club, after a pub, then a taxi home, her hand on his thigh, like a question, evaded. The sky, black and blue.

'Toast?' he said, the last thing he wanted. Sweat was collecting on his upper lip.

She looked at him and put her mug down, holding her hand out as if to shake his.

'Clare,' she said. 'We didn't do anything.'

'I remember your name, Clare. I wasn't that drunk.' Relief made his heart pump faster.

'So, you remember telling me all about Grace? In Greece?'

'Of course.'

'I hate her.'

He tried to make his face neutral in case she wasn't joking. She took her mug to the sink.

'You wouldn't do anything,' she said, running water into the mug. 'I tried.'

She put the mug upside down on the wire rack and turned to him, touching the collar of the shirt she was wearing. 'Can I use your shower? Or is it too painful because Grace used to shower in it? Before she went to Greece?'

'Very funny.'

They grinned at each other.

'I'm not good at whatever dance you're supposed to do the morning after nothing happens,' she said.

He laughed to show that he wasn't either, but then she had to go and confuse things by looking at him for a second longer than she should have done, so now it was awkward again. She must have seen the disappointment in his face.

'Who are you?'

Grace opened her eyes. A little girl in a red swimming costume was standing so close that Grace could feel her hot breath.

'Let our visitor wake up before you interrogate her,' said Sasha, coming out from the apartment.

Grace sat up on the sunbed, straddling it. This morning's boat trip may as well have been a sleeping pill, and now she felt groggy out here on the terrace, one beer too many, the heat shimmering around her like a fever. She tried to shake off the paranoia she always experienced when waking up in public.

'I brought you some water,' said Sasha. 'Katie, this is Grace. Grace, this is my daughter.'

'I still feel like I'm on the bloody boat.'

Katie moved to Sasha's side and leaned into her leg. It made Grace feel off-balance.

'I'm four and three quarters,' said Katie.

'Thanks for the water.' Grace swallowed some, feeling a tug of irritation. She wondered why you were supposed to lavish kids with unwavering and relentless adoration while they did whatever the fuck they wanted, like shout at you or pull the cat's tail or run into things. Nathan loved kids of course. She'd seen it. They were in the park near the swings when a little girl appeared, lost, a twig in her hair, and had latched onto Nathan. That was that. He'd taken the little girl's hand in his, fluent in a language Grace could not understand a word of. They're just little people, he'd said afterwards, shrugging his shoulders as though he shouldn't really have to explain this to an adult.

'Why won't she talk to me? Is she ill?' said Katie, looking up at Sasha.

'I'm not ill,' said Grace.

Her not liking kids had burrowed itself inside all the arguments she and Nathan had.

'O-K,' said Sasha. 'Let's go and find Mr Frog, shall we?'

'Why?' said Katie, 'I was only – '

'Because that's what we're doing. Inside.'

Grace heard the annoyance in Sasha's voice and knew it was aimed at her. This was a new one, sabotaging a friendship with someone who wasn't even your friend yet. Where were her real friends when she needed them, so she could really fuck things up? Grace got up and walked to the whitewashed terrace wall that came level with her shoulders. She looked down on the view. They were up pretty high, she could see to the harbour where they'd been this morning and the winding track that

Sasha's moped had putt-putted its way up. She searched for the little apartment block where she was staying but they all looked the same from up here.

The ache of missing Nathan wouldn't leave her alone. She thought about what happened the night before she left, him standing there in his thinnest pants holding a hammer in case the mouse she insisted she'd seen (she had seen) came back out from under the sofa. 'Don't you dare fucking try to work me out,' she told him, horrified at herself because that was exactly what she had allowed to happen. He had laughed a joyless laugh, basically just an exhalation, and she knew that if she didn't go, he would.

She heard Sasha's voice from somewhere inside the apartment, not the words, the tone, quite loud at first then too quiet, and she got the creeping sense she had become the uninvited and, perhaps, they were waiting for her to leave. Once the thought took hold, she couldn't shake it. She stayed a little longer, waiting for Sasha to come out, then a few minutes more. She pawed about in her bag for coins to call Nathan and when Sasha did come out, carrying two more beers, apologising ('She's meant to be with her father today'), Grace was so strung out she desperately wanted to be away from there.

4.6: POLINA VISITS ISAAC.

'I didn't know her, I think we were in different years at school. Well, good for them, Mum. No, I didn't know her either. Can I call you back?'

Polina was stuffing papers in her bag as she passed Isaac's room. She stopped to look at his desk and thought about the locked drawer. Her throat felt dry. To get out, she had to go via Leon in the clerks' room.

'It's not a bed of roses this end,' she heard him say. She

waved and tried to hurry past, but he put his hand over the mouthpiece.

'Are we sure we're on top of things, Polina?'

It wasn't friendly. He seemed to require an answer.

She said: 'I'm going to swing by the hospital to see Isaac. Do you want me to give him a message?'

Leon flashed her a look. She recognised it from her mother. It made her want to duck.

'Why don't you tell him not to hurry back.'

Outside, a lone photographer took her picture. Every day for the last month there'd been someone outside. This one looked freshly divorced.

It embarrassed her to watch him sleep; she didn't want to know what he looked like when he did things that weren't work, when he slept, or when he had sex with Leon's wife, or when he held up a petrol station with a water pistol. Polina looked at her watch. It was bad enough she had seen the T-shirt tan lines on his skinny arms. She sucked one of the grapes she'd brought for him, holding it intact in her mouth for as long as she could manage and timing its lifespan in bleeps from his machine: sixteen. If he wasn't going to wake up, this was a waste of time; she could be at home, where there was wine. Maybe she could leave him a note?

She straightened one of the orange box files he had piled up by his bed, straightened it again and then popped open the top one and speed-read the first couple of paragraphs.

'You going to represent me?'

His blue eyes drifted until they found hers.

'You couldn't afford me,' she said, closing the file. Her hands shook a little. She was very tired. 'You're suing the police?'

'I might.' He frowned as though trying to focus on someone he'd just spotted a long way off.

'Shall I help you sit up?'

He exhaled. 'No.'

She resisted talking over the awkwardness of him struggling to sit up until, eventually, he got himself into a kind of ready-to-toboggan position.

'Does that bleeping drive you mad?' she said.

He didn't answer. She thought she could feel him trying to swim up to the surface of his thoughts and break through. Or perhaps it was just a silly question. He never answered those.

'Would you like a grape?' she said.

'We're hoping for a smallholding,' he said, clearly.

'Are you?'

'Anita wants chickens.'

His eyes, without warning, over-flowed with tears while the rest of his face stayed motionless as though it had absolutely no idea that that had been about to happen. It was so disconcerting she didn't know whether to call for help or pass him a tissue. He pressed the little device she'd just noticed in his hand and she half expected security guards to come and escort her out. When he kept crying, she looked around for tissues but couldn't find any, so she leaned forward and wiped his eyes with the backs of her hands.

'Does it hurt?' she asked, once his shoulders had stopped their shuddering.

He closed his eyes, a long blink. 'You probably think I've gone mad.'

'You don't have to tell me anything.'

'That place is toxic,' he said, after a pause so long she wondered if he'd fallen asleep.

She nodded, unsure what he was talking about.

'Be careful.'

'Me?'

He pressed his buzzer. She allowed herself to imagine what morphine might feel like travelling in thick, slow rivulets through her body.

178

—◇—

'You didn't need to do that, with the wine.'

'Was it that bad?'

Grace could feel the warm sun stretch her scalp.

'Paraffin,' said Sasha. 'But I drank it anyway. Look.'

Sasha pushed her sunglasses onto her head and pointed to her eyes.

Grace had walked back up the track last night with a note and a cheap bottle of wine (she was almost out of money). She heard men's voices coming from inside Sasha's place, theatrically raised as though they were reading from a script requiring gusto. No sign of Sasha, so she left the bottle on the step.

'Who's looking after Katie?' said Grace, the coldness of her frappe, sucked through a straw, squeezing her hangover tight like a fist.

'Her father. I've got a job this afternoon.'

Grace wanted to ask about the father but felt she wasn't back in credit with Sasha yet. She also knew you were supposed to save up to ask those kinds of questions, although she'd never understood why.

You were either friends or you weren't; what was the point of preliminaries? She'd never had the patience.

She thought of the beach hut, Polina and a bottle of Thunderbird, that vile paint-stripper they both pretended they loved when they were, what, fifteen? She remembered Polina's tone, close to horror as something occurred to her about Grace: 'You don't want to have sex, you just want to have had sex.'

'I want to get on with it. Don't you?'

They'd been doing handstands against the wall of the beach hut at the time; for a while they conducted every conversation upside down. Grace claimed it got you drunk quicker.

'I don't know,' Polina said.

'I'm definitely going to do it with Justin.'

'So how long have you been married?' Grace said to Sasha.

'Is that what you've been mulling over? I've been watching you thinking.'

'Tell me to mind my own business.'

'He's not my husband. We're single.'

Sasha hesitated. There was something important in this if Grace could just work out what it was.

'Two more!' The waiter looked delighted as he carefully positioned the iced coffees in front of them. 'One and two,' he said, standing back to look at his handiwork.

'I don't think we – '

'On the house.' He pointed towards a man, the owner perhaps, who was hovering close to the door of the café waving shyly at them. Mostly at Grace.

'It's your lucky day,' said Sasha.

They started on the new coffees, but Grace sensed that shift in the air that signals when someone is winding up to leave. She didn't want to be alone with her thoughts just yet. She said, partly because it was true but mostly to prolong things: 'You should have told me to sling my hook the other day. I'm afraid I'm not that into kids.'

'You can say that again,' said Sasha, laughing, and then, as though she'd let her guard down at the end of an interview: 'You don't meet many adults who are jealous of four year olds.'

'I wasn't jealous,' said Grace, stung.

'OK, wrong word.' But Sasha's shrug said right word.

'She's such a cute kid,' Grace tried to grin in the goofy way she'd seen parents do when thinking about their children.

'It doesn't matter. Look, I have to go. I'll get the bill.' She raised her hand for the waiter. He took his time; the eager one from earlier had disappeared.

'What do you take photos of?' said Grace. This wasn't turning out the way she'd planned. Jealous?

'See, I don't take photos, I take verbs,' said Sasha. She seemed to be waiting for a response. It didn't come. 'Which is photo-journalist speak for "I'm a wanker".'

Grace took the business card Sasha handed her.

'When are you off?' said Sasha.

'Tomorrow.'

'I'll look you up when I'm in the UK, shall I? I'm over there quite a bit.'

'Why would I be jealous?' said Grace.

'Gotcha,' said Sasha, clicking an imaginary camera. When Grace didn't react, she said: 'Look, Grace, you hit the point sooner or later where you have to leave being a kid to the kids.'

The keys in her mouth tasted like rotten fruit as she pushed open the front door with her foot and let the bags in both hands fall on to the kitchen table. Except 'fall' wasn't quite right because there was no abandon in the slow motion precision necessary to protect the bottles in the bags from the hard wood table, a carefully choreographed move she'd practiced so often it had a certain dignity, as though the bottles were stiff-boned relatives and she was easing them into their baths. An apple rolled onto the floor. She ignored its cry for help.

All was calm inside the freezer, the vodka just where she left it, banked up against the ice crystals like a gleaming skier. As she reached through the smokiness for it, her heartbeat got faster. She could use a glass, barely clean, or she could drink straight from the beautiful clouded bottle. She tipped her head back and swallowed, the burn ripping her throat.

While her bath filled, Polina ran back downstairs to pick up her wine glass and the half empty (half full?) bottle of red. It struck her that one of the luxuries of being single was running up and down the stairs with no pants on without losing your allure. 'Bert! Allure.' The cat was stretched horizontally on the stair as though intent on pushing the banister further away from the wall. She nudged him with her foot. He ignored her. 'Do I have it?'

An hour later she was still in the bath trying to forget the whole day. Late to court, sobbing client (that client was always sobbing) and a slack-jawed judge who had told her off: 'Miss West, you have let this court down.' Back at chambers, Leon had to stick his oar in, which meant someone must have complained about her: 'Are we sure we're on top of things, Polina?' Which meant there'd be words. Which meant she was in trouble. She reached for her glass. Her mother's call, which came just before she'd left work to see Isaac, was a whining, when-will-my-only-child-come-and-see-me call, as though Polina had nothing better to do than visit her mother to be told about people she didn't remember from school who, having never moved beyond a six-metre radius of where they were born, got married and had some kids. 'Yes, you're a clever girl,' her mother had said, as though grudgingly conceding a point, 'and you've gone for a career. But must it be either or?'

Polina felt slightly better as she stepped out of the bath. She still had about three hours of work to do, which was nothing, and was giving herself the bullshit and control pep talk while thinking she should eat something, some soup, except there wasn't any soup, when her left foot, instead of finding the stone floor as her right had done, found nothing. She fell, and kept falling, and there was a rushing sound, like interference, whooshing and swarming around her head. Polina had just enough time to be curious about that sound because she'd heard it, years ago when she fainted in the science lab at school during the dissection of a heart, and Miss Wood, Mrs Woods – what was her name? – had been so kind, helping her up and stopping the others laughing. 'She swooned,' someone had said, 'Because she loves Mrs Wood!' Except this was different now because Polina was alone as her head hit something hard on the way down and the sound of a huge wave broke over her.

The room hummed like a tuning fork and, inside her head, another throbbed at a different pitch, in and out of time with her heartbeat. It was too cold to be lying naked on the stone floor. She poked her tongue out to taste the blood.

Her-teeth-shivered-she-couldn't-string-a-thought-together-that-made-any-sensible-to-try-and-get-up. Am I due in court? She tried to roll onto. Her black. It all went.

On the balance of probabilities, what had just happened was she'd passed out. The burden was on the claimant to prove it. Was she in court? In her mind she saw her music teacher from middle school, Mr Hancock, one of the best, his image floating precariously in the corner of the bathroom. It was odd to see him there after all these years, tugging at the fraying hem of his navy blue jumper, while she tried to keep order against the noises in her head, unruly glockenspiels, recorders, the things they let kids loose on. Her need for her mother was sudden and primal and pathetic, the tears rolling down each cheek and in and out of her ears. Can you hear me? She willed her message telepathically, I don't know what to do. At the same time as Mr Hancock said 'Lines of the stave are EGBDF', all the oxygen and light in the room got compressed to the size of a Polo mint. Polina tried to go with it through the hole but the hole disappeared too fast.

She woke again, which meant she'd passed out again, and pushed her way backwards towards the bedroom, legs bent, legs straight, legs bent, legs straight. The carpet fibres slowed her progress and scratched her back, and she was sweating as her arms were doing spastic angel wings in the blood (there was blood!). Someone was going to have a fun time cleaning this lot up.

She was too cold. Out loud, when she meant to say help, she said toast, and a memory swung in front of her eyes of a boy tucking his shirt into his jeans, and a fir tree air-freshener on a fraying string, the image so bright she thought she smelled lavender. Get to the phone. Call Grace. Call Grace.

There was supposed to be a map here somewhere. With one hand on the steering wheel, he pushed the mess on the passenger seat to the side; two empty Coke cans, a used-up pen, a little green comb from a Christmas cracker, and *Gooch: My Autobiography*. He wished he'd had the heating fixed ; the van was freezing.

Earlier that evening, he'd picked up the phone, hoping it was Grace. Instead, a woman's panicked voice had said: 'Is she there? Can I speak to her?'

'Who is this?' he'd said.

'Are you Nathan?'

'Do you know what time it is?' he said.

'What time is it?' She wasn't joking.

'Er … hang on.' He'd started to push up his sleeve to check his watch.

'Tell her "toast"? It's Polina.'

Nathan yanked open the glove compartment with one hand and flailed about in it, keeping half an eye on the road as he tried to locate the pocket-sized *A-Z* he was sure was in there, though most of its pages were missing. Grace called it his A-B. He pulled out his lucky cigarette, concertinaed and soft and, as if by magic, his lucky red disposable lighter glinted at him from the footwell of the (lucky) passenger side.

'Do you need an ambulance?' he'd asked Polina.

'I just need her to come. Please.'

So, this was Polina. 'She's away, like I said.'

'What time will she be back?'

'I don't know,' he said, truthfully.

'I don't know what to do.'

He took a deep pull on his cigarette, the sensation clearing his head and making sense of the idiocy of driving at night to somewhere he'd never been to help a woman he'd never met.

Why had he ever given up smoking? A police car appeared in his rear-view mirror, signalling for him to pull over. He took another deep drag and wondered if police officers actually said, is this your vehicle, sir?

To Polina, he'd said: 'Don't you have anyone closer who can help?'

There had been a long pause.

'Are you OK?' he'd said.

'Not really.'

He wasn't exactly sure what prompted him to say: 'I could be there in a couple of hours.' It felt reckless and heroic. He'd play that down or pretend he'd never even considered it that way when Grace thanked him. If she came back. Please let her come back.

'Is this your vehicle, sir?'

The policeman let him off once Nathan promised to get the brake light fixed; he promised that a lot. No sooner had he set off again than he got lost driving the wrong way down a one-way street, some wanker in a yellow sports car following him into a side street on his bumper for two long minutes.

From the address, he'd expected a modern, industrial façade but this was a three-storey Georgian house. Polina's flat was on the ground floor, with a flat above and another down some mouldy steps to a separate basement entrance. He remembered the basement flat he'd shared with a mate and a spider the size of a tennis ball, which lived in the bathroom and only showed itself when you'd settled in for a dump and couldn't escape. It sometimes liked to lift one leg provocatively. The damp in that place was so bad it made condensation trickle down the inside of his bedroom wall.

'You really didn't have to come,' Polina said. He'd waited nearly five minutes for her to answer the door, but here she was, her breath sawing in and out and her face swollen and puffy on one side.

She'd cut her top lip clean down the middle, as though with a cheese wire. He could smell the alcohol coming off her. She said: 'Do you mind if I sit down?'

She fainted backwards into the hall and he got to her just before she cracked her head on the wall.

'I'm firefighting here, Polina,' said Leon, at the other end of the line, with too much bonhomie.

'Are you?'

She tried to sit up in bed without making bed-rustling sounds. She looked at the clock. 8.32am.

'That solicitor who only instructs you,' said Leon, 'has instructed someone else. It was always going to happen. I said, "Can I help it if they're dropping like flies?".'

'I should be back soon.'

'And as long as you're not shagging my wife, you'll be welcomed back with open arms.'

She heard one of the junior clerks laugh.

'You're not, are you?' said Leon.

Perhaps he wasn't joking.

'Am I shagging your wife? No.'

'I'm only pulling your leg, Martina.'

Another guffaw.

'Listen, the other phone's going. Do we have an ETA Polina? It's been over a week.'

'The doctor wants me to – '

'We're going down that road, are we? You're self-employed; a sick note is a death certificate.'

Her face throbbed.

'Bit of friendly: get back on the horse,' he said. He hung up.

You couldn't unsee the empty vodka bottles stacked under Polina's stairs; different brands, which somehow was the most shocking part. The memory of them neatly balanced made Maggie's mind go blizzard white.

Everyone looked younger and more hopeful when they slept, Maggie thought, as she stood at Polina's bedroom door. Wasn't it strange that you knew the rise and fall of your daughter's breath better than your own and yet, on the inside, she was all closed doors. It was too late, wasn't it, to do a motherly thing like push the hair out of Polina's eyes or sing to her without embarrassment (a skill she'd never really mastered). Polina had loved the songs Howard used to make up for her, sea-shanties with rousing choruses that made no sense to Maggie yet reduced Polina to a mess of giggling. After he'd gone, Maggie tried to replicate them but you needed not to care how you sounded and she wasn't good at that. You knew you were dying inside when your own daughter told you not to worry, songs like that were for babies. Sometimes Maggie would sit on the bed long after Polina had fallen sleep, sliced through with gratitude and guilt over who was comforting whom.

Her private joke back then, unoriginal and shared with no one, was that when it came to being a mother, like a stopped clock she was right twice a day, when Polina was at school and when she was asleep. Otherwise, Maggie was unreliable and too tightly wound; it wasn't the job for her. She remembered her own disillusioned parents as forever reeling from the unfairness of the blows life dealt them, forced together and apart by their shared suspicions of other people's motives and their enmity for one another. What did that do to a child? She was never going to be like them, she told herself. Their house was sad and small. It held you in like a corset and taught you that life wasn't meant to be fun. There weren't many books, and no fiction at all except what was there by accident (someone at work told Maggie's father that *The Canterbury Tales* was an illustrated history of Kent). Maggie moved towards Polina's bed.

'Mum?'

'You're awake? Would you like some water?' Maggie sat down, gently.

'Don't worry about me.'

'Do you remember that song about seagulls your dad used to sing?'

'Please don't sing it.'

'No, all right.'

Polina's eyes sparkled with a smile.

'You could have broken your nose,' Maggie said, tracing the scoop of violet under Polina's eye.

'I'm very lucky.'

Perhaps a psychologist could tell something about Polina from the careful way she'd stacked those bottles. But what would that achieve? 'They're working you too hard.'

Polina shook her head. 'They're not.'

'This is my fault,' said Maggie.

4.10: DOUG AND AMY: BONFIRE PARTY ANNOUNCEMENT.

Amy came into the kitchen rubbing her hands together. 'Your dad wants to pop out for more wine, so I'll have to man the fort.'

So far there were six guests to eighteen bottles of wine, Grace was mulling cider and she'd seen champagne under the stairs. 'I think there's enough booze, Mum, even for Dad. It's only a bonfire party.'

The doorbell rang again and Amy clapped a hand to her forehead. 'Oh God.'

'What? It's a party, you invited people.'

'If it's Caroline's mother, keep her away from Doug.' She pointed at the cheese scones Grace had just made. 'Are they a bit small? I was going to make some myself today, but I literally haven't had a minute.'

Thank fuck for that, Grace thought, as she stirred the chilli jam. She said: 'Remember the bonfire party?'

'I remember a three-hour wait in A&E and Doug threatening to sue because they wouldn't take his blood pressure. Do you think jam goes with a savoury scone?'

'Watch this, will you, I'm just going to make a quick phone call,' said Grace.

Tucked in the stair alcove, the phone under her chin, she said: 'Please come and save me.'

'You know I would but I'm rewiring a house,' said Nathan.

'You're washing your hair.'

'I'm rewiring my hair. Are they arguing?'

'She's disrespecting my cheese scones.'

'No one disrespects your cheese scones and gets away with it.'

'She asked me to do the catering for this.'

She could hear from the pause that he was smoking.

'I like your cheese scones,' he said.

'Dad's going to do something embarrassing soon, I can feel it in the air.'

'I can feel it in my hair.'

In the dining room, Caroline's mother was standing by the Hula Hoops talking to a thin-looking Maggie. There was no chilli jam. Amy had burnt it.

Grace put the scones on the table. 'Go on, I dare you, Barbara,' she said. 'A Hula Hoop on each finger.'

Barbara smiled her tolerant smile at Maggie. 'Will Polina be home for Christmas? Has she found a young man yet?'

'She's a barrister, she's extremely busy,' said Maggie, looking at the scone on her paper plate.

Grace said: 'What's your secret, Maggie? Is it yoga? Look at you. Extreme ironing?'

'Worry?' said Barbara.

'I'm fine,' said Maggie.

Barbara rooted round in her bag. 'Caroline's latest,' she said, proudly. Grace and Maggie peered at the dog-eared photo in its cardboard frame; the baby's face looked startled and spiteful.

'You can really see Caroline,' said Grace.

Maggie muffled a cough.

'Who wants some mulled cider?' said Amy.

'Just put it on the table, Mum, let people help themselves.'

'That scone was nice if a teensy bit dry,' said Barbara, dabbing the corners of her mouth. 'It needed, perhaps, a dip? Something to spread on it? But you're the expert.'

'That's what I said,' Amy said, slopping cider from the bowl as she set it down.

'I'll start the ball rolling, shall I?' said Grace, helping herself to a mug filled almost to the brim. With Barbara's eyes on her, she went back and added more. 'I'll just go and check on the bonfire.'

Barbara said: 'I'm so pleased you and Polina have finally made up after all this time. What was it, a lover's tiff?'

'Dad, come and chat to Barbara,' said Grace, grabbing Doug's arm.

She'd been in love with that tree once. Grace looked at it now, its pale grey body electrified white each time a rocket went up. What had possessed her to jump?

Maggie was next to her, from nowhere, and linked her arm through Grace's. Grace wasn't sure how to feel about that.

'I always thought it was taller than that,' Grace said, a kind of holding sentence until she could think of something better.

Maggie seemed to be feeling about for words. Their linked arms phase had gone on too long, so Grace tried to extricate her elbow inch by inch without making it obvious.

'I haven't been well,' Maggie said, eventually. 'It makes you look at things differently.'

'Is that good?' Grace said.

'I don't know yet.'

You could always rely on Doug to spoil things. He was in the dining room tapping the side of a wine bottle vigorously with a teaspoon, while Barbara pulled a Hula Hoop from one finger with her mouth. The mulled cider on the table next to her was nearly gone. It was almost too much for Grace to have to witness without Polina there.

'We have an announcement,' Doug slurred.

He held out an arm to Amy and she moved across to him, taking his hand. Something about that made Grace feel uncomfortable, the maternal flavour of it, Doug the over-indulged son.

'We're going to do something very special,' he said.

'You're all invited,' said Amy, flushed.

'Yes, to the after-party, not the actual …' Doug said, quickly. 'We're going to renew our vows. Next year. I love this woman!'

They weren't holding hands anymore because Doug had moved his hand to Amy's arse. Someone was clapping much louder than everybody else. It was Barbara.

4.11: POLINA. ED. AYSHA. SAM.

Ed's new glasses made him look like his own younger brother, the less cautious one.

'It's nothing. We were passing.'

Polina felt self-conscious in her dressing gown with the cord pulled tight around her waist at 3.15, all the dirty washing-up just sitting there, dirtily. She hadn't washed her hair for days.

A (new?) blue beaded bracelet on Ed's wrist caught her attention, the way it trapped the fine golden hairs that stood up on his arm, as though affronted, and the soap smell coming off his skin struck her as passive aggressive, though she couldn't say why. When you hadn't slept it skewed things. The vegetables kept on coming: a frilly-edged lettuce, carrots, a cock-shaped courgette.

'All from our garden,' said Ed, and he bent to pick up the courgette he'd just dropped.

Loving him had never been the difficult bit but loving him enough was impossible; even now she felt ashamed. There was a time-lag whenever they saw each other, a polite delay between what he deserved and what she could give.

'Is Aysha … ?' she said.

'In the car. I wasn't sure you'd be up to visitors.'

From the never-ending box, he pulled out a packet of ginger nut biscuits, which weren't home-grown, thank God, because the goodness of it all was starting to make her head swim. And then came a clay mug with pink geraniums poking out from it.

'Have you got a coat stand in there?'

'Shall I bring them in?' said Ed, nodding towards the car.

Polina looked at her table, covered in things that weren't hers. She felt so tired she wanted to laugh.

'It's too soon,' Ed said.

'Go and get them,' said Polina.

He was at the kitchen door in two big strides and at some point in the last few years when she hadn't been looking, he must have grown into his body at the same moment she grew out of hers. She heard him put the front door on the latch. Any minute now she'd wake from this dream fully clothed and clean and tipsy.

'You'll love Sam!' he called.

It had been almost three weeks since she fell. Since then, she'd been living in a disquieting fug, sleepwalking through the days. Three times a week she ordered Chinese takeaways, sometimes more, and she'd started watching daytime TV but with the sound down – a pathetic concession to her soul. Work calls were ignored and vodka was a laser beam of sense in the gloom. Shots in the dark.

What was taking them so long? She looked around for the bottle of port that she remembered at that moment having drunk when the wine ran out.

Sam came in first, robotically shy and looking a lot like a blonde Michael J Fox. She liked him immediately.

'Anyone cold?' she said, noticing she was shivering.

'She's in her pyjamas,' Sam whispered.

'How are you feeling?' said Aysha, at the same time as Polina said: 'It's so nice to finally meet you.'

'You're out of milk,' Ed called from the kitchen.

'Sorry!'

'Shall I say my joke?' said Sam. He sat on the floor and stretched his arms towards his toes.

'Not the donkey one,' said Aysha.

'What do you call a three-legged donkey?'

'I don't know,' said Polina, startled by the sudden change of gear. 'What do – '

'A wonkey.' He bit his top lip to keep the pride in.

'Very good,' said Polina.

'Be there in a minute,' Ed called.

'Have you thought about trading him in for a faster one?' said Polina, nodding towards the kitchen.

'I know! I think he's hand-picked the tea from China for you.'

Polina heard the tiny catch in Aysha's laugh. She picked up the clay cup full of flowers and breathed in their scent.

'Did you make this?'

'Mummy used to be a dancer but somebody dropped her,' said Sam.

'Oh.'

'Not on purpose,' said Aysha. 'I don't think.'

'It was a present from my mother,' said Polina, mortified as Ed brought in a large rectangular plastic tray depicting a lurid woodland scene. There were nymphs; it was like a jigsaw your granny forced you to do. She raised the cup to her lips and blew on the hot black tea to try and disguise her shaking hands.

'Are you feeling any better then?' said Ed.

'You look pale,' said Aysha.

Polina saw Ed glance at Aysha as though this was something they had agreed not to say.

'We'll leave you in peace soon, I promise,' said Aysha, raising both arms to pull her dark hair into a ponytail. Polina imagined Aysha's hands cupped around a snowman-shaped body of clay with the wheel going round.

'Sam, put that down,' said Ed.

He'd found a plastic magnifying glass she had no idea she owned (it might have come free with a magazine she hadn't ordered) and was moving it quickly up to and away from his eye. The sight of his gargantuan eyeball made her queasy.

'Can I do investigations in your house?' he said.

'Why not?'

'Just for a few minutes!' Ed called after him.

Now it was just the three of them and she felt like a gooseberry in her own house.

'I saw it on the news about that barrister you work with,' said Ed.

'Isaac.'

Aysha said: 'Something like that would have tipped me over the edge.'

Ed took a quick slug of tea. 'I hear Nathan came round? You know I'd have come, if I'd known.'

Aysha blinked.

'I saw Grace at the weekend,' Polina said, remembering. Grace in the flat had made the light lighter. Simple. She'd said: are we all square?

'I found this!' said Sam, running in. 'There are loads of them under the stairs.'

There weren't loads of them because yesterday Polina had

taken a full box down to the recycling bin. Aysha immediately took the empty vodka bottle from him and tried to hide it under her jumper.

'Damn! My secret is out,' Polina said. It was hard to stop laughing when no one else was joining in. Ed touched his glasses.

'Why don't you pop this back, Sam,' Aysha said.

'We're all the same, I'm afraid,' Polina said, still laughing. 'It's the profession.'

'Then you need to get out,' Ed said. He sounded disproportionately, farcically concerned and it nearly set her off again.

'I plan to,' she said. 'I'm going to take some time out, maybe teach a bit. Travel.'

This was news to her, but it sounded appealing.

'Good,' Aysha said.

When they left, soon after, the washing-up all done and stacked neatly in the rack (Ed insisted), it was only Sam who turned back to wave, and she loved him for it, the feeling in her chest like the downward whoosh of a swing.

—◊—

Polina thought she must be imagining things until she heard his voice again. He sounded like someone doing a very good impersonation of the old Isaac.

She stood outside his open door and watched him talk on the phone, both legs on the desk and his bright red socks on show. You'd never know he was held together with pins. One hand did a loop the loop motion in the air as he spoke. He spotted her and clicked his fingers, pointing at the seat on the other side of his desk. She wondered what he was taking to enhance this performance. It went on for a while.

'Don't go all hortative on me, Polina,' he said, folding his arms on the desk once the call was done so he could lean across to her.

'I thought you'd left,' she said.

'I thought you'd stay.'

He pushed a hand through his hair and sat back on the chair. 'How long will you be away?' He directed this question at the computer screen.

'I don't know yet. You said this place was toxic.'

'I tergiversate.'

'She went back to Leon, didn't she?' said Polina. He didn't say anything. 'Isaac?'

He half stood. 'Thing is, Polina.' He sat again. 'And you'll find this out for yourself one day if you're very unlucky. If you're looking for a deus ex machina,' he chopped at his desk with the side of his hand, 'a fucking chicken farm is not it.'

She shook her head.

'Are you going to say anything?' he said.

'You can't stay here with him, can you?'

'I just might,' he said, and his brief smile faded to mild distaste, or disappointment, as though he'd popped what he thought was a grape in his mouth and it turned out to be an olive.

REMOTENESS

5.1: WAS THE TYPE OF LOSS REASONABLY FORESEEABLE OR TOO
REMOTE?
5.1.2: IS THERE ANY POINT BLAMING SOMEONE ELSE?
5.1.3: ED DOESN'T WANT TO GO TO THE PARTY.

Aysha's CD started up from the kitchen just as Ed stuck the
toothbrush in his mouth and hugged Sam, who was pretending to shave, the bathroom barely big enough for both of them.
It was one of those moments you can't plan, where the mist
clears. He didn't mean to cry but he could feel the tears coming
so he clung to Sam, who hugged him back as though he knew
something Ed didn't. When the feeling went thin, Ed thought,
I don't want to go to the party.

In a few hours, his parents would be flushed and evangeli-
cal about their renewed vows. Ed pictured Doug, drunk then
nasty, the guests bemused about what they might have done to
offend him because he'd seemed all right a minute ago. Even
thinking about Doug made Ed tired. He wondered whether
Polina might be at the party and, straight away, despised himself for his own hopefulness.

He hovered outside the kitchen listening to Aysha sing, 'I've
Got You Under My Skin'. She turned and saw him. Normally
she stopped when she had an audience but today she kept singing, he didn't know why. He smiled.

She handed him the clay bowl she'd made for his parents and
asked what he thought. What he thought was that he should
stop behaving like a spoilt child, but he was dreading the party.
'They'll love it,' he said. His parents wouldn't understand the
bowl. Doug thought his pine cone collection was avant-garde.

'Who renews their vows except desperate people?' he said, raising his eyebrows. When she didn't respond, he said: 'We don't have to go.'

Aysha sighed. They'd been here before. 'We do have to go.'

'I might take the bike,' he said, testing the line, not sure yet if he would or he wouldn't.

Sam came in, pinging his elasticated tie and whistling out of tune, and maybe the combination of Ed's mood and Sam's chirpiness needled Aysha because she was sharp when she said: 'Ed, do what you want.' He didn't know what to do with that. He said: 'I will, then!'

It was a relief to be outside and to start up the bike's engine. He loved the ripping noise it made. He pulled his helmet off as soon as it was on, held it level with his face and looked at its implacable expression. He should go back in and apologise but he didn't, he pulled away, fast.

5.2: THE PARTY.

Polina noticed two things, one after the other: Grace's speed as she moved around Amy's kitchen and the other woman with her.

'All I do is cater for my parents' parties,' said Grace. 'I've really carved a niche for myself. Pols, this is Sasha, my friend from Greece.'

'That's a lovely dress,' said Sasha. 'May I?'

Sasha took a photo before Polina could answer, her camera on a pale leather strap over one shoulder. She looked at home in her clothes, a faded black T-shirt, tightish jeans of indiscriminate indigo/black/blue, sunglasses on top of her dyed blonde hair, and she had that gift of being able to wear make-up but making it look like an accident. Polina looked down at the olive green dress she'd bought yesterday from an unfriendly shop for more than she could afford.

'Sasha is a photojournalist, Pols. She takes verbs. Not a clue what that means but you went to Cambridge so maybe you can explain it to me. She's also a part-time lesbian so you'll probably fancy her.'

'I'm not a part-time anything,' said Sasha.

'Right,' said Polina, caught off-balance because Sasha was so exactly her type she couldn't look anywhere except at the freezer door, which she headed towards as though she'd planned to go straight there all along.

'Sasha's really made an effort with her outfit, as you can see,' said Grace.

'I didn't know I was coming to a party, did I?'

Polina poured herself a shot of ice-cold vodka and knocked it back. 'Anyone else?'

The aroma of roasting chicken filled the kitchen as Grace pulled open the oven door.

'I've never been here and not lied about the food,' Polina said. 'That smells fantastic.'

'They wanted chicken supreme but chicken supreme is for men in flares wearing medallions, so we're having my version.'

'How long are you over for?' Polina said to Sasha, who was leaning forwards on the counter to take a close-up of some cutlery. Grace opened a drawer and started rooting around noisily.

'It's a week-long assignment,' Sasha said. 'Any longer and I miss my daughter too much.'

'Serious question: has anyone seen Mum and Dad?' said Grace. 'They seem to have vanished.'

A daughter. Polina let herself drift for a few seconds.

'We were just going to open some wine if you want some?' said Sasha.

'Love some,' said Polina.

Aysha popped her head round the door, looking healthy and flushed like she'd just jogged up a hill. 'You haven't seen Ed, have you? He should be here by now.'

'Come and have a drink,' said Polina.

'Can you send him outside when he gets here? I really need to talk to him.'

Grace wiped her hands on the tea towel. 'Almonds with sea salt and chilli, olives in a secret marinade. Can you two hand them round out there? Tell me if Nathan's getting overtired.'

'I'm worried Nathan won't recognise me unless I'm lying in a pool of my own vomit,' said Polina.

'We can arrange that,' Grace said. 'I'll get mum to whip you up something tasty.'

Polina turned back from the kitchen door to pick up her glass, lifting her middle finger in response to Grace's exaggerated double thumbs-up.

'You're Jimmy Krankie,' Polina whispered.

'Fandabidozi.'

'You're a lawyer, right?' said Sasha, once she and Polina were outside. 'I could do with some advice on a custody thing.'

'That's not really my area,' said Polina, the opposite of what she meant to say. She looked at the ground and willed it to bury her.

'OK.'

Nathan and Sam were throwing a rugby ball, hard; someone was going to get brained.

Polina said: 'But what I mean, in a general sense, is that I could probably – '

'Could you?'

—◊—

5.3: ED?

'Can you tell me your name, son?'

'Dad?'

From nowhere, Ed gets it, the joke, and all he can manage is a feathery laugh that tickles and bends the air upwards into a lopsided smile until he's forced to choose between laughing and breathing, so he stops laughing. He opens his eyes to a stink of petrol. He needs to cough but he can't because his lungs have shrunk to the size of dolls' teacups. Something is crushing his chest so effectively he's too shocked to wonder what it is. He shivers and is scared to shiver. He doesn't want Aysha to know he's frightened, so out loud, as though she can hear, he says: 'I'm crying laughing.' He means the words as a gift and is wary of saying I love you or you'll be all right, in case they mean he's already dead. Is that the joke?

Two paramedics struggle to pull the motorbike off his body. They've never seen anything like this, they say. He hears them, on and off. Some combination of the speed he was going and the weather conditions, the log across the road: shouldn't the council have moved it? And no bloody helmet!

The joke is back, blacker, and he's careful to respect it, laughing lightly round its edges as though the joke is all that's holding him together, as though he's the joke – maybe it's not a joke? His heart bangs with hope and he can't make it stop. What if this is real?

'How many fingers am I holding up?'

Ed's got questions of his own but he can't remember what to do to get them out. It is late afternoon and they'll be wondering where he's got to. He thinks about Doug's pinched face.

'I'm Bill. What's your name son?'

Something crumbles, he hears it go, little stones, and it's comforting at first, like ramblers on a cliff path, but the noise swells until he can't hear properly and he's coming loose from himself. There's still so much to say. Music, I love music; do you, Dad? Mum never told me your name. I like Bill. I'm married (but not to the love of my life). I have a sister; did you know? Her name's Grace. You'll love her.

'Try and stay with me.'

Ed wants to say, 'I'm not going anywhere', except that's a lie because he thinks he's already gone, or he's going, which might be the same. It's sleep, coming for him, and he would try to resist but he doesn't know how. A thin voice somewhere down below him mimics his own.

'I'll try, Dad.'

His tears have dried; better than that, he hasn't even cried yet. Ed watches his bike disentangle itself from his limbs. Black blood unpools from the road and disappears back into his wounds, that stop their gawping like lips sealed. A bruise on his knee changes its mind. He's on the saddle, flying backwards, the bike's engine groaning in reverse. 'Look, Dad, no hands!' He grips the handlebars and the front wheel rears in anticipation of the log it hasn't hit yet. Aysha's clay bowl reassembles itself around one seemingly magnetic shard and loops elegantly back into the seat of his motorbike.

Ed remembers he's late, buzzing backwards towards a vanishing point he can't see, getting slower.

There were the rumblings of an argument. He can see its end but not how it started. He's metres from the houseboat, furtively pulling on his helmet then pushing it off as he kicks the bike rest to the ground. His anger is already subsiding and he wishes he hadn't said the things he hasn't said yet. Nothing a bike ride won't fix, he thinks, disappointed because the ride seems to be over and he doesn't even remember it. He backs towards the door, a tissue-wrapped bowl under his arm, and unzips his jacket.

Music plays in the kitchen, 'I've Got You Under My Skin', and Ed shouts: 'I will, then!' It rocks him; he doesn't know why he said it. Aysha says: 'Do what you want.' And now Sam is moonwalking backwards out the kitchen door. Ed wants to point at him: 'Who's this, Michael Jackson?' But he can't move his arms or form the words, and instead something tugs at the air around him when he says, 'I might take the bike,' and it's lost before he can understand it. 'We do have to go,' Aysha sighs. 'We don't have to go,' he says. 'Who renews their vows except desperate people?'

He examines the bowl that Aysha has made. He thinks of

her hands holding it steady as the wheel spins clockwise, anti-clockwise. 'They'll love it,' he says, just before Aysha asks him what his mum and dad will think. He feels sad with dread and he doesn't want to go. The song sucks towards its beginning and Ed hovers outside the kitchen because she'll stop singing if she knows he's there.

Reasons to go: he'll see his sister; Polina might be there (don't be stupid); it's a party. Reasons not to go: Doug. Must every road lead back to him, Ed thinks, trying hard to pull himself together.

She's got her CD on in the kitchen, maybe she'll sing soon, he loves it when she sings, and he tells himself a party might be fun (but he knows it will be awful.) He needs to hug Sam and he laughs when Sam pretends to struggle because they're lovely these moments, the best, except Sam must have heard the change in Ed's breathing because he hugs Ed tighter without looking up. Ed wants to thank him but doesn't trust himself to speak, and he'll get toothpaste down them both if he talks with the brush in his mouth. I'll take this, he thinks, not the big scenes. When they talk about love – as his parents are bound to do, once Doug's drunk – I'll play this back and back and back.

GRACE
(From downstairs.) Mum!

AMY
They're waiting for us down there.

DOUG
I should remarry you more often.

203

GRACE

(From downstairs.) Mum! Can you come down?

AMY

(She steps into her dress and reaches her arms round the back.) Zip me up, will you?

DOUG

Or you could come back to bed?

AMY

I don't want people wandering in here and seeing you in your pants.

DOUG

(Getting out of bed quickly in just his pants and embracing Amy from behind.) I could (only half joking) whip them off?

AMY

(She manages the zip herself.)

GRACE

(Opening the door without knocking. A policeman just behind her.) I'm not sure if they –

POLICEMAN

(Stunned.)

```
                    DOUG
        Are you the stripper?


                    POLICEMAN
        Mr and Mrs Mullin?


                    AMY
        Not Ed? (She reaches backwards to
        steady herself but there's nothing
        there.)


                    POLICEMAN
        I'm so sorry.


                    GRACE
        Mum, sit dow …


                    DOUG
        … normally two of you?


                    POLICEMAN
        … colleague, sir, but we …
```

—◊—

5.4: TWO MONTHS LATER.

'Have we missed it?'

It was the first thing Grace had said for over an hour and it woke Polina from the memory she'd been letting play itself out, the one where Ed told her to fuck off.

'I wasn't looking,' Polina said. 'Can you slow down a bit?' They'd been driving nearly two hours and the stale air inside the van was making her feel sick.

'You're meant to be navigating,' said Grace.

Cigarette smoke had been absorbed over time into the fabric of everything Polina touched, the seat, seatbelt, the dashboard, the handle on the passenger side. A dirty beige halo stuck to the roof above Grace's head.

'I can't get this window open,' Polina said.

'Don't even try, it's held together with nicotine.'

'Pull in here,' said Polina. 'I think this is it.'

It looked like a derelict shop, cardboard taped to the inside of the front window on the ground floor and the glass punched through in a couple of places as though stones had been thrown or stray bullets fired from a passing car. There was graffiti all over the side wall, purple D-shapes reproduced again and again like bacteria up as far as the first floor, and damp post spewed from the letterbox, all of it rubbish, as far as Polina could tell, sodden flyers, pizza adverts, opportunities for which The Occupier of Carnegie House had been specially chosen. There was nothing addressed to Carl, but he'd drifted in and out of this place, Ed had said, a kind of halfway house for the halfway homeless.

Grace peered through the glass at the front, her hands a visor. She knocked, not very hard.

'Do you think anyone still lives here?' said Polina.

Back in the van, neither of them said a word. What was there to say? When Grace revved the engine, Polina knew without asking where they were headed. She took a deep breath of un-fresh air and wished she hadn't.

'We may as well eat this before it gets cold,' said Grace, and she tossed a warm foil package onto Polina's lap.

'You did us a packed lunch?'

Polina opened the parcel and closed it again when the smell of bacon got tangled up with the smell of old cigarettes.

'Give us a bite,' said Grace. 'It was Carl's favourite.'

The white of the fried egg had puckered around the yolk, which had shrunk and dried into a mustardy dome.

'Have all of it,' said Polina.

'As in, it was Carl's favourite thing to steal from our house.'

They parked in the little car park you didn't have to pay for out of season and Grace said: 'You think this is a stupid idea, don't you? As if Carl would be here, right?'

Polina nearly tipped herself head first into the side of Grace's left shoulder as she leant across to give Grace a hug. 'Come here,' she called across the chasm between the seats.

Grace laughed. 'What are you doing?'

'What does it look like? Trying to mount the gearstick, of course. It's what lesbians do.'

'In the dry season?'

'Exactly.'

Carl wasn't at the beach hut because the beach hut wasn't there anymore. There was a gap where it should have been, like a freshly extracted tooth. Its absence hit Polina like fear, like being suddenly lost. 'Where's it gone?' she said.

Grace looked small, like a child, as she straddled the smooth concrete seawall they used to pretend was a whale's back and covered her eyes with her hands. Polina had to look twice to make sure the crying was real. Grace cried the way men cry, not at all then too much and not with tears but dry sobs.

The grey of the sky, indistinguishable from the colour of the sea, reminded Polina of the dizzying feeling of floating on your back on overcast days, she and Grace feigning fearlessness (perhaps Grace wasn't feigning) and both of them shutting their eyes for a count of ten. When you opened them, you could kid yourself if you concentrated hard enough that you were in the sky looking down at the sea. She could still see Grace's expression as she'd surfaced from the water back then, wearing Ed's face mask, her arms held much wider apart than the length of the grey mullet she said she'd just seen under there. Was that the summer Grace had invented Horizontigo? (It's like Vertigo but more serious and I get it a lot when I do long-distance swims.) Polina had grabbed the mask and dipped under, caught sight of the swish of something in the churned up water, a pair of sand-coloured eyes. She'd had nightmares for weeks.

'Did we make it up?' said Grace, motioning with her runny nose in the direction of the beach hut.

Polina joined her on the seawall. I should talk about Ed, she thought. I'm supposed to say something comforting. Maybe he'd have found it funny, the missing beach hut; he'd have said it didn't matter, it was just a beach hut. He'd have said that Carl, if he wasn't dead himself, which he probably was, would already know on some cosmic level about Ed's death, so there was no need to worry about letting him know, if that was why they were here, and definitely no need to hang about where the beach hut used to be on the off-chance that probably-dead Carl might choose that moment to do what he'd only ever done once or twice before, which was to stroll past nonchalantly, wearing shorts in the winter and waving his royal wave.

After they'd done it in the beach hut, Polina had lost her nerve. What she'd wanted was to tell him how profound an experience it had been, that what they had done was meaningful for her and precious (even magical?). But she couldn't find the words because words won't come when you grasp for them. He'd given her a gift. How could she tell him that? And what would he have said in response: 'I made you gay? Gee, thanks.'

So, she'd never mentioned it again, pretending it was kinder that way, even when he tried to talk about it, which was often, even after his concern started sounding like hurt and then moved from disbelief into something more brittle, so now they couldn't talk about it if they'd tried. She wished she'd told him the truth, that he kept her from feeling alone. That she loved him back.

Her current problem was that the cold of the concrete was starting to penetrate her arse-cheeks and was so painful and distracting, she had to move her weight from one side to the other to retain some feeling.

'I might go travelling for a bit,' Polina said, out of nowhere.

'Do you need a shit or something?' said Grace.

'My arse has gone numb.' Polina stood up from the wall and

shook one leg at a time as though she was dripping wet.

'You're running away? Again?' Grace said.

'I'm not running away.'

It was suddenly difficult to hear over the rasp of the waves.

'What about your meetings?' said Grace.

'I'm much better now.'

They got back in the van, slamming the doors shut against the wind. Grace started the engine and clicked the radio on; a sports station shouted a football match.

'Let's go home,' said Grace. She sounded very, very tired.

'Yeah.'

'Find something else, will you?'

She backed out of the car park and Polina fiddled with the radio but there was either loud buzzing or the football match, loud and clear.

'Is there a bee in here?' she said.

'Just turn it off,' said Grace. 'Please.'

They drove in silence for the first few miles. Polina balled her scarf up around her neck to block out the smell. I am not running away.

'Will you go to Greece?' said Grace, eventually. 'On your travels?'

It crossed Polina's mind to pretend the idea hadn't occurred to her.

'Say hello to Sasha from me,' said Grace. She reached across and patted Polina's thigh.

'I will.'

—◊—

5.5: DOUG'S LOSS AND AMY'S REMOTENESS.

He'd been doing all right before he bent to pot the ball. Dave patted him gently on the back.

'Don't let me put you off.'

'Very funny,' said Doug. It looked easy on television.

The low ceiling in the snooker hall had made him feel dizzy in the past so he was being extra cautious and taking his time, but the back of his head still felt unnaturally warmed by the trough of strip-lighting that illuminated their table, the kind of lighting that set the mood at 2am whatever the real time. He pulled back his arm and pushed the cue through. As it skimmed his chin he suddenly remembered the way Ed used to pretend his snooker cue was a bass guitar, and the memory caused something inside his body that was holding him up to slide downwards. He wasn't surprised so much by missing the cue ball and gouging the gauze, leaving a blue chalk skid mark, as how he came to be on his back on the prickly lager-sodden carpet, sobbing like a baby into Dave's big dark face.

'Are you all right, mate?' said Dave.

'I'm fine.'

Amy had made him go out, it was her fault. She said he was getting under her feet; she said she couldn't think straight with him there. That'll be the pills, he said. If I promise to go out will you promise to wash your hair?

The snooker hall was too quiet and too menacing and smelled stale like it had been pumped full of burps. Then there was Dave, who'd been Doug's best man and whose reconstructions of heated conversations he'd had used to impress Doug until gradually, over the years, he'd finally cottoned on that Dave was a fantasist, never actually complaining and not giving waiters a piece of his mind. He once convinced Doug he'd told their mutual friend Colin to fuck off on the steps of The Pink Flamingo. *I said Colin, if you're going to talk like that you might as well fuck off! You never told Colin to fuck off? I did, mate!* Doug had felt buoyed for weeks imagining Colin's startled face being told for once in its charmed life to fuck off. But it turned out Dave hadn't even been there that night, it was Nigel and Colin, and actually it was Colin who told Nigel to fuck off, not the other way round, and it wasn't even fuck off, it was back off. As Nigel said: 'I hate to be the bearer of bad news but no one said fuck off to no one.' It was hard to explain the depth of the betrayal Doug had felt about that; it got mixed up with embarrassment about his own gullibility. Plus, he really wanted someone to tell Colin to fuck off. He lied to me, he'd told Amy. She didn't seem to understand. People in glass houses, she said.

This morning was the first time since Ed that Doug had got himself fired up in a good way. Fuck, he'd like to bottle that feeling; the sweat pouring off him like brine, he'd done fifty sit-ups before Amy was even awake, grunting hard on the out-breath so she'd wake up and notice. Maybe she'd even react. She'd been in bed for three days.

'What time is it?' she asked, eventually, so groggy she could barely see. Her lack of effort had begun to make him feel physically sick.

On the steps of the snooker hall, which was part of the leisure centre complex with a swimming pool and a training pool (with rats, he'd heard), he gulped down fresh air. Two women gave him a look. He was barring their entrance and the braver one with the towel rolled up under her arm said 'Excuse me' in that sneering way older women seem to think repels imminent male attack.

'I think they'll want that back, mate,' said Dave, wheezing. 'You can't take it off the premises, the woman said.'

Doug realised he was still holding the cue. It felt good in his bunched fist. 'I'm coming down with something,' he said.

'Shall we call it a night?'

There were a few stars out already. Someone was noisily parking their car, its dark blue the exact same dark blue as the short-sleeved shirt he'd bought for the party. Amy called it natty. He hadn't been able to do anything with it since then, couldn't wash it or throw it away, so it remained hanging like a natty hair shirt down the bad end of the wardrobe with the other things he'd never wear again.

'Who is that reptile on reception?' Dave said. 'Did you clock her? I said, "Does he look like a thief? He'll be back in a minute. Chill out".'

Doug thought, you did not say chill out.

'She said, "You can't take equipment off the premises", and I said, "The premises include the steps".'

'You're right, Dave, let's call it a night.'

He thought he'd feel better once he was back in the car but when he started the engine, its growl was his own anxiety and he wanted to jump back from it.

He had a recurring dream when he was a boy of a runaway car picking up speed. His mum popped out for something and the car started moving with him in it, so he slid across to the driver's side and took the wheel, turning it side to side like they do in films. When he pressed at the jammy air with his feet, his legs didn't reach the pedals.

Having parallel parked the car, the prospect of silence when he turned the engine off was too much, like the roar that came when you woke from a deep sleep, so he let it run, and when he couldn't bear that either he turned the radio on, then up. Paul Weller. He couldn't turn it off; what kind of sick joke was this? He couldn't turn it off because last time he'd heard this one they'd been sitting in the car, Ed in the passenger seat. Had they been on their way back from somewhere? Where would they have gone, just the two of them? It had been raining; he remembered the squeak of the windscreen wipers as they moved right to left, erasing whatever the last person just said.

'Is this "Wild Wild Wood"?' said Doug.

'It's not Wild Wild. It's just Wild,' Ed said.

'I'm trying to make it exciting. It being the most boring song I have ever heard.'

Ed shook his head with irritation.

'They all sound the same,' Doug said.

'Just turn it off.'

Doug had parked here a dozen times over the years, maybe

more, always scanning the road surreptitiously for a girl with a limp – ridiculous – and praying he didn't see her. It was dark now, the street lamp had blown, but his car door made a comforting, grown-up sound as he pushed it shut, the sort of dampened crunch you'd expect to hear from the closed car door of a TV detective, part heavy boot on gravel, part needle being wrenched from a record. Somehow, it gave him the confidence he needed to scan the road up and down. It had to be one of these houses. A dog's whining sent his heart thumping with hope until he remembered the dog he'd nearly run over would have to be thirty years old by now. He made himself breathe in and out. It was a start. Perhaps the people he was looking for were dog people who replaced the old one with a new one each time.

Before he could talk himself out of it, he knocked at what he guessed was the house of the whining dog, though the whining had stopped, and took a step back. He saw the bell he'd missed and pressed it. The dog went crackers. There was shouting and, in a daze, he stepped sideways over a low brick wall that separated the house from its neighbour and knocked there. Lights were on behind the curtains and he thought he could hear a TV and see the outline of someone lounging in front of it. It made him think about Amy, who was at home right now doing the same. He pictured her as she was when he'd left, curled up on the sofa, same as every night, pale and childlike in that dressing gown he couldn't stand, clutching a glass of milk while she watched *Pretty Woman* or *Beaches* or *The Lost Boys*. He searched for tenderness but all he felt was chest-tightening fury; she'd be mouthing the words for fuck's sake. Then the door opened, he'd forgotten there was a possibility it might, and the woman standing there stared with the same bemusement she must have seen in his face.

'Frank,' she called back into the house.

Could she be the mother? Maybe. She looked the right age for the mother.

'I wondered whether you remember a little girl?' he said. He held the flat of his hand at the level of his thigh and looked at it. 'Sorry to trouble you.'

'Frank!'

'Where's the fire?' a voice called from upstairs.

Doug heard the slow, soft footsteps of slippered feet.

'I'm trying to trace a girl who was run over here in the road,' he said. 'About thirty years ago.'

'What's this?'

Frank appeared. He looked from the woman to Doug and put a protective arm round her. They looked stiff, posed for a photograph they didn't want taken.

'He says a little girl was killed in our road thirty years ago,' she said.

'Like I said, I'm sorry to trouble you,' said Doug. He didn't sound like him.

'Bit late to be calling now, isn't it?' said Frank.

'I'm trying to trace her,' said Doug. 'She wasn't killed, she was injured. That's all. Not too serious.'

'We don't know anything about it,' said Frank.

'She'd be about the same age as, or older, than my son would have been. If he hadn't – '

He put a hand to his hair. Was he having a stroke? The hard edges of the woman's face melted and, when she spoke again, her voice was so quiet he barely heard her. 'Was it suicide?'

'Margaret!' said Frank, rubbing his left arm nervously with his right hand, up and down.

Margaret looked like she wanted to invite him in, he could sense it in the minute concaving of her stomach, like a pre-bow, but he didn't want to go in. Frank said, 'We can't help you,' and shut the door, not hard, in Doug's face. He wiped his nose on the sleeve of his coat and, after watching the curtain being twitched a couple of times from the inside, turned and walked away.

Amy didn't say a word, even when he sat close to her on the

sofa. He wondered whether she'd pick up on the peculiar energy he was throwing out – relief, elation, guilt – and if she'd suspect him of having an affair. He was sweating though it was cold outside.

'I took the snooker cue by mistake. I had to return it.' He was still out of breath.

'You're cold,' she said, and she felt for his hand without turning her head from the screen.

Tonight, it wasn't milk, it was wine. He registered that as a tiny step forward.

He'd driven back, left the snooker cue poking out of the glass-panelled door, tip first, like the thin barrel of a gun pointing up to the sky. It had taken a while because his hands wouldn't stop shaking and the glass in the leisure centre door was much tougher than it looked. He'd had to heft the butt of the cue in the same spot over and over until finally the glass curtsied in a little circle around the point of impact, cracking inwards like thin ice. 'There,' he said, feeling relieved beyond belief, like the best piss after the longest wait. They didn't have a security alarm, which surprised him; he could have been anyone.

5.6: AMY AND THE MYSTERY MAN.

She woke again, or fell asleep, there was no difference – another revelation but there was no one to tell, where was Doug? – and in her hand she held the blurry Polaroid Ed took years ago of her and the mystery man. She sniffed it. It used to smell of marker pens.

                                AMY
            You couldn't talk him round?

MYSTERY MAN

You know how stubborn your father
can be.

AMY

Did you even try?

MYSTERY MAN

How is Ed? How's Doug?

AMY

He'll never speak to me again, will
he?

MYSTERY MAN

You have your own family now.

AMY

Doug's not all bad.

MYSTERY MAN

I've never yet met a person who
is.

AMY

(Saying nothing.)

MYSTERY MAN

(Nods at the flask.) Any more tea
in there?

AMY

I never told anyone about you. Except Doug and even that wasn't the
whole truth.

MYSTERY MAN
(Holding aloft his flask cup of tea.) To Perth! Land of the culturally barren but with excellent wheelchair access! I'll send you a postcard.

AMY
Was this all Julie's idea?

MYSTERY MAN
My wife remains an enigma wrapped in a wheelchair. (Pause.) I want to give you something. For Ed. (He hands her an envelope.)

AMY
I can't take this.

MYSTERY MAN
It's for him, not you. For college, when the time comes. Or a car, or whatever floats his boat. A boat.

AMY
It's too much.

MYSTERY MAN
It's also a thank you.

AMY
What for?

MYSTERY MAN
You know what for. It would have

killed your father if he'd known
about us.

                    AMY
I have to go.

                    MYSTERY MAN
Take it, please.

DEFENCES

6.1: IT WASN'T MY FAULT IT WAS YOUR FAULT.
6.1.2: POLINA. WHICH DEFENCE TO RUN? CONSENT? CONTRIBUTORY NEGLIGENCE?

7.30am. Polina was in the Post Office shop again, this time buying two newspapers and some half-price milk chocolates. She made smalltalk with the shop assistant while rattling the chocolate box. This weather! He agreed. The spirits were on the shelf behind the counter, with the razor blades and the paracetamol, and she looked everywhere but there. Oh, and some vodka, if you've got any? She tried to make it sound like an afterthought, something forgotten from a shopping list, knowing as she did so that he must be able to see right through her, because she'd been here before and had the same conversation with the same man. She was almost ashamed enough to leave empty-handed. She banged her forehead with her open palm as if to say, I'd forget my head.

6.2: DOUG AND AMY – BENEFIT GIG.

'Why did we never go to one of Ed's gigs?' Amy said. Doug noticed a blackcurrant half-oval stain on her top lip as she sipped from her wine glass. He shoveled down a handful of peanuts. At least it wasn't a milk moustache.

Everything should be all right as long as he didn't have to talk to anyone. Grace had the café looking really nice; it felt different at night time, there was a bar, she'd put candles on the tables and red tablecloths, and there was even a small stage in one corner where the band were warming up. He'd nearly gone to a gig once. He took two trains into London, only his second time there, and had called a helpline the day before to double-check the times. Although both trains were on time, he was late to the pub because Kings Cross was very confusing and he didn't want to ask directions in case it made him a target for mugging. He'd walked mock-confidently for half an hour in the wrong direction and when he finally found the place, his neck was sweating inside the collar of the smart-casual mistake of a shirt he didn't know why he'd chosen. Light-headed, he'd tried to peer through the steamed-up pub window, and a couple, arm in arm, pulled open the heavy door and held it for him.

'Coming in, mate?'

The music lurched at him from inside the pub, making him take a step back.

'The bass player's my son.'

'Great stuff.'

What if Ed didn't want him there? He let that thought sink in for two more songs. By the end of the third, he'd stopped trying to see inside the pub and was working up some real resentment towards Ed. Who did he think he was? Doug had every right to be here. When the door opened again, it was Ed's friend, Jonty, stepping outside in a long brown leather jacket.

'Douglas?' Jonty blew smoke like a blessing into the air above Doug's head.

'I can't stay,' said Doug, and his legs shook as he hurried away.

In the café, Doug watched Grace hold up a bucket to two men who'd just arrived, both Ed's age. His friends? One said, 'Cosy in here', and something more that Doug didn't catch because the band started 'Superstitious' at that exact moment. It unnerved Doug it was so very loud. Grace kissed the men on both cheeks, like the din wasn't bothering her, they put money in her bucket and then Aysha came in, and she and Grace held each other for a long time. Doug couldn't watch that.

'I'm off to the gents,' he shouted to Amy.

'What?'

At the bar, he asked for a beer and the woman who served him had sympathetic eyebrows that looked as though they planned to rendezvous shortly at a point in the middle of her forehead.

'You're his dad,' she said, reaching her hand across to touch his arm. 'Ed practically lived round at ours when they were at school. I'm Mack's mum. Jean.'

'Doug.'

Who was Mack?

She clicked her fingers. 'Now he's gone, like that.'

'Yes.'

'Aidan and I put £50 in the bucket because you live in A&E when you've got kids, don't you?'

'You do,' Doug said. He couldn't go back to the table because Aysha was now sitting there with Amy. The band were taking a break. 'Gottle a geer,' he said and raised his bottle to Jean.

Her eyebrows going into overdrive told Doug that someone was behind him. Before he could turn, he felt himself being lifted off the ground by a man's arms around his waist. A foot off the ground and kicking his feet about, Doug tried to signal with his eyes to Jean that this was fun and even got as far as a tight, 'Ha ha ha!', before Jonty dumped him back on his feet. His leather jacket smell was very pungent and Doug exhaled hard, praying his allergies wouldn't flare up and/or he hadn't cracked a rib.

'Holy shit!' said Jonty, whipping Doug round by the shoulder to look him up and down.

'How good is Jonty on gee-tar?' said Grace, appearing from somewhere behind Jonty's back.

'Ha ha!' Doug squeaked.

'This guy,' said Jonty, pointing at Doug, full of emotion. He put his arm round Grace and pulled her in, starting to cry.

'Let's get this man a beer, Joan, quickly,' Doug said, and he punched Jonty hard in the arm.

'Dad, relax,' said Grace.

'I am relaxed. I'm very relaxed.'

'Jean,' said Jean.

Jonty was mopping his eyes with the heels of both hands.

'You going to play some more for us, Jonty?' said Grace.

'Play all night if you want.'

'I expect there's a noise curfew of some sort though, is there, around 11?' Doug asked Grace. She looked at him witheringly and he tried to turn it into a joke. 'Bloody noise police!'

Three hours later and the band were packing up.

'How many beers have you had?' said Amy.

'I'm telling you, I went to his gig! I kept the train ticket. It was great. We had a great time. Do you want to see the train ticket when we get home?'

'I didn't know.'

'We had a great time,' said Doug.

'So you said.'

'I'll show you the train ticket.'

'I don't want to see the train ticket.'

'Well, there you go then. Shall we have another drink?'

'The bar's closed, Doug. We're leaving. I just want to ask Grace how much they've raised. You coming?'

'I'll wait outside.'

The fresh air made his head thud and he put a hand to one eye while nodding at the last few as they left. The thought of going home where Ed was still dead made him feel so weak he decided he should probably find another bar.

Grace came outside rattling keys and calling, 'Everyone out!' To Doug, she said: 'Have I got mafia parents? Mum's just donated an envelope full of cash.'

'Has she?'

'Settle an argument for us, Jonty,' said Amy, in an over-loud voice, appearing arm in arm with Jonty and looking pleased with herself. Doug swore under his breath.

'Amy, time to go, my love.' His jaw was tight.

'Did Doug come to a gig or not?'

'Our taxi's here,' said Doug, jauntily.

Those three seconds during which Jonty blew a smoke ring went on and on and on.

'Well, yeah …' said Jonty.

'See!' said Doug, grinning and genuflecting. 'Let's leave the man alone, Amy. I need to talk to you. About money. Grace, are you coming with us?' He couldn't stop. 'Or making your own way? Shall we find a bar?'

'Yeah he did or yeah he didn't?' said Amy, narrowing her eyes. Jonty's head was doing a kind of so-so wobble.

'Ah, man,' said Jonty.

—◊—

6.3: POLINA AND SASHA IN GREECE.

Three tethered fishing boats plopped up and down, their colours, turquoise, stripes of pink, like ageing homosexuals dressed with fastidious abandon.

'It sounds like applause,' said Sasha.

'What does?' said Polina.

'When the sea scrapes the beach. Listen.' Sasha picked up her camera just as the moon streaked the water. All the stars had gone, and above them was a dome of black, a layered, diaphanous blackness you'd never get at home. They huddled side by side on the beach.

'Are you cold?' Sasha said, putting her arm around Polina's shoulders and pulling her close. Polina was so cold she couldn't feel her feet, but it was worth it for the sensation of Sasha's arm, her fingers almost close enough to kiss.

'This was a bad idea,' said Sasha.

'It was a great idea,' said Polina. She pulled out the bottle of white wine she'd half buried in the pebbles and offered it ('Tada!') but Sasha shook her head and suddenly got to her feet as though the sight of the bottle irritated her. Polina took a quick swallow while Sasha wasn't looking.

Polina didn't know where to look while Sasha undressed, quickly and messily, everything off and dropped on the pebbles in under a minute, so she focused on the camera, which was really an excuse to look at Sasha's pants draped over it as if to protect the camera's modesty. Were they dark blue? It was hard to tell in the dark; they looked plain, no frills or bikini-tie bits. She took another slug of warm wine. If Sasha was not at all self-conscious about taking her clothes off in front of Polina for the first time, didn't that make them more like sisters?

Sasha ran down to the sea over the pebbles, making it look easy, and was soon in up to her knees, then her thighs, without hesitation and without making a sound, denying Polina any chance to study her body from behind. She turned as though she knew Polina would be watching and called, 'Hurry up!'

'Shit.' Polina pulled at her T-shirt to get it over her head. Her bra chose this moment to be fiddly.

'I'm not doing this by myself!'

Polina gasped with the cold of the water, unexpectedly Britishly cold, as the ground under her feet didn't slope so much as disappear from under her, like stepping into a bowl. She grabbed for Sasha's hand and immediately lost it, then dunked her head under the water to give the impression that swimming at night wasn't something that scared her. When she came back up, she caught a flash of what might have been Sasha's white arse as it curved and sank into the black.

'Here!'

Polina turned and Sasha's face was so close to hers it blurred. When they kissed, Sasha's mouth was edgeless, underwatery. Polina's foot found a little hold in the sand and she pushed down on it for purchase, but this propelled her upwards too hard and fast against Sasha's chin, a kind of slow motion chin-butt.

'Shit! Sorry. Sasha?'

They lost each other, so Polina flipped onto her back and

floated to let her heart slow down. She could hear Sasha laughing. It sounded like it was coming from the sky or rebounding off the ceiling of the sky, but she didn't want to laugh if laughing meant this was just a game. She turned onto her front and saw Sasha swimming hard towards the beach, each arm spearing the water, so she followed as fast as she could with her splashy, childish crawl. Please don't let this be a game.

Now they were in shallow water and both could stand, but it was too exposing for Polina, like someone had ripped the sheet away, so she kept swimming as long as she could though the stones were scraping her belly and pushing her towards the beach. Then they were both standing, wading in, Sasha just ahead, her balance much better than Polina's, whose mind raced for something to say before the chance was gone or Sasha came to her senses.

'Fuck this,' said Sasha, stopping suddenly and turning to face Polina full on. Without hurrying, she raised both hands above her head to wring out her hair. The movement lifted her breasts and exposed the inward, uneven curves of her torso, and Polina didn't want it to look like she was ogling. Sasha said: 'Can I make it any clearer?'

The next afternoon, Polina got to the taverna first, a tiny place tucked into the wall of the beach. It was a different beach from last night, less rocky and dramatic with a handful of sunbathers laying back in the sand in white bikinis or tiny trunks. Polina ordered an ouzo to settle herself and a beer for after. Sasha had left early that morning to get to a job and Polina had felt the warm thrill of watching her ride away, still basking in the smell and the heat from the bed they'd fucked in. But the sensation faded too quickly, and with it her utter sureness they would do it again, replaced instead by a creeping dissatisfaction mixed with doubt that now followed her around like hunger.

She found a bottle of retsina open in the fridge and poured a glass or two to drink with some dry crackers from the cupboard. Her mood slipped another notch when she poked her head into what must be Katie's room, taking in the crayoned pictures and scattered books, the bits and pieces of Sasha that had nothing to do with her.

By the time Sasha arrived at the taverna, Polina was half-way through her second beer and so on edge she couldn't even make eye contact.

'I got stuck at work,' Sasha said. She sat down and touched Polina's cheek for a second. 'And Katie's got a bug.'

'Oh no,' said Polina.

The touch on her cheek wasn't a sexual touch, it was a friendly touch, definitely; all the chemistry had gone and last night meant nothing.

'And her father's being a fucking idiot.'

'Oh.'

Sasha stopped rubbing her temples and looked at Polina. 'It's not you.'

Polina raised her hand for two more beers, so relieved she could have cried. She noticed Sasha's glance at the bottle and the glass already on the table.

'What are you doing later?' said Sasha, to the fresh beers.

Something was amiss. Was it to do with beer?

'I only really drink beer on holiday,' Polina explained.

'Does your drinking ever scare you?' said Sasha.

'We can just have coffee if you don't want a beer?'

'You know that's not what I'm talking about; I know you do.' Sasha sounded hurt.

'I'll replace the retsina.'

Sasha shook her head and held her hands up as if in surrender.

Polina rolled her eyes at the sky and tutted. She made herself not reach for the beer. She reached for it.

'So, are you busy tonight?' said Sasha.

—◊—

He looked like someone had taken a bicycle pump to him. Not only his belly but his head and neck had inflated too, and the force of the pumping seemed to have pushed the hair from his scalp. His teeth were the same as ever.

'Howard?'

Maggie was so shocked, she almost drove the car over his feet. What was he doing standing on her drive? She rolled down the window.

'Margarita! You look wonderful. Where have you been?' he said, which was such a surprising thing to say after more than twenty years that she told him the truth.

'Hospital.'

'Nothing serious?'

'Breast cancer.'

'Sheesh. We need a cup of tea.'

'Why are you here?' she said.

'Are you going to get out of the car?'

'I can't, I'm going straight to work,' she lied. 'And then I'm going straight to bed.'

'Are you? Count me in, my darling.'

'She's kicked you out, hasn't she?'

'Who told you?' Howard looked left and right, suddenly serious as though he was being watched.

'A hunch.'

'We had a good thing there, Mags, while it lasted.'

She wasn't sure whether he was referring to her or Kerri-Ann.

'Look,' she said, glancing at her watch. 'Can I give you a lift somewhere?'

'A cup of tea would be better. Or something stronger?'

'I can't.' Then she noticed the holdall by his feet. He followed her gaze, smiling sheepishly. 'No,' she said.

'A night? Two nights tops. I just need the headspace, Maggie.'

'I'm going to be late.'

She wound up the window.

'I still think about you, Maggie. How's Poli?'

'You're twenty years too late.'

She reversed and shoved the car into first gear, ready to go. He was motioning at her to wind down her window again.

'What?' she said.

'Do you need someone to come to the hospital with you?'

'That was my last appointment,' she said.

'Shall I come back later?'

'You're unbelievable.'

She drove round the block a couple of times, the long way round, to give him time to leave. Then she went inside, checked the locks, went upstairs and took her clothes off while her bath was running. The shaking slowed when she leaned her forehead against the bathroom mirror and, as everything steamed up, she cried.

—◊—

6.4 POLINA: A SLIP NOT A FALL.

It was a little slip, not a fall. Everyone slips.

There was a party, an invitation from a solicitor she still knew, and she'd worn a red dress she'd bought years ago for some occasion and then lost her nerve, so this was its first outing. She'd looked good in it, as good as it got for her, as in she didn't much care how she looked which also doubled as confidence. Someone's musky perfume had quickly given Polina a headache and she'd said, 'But sir, your cologne!' but, unfortunately, the woman hadn't found this anywhere near as funny as Polina, which may have been when the light hysteria set in, akin to panic but lighter, panic-lite, you-won't-believe-it's-not-panic, the kind of fluttering that was contagious if you were with a friend, only she wasn't. She recognised the feeling straight away as the forerunner to that moment – had it already passed? – after which it was too late to step back, or at least that was what she always told herself about three drinks in. Somewhere in her eagerness to know if the moment had passed or was passing, she realised she'd stopped mingling and was standing at the bar, letting her eyes read the shelves left to right, her hand on her chin and the anticipation kicking about inside her like a cat in a bag.

The barman said: 'What can I get you?'

But that was no explanation for how she found herself in a field with someone who dribbled brandy from his mouth into hers, his party trick, and left before she could find the words to protest. She'd got up and staggered, the dress ripping like every fucking story you read about a woman in a dress on a night out. One of her shoes was gone. She'd pressed her face against a long window, all that glass low to high, and a dozen faces looked back at her, men in suits, their features ghoulish and unfriendly. It was raining and she coughed and couldn't stop. Help me. This may have been a different party, come to think of it.

A replacement dress arrived in the post a week later and she didn't know who to thank, how they knew where she lived.

At her first meeting, after she'd introduced herself with eyes lowered and they'd repeated her name, she described the party and the dress as her lowest point and thought she was doing very well indeed at 'being candid'. She felt she'd judged the mood of the room just right and even started to enjoy it, adding little pauses and authentic-sounding details here and there, like how the dress label had made her neck itch all night, the party guest with halitosis who'd suggested she tone it down and, why it should be that a drink spilled on the wooden floor had rendered that floor both slippy and tacky at the same time, but she sensed from their reactions when she looked up that they weren't with her. You could make it all doom and gloom or you could laugh at yourself, what did they want? Some of

229

them were shuffling, not meeting her eye, or they glanced very quickly across at one another. Had she got the rules wrong? She was new here, they knew that, did no one have the decency to help her out? The only other woman, whose bedraggled fox fur curled round her neck looked even more inebriated and bored than she did, began contemplating the nails of one hand, pulling her gaze back from them as though struggling to focus. Polina pitied them, all of them. She wanted to ask: *Am I not alcoholic enough for you?*

It took five months for her to admit what a fake she was. Her lowest point was lower by the time she went to her second meeting, so she apologised straight off for last time, to clear the air. I was acting, she said, and she meant it, though scanning the horseshoe of faces she realised there was no one here from last time. She'd half expected to see the curled fox, now without its owner and bravely doing the twelve steps alone. A purple-faced man with a voice uncannily like Roger Moore's, his trouser legs rolled up to reveal slim, hairless ankles, told her: 'Don't worry about it, dear, we all lie at our first meeting.'

Doug woke up that day with the clear idea that he must learn to play the bass guitar. It had come to him in the night. He got Amy to look up local teachers in the Yellow Pages and booked multiple lessons with each of them. He recognised, quickly, the potential he had to be a very talented musician. He bought an expensive bass guitar and amp. So important, the amp, and this one was quite a lot better than the one Ed used to have.

Some days were better than others. Some days weren't days, but parts of days, mornings, afternoons, noons, mid-afternoons, which you subdivided into parts, hours, minutes, each minute a cluster of moments. The thinking goes that if you can make it through a moment, this moment, if it's not unendurable, then the possibility of the next being similarly do-able is so high as to be a dead cert, more or less, and in the time it takes to mull that over, to think about whether you buy it, that next moment, now in the past, has been endured too, and before you know it you've strung some moments together like fairy lights. The more lights, the brighter you feel.

But some days, vodka was the only thing that quieted the noise. Polina often wondered whether she should have sued the council for their negligence in leaving a log in the road, but she didn't and, anyway, it didn't matter now. Most people drink to forget. She couldn't remember why she drank. Not that she really drank – she had breaks, she ate, she went to work, she slept. It wasn't a perpetual state – she sometimes had a drink, which has quite different, not the same at all.

6.5: MAGGIE FINDS AMY.

Buster flicked up little pebbles with his back legs, delightedly, while Maggie crouched, revolted, a poo-bag fitted over one hand like a puppet bird as she pecked up the tubular segments of shit. Buster wasn't her dog, she'd borrowed him from Geoff to see if she could hack it, and she couldn't, not if they did this every day.

The early morning air was grainy, it had an abrasive texture like a salt-rub, and seagulls cursed as they circled in the damp above her head, so she held the bag of dog poo up towards them and waggled it threateningly. Maggie wanted to call out to the old woman she could see in the distance, tip-toeing gingerly over the stones towards the sea, to tell her not to go in. The October sea was not your friend, still and alluring as it looked. She'd find out soon enough.

Buster cleared the seawall easily and ran ahead to bark at the seaweed on the next beach along. She followed him, but it wasn't easy; she had to straddle the wall as though it were a Thelwell pony and there was quite a drop down to the stones on the other side. She'd already lost the bag of poo somewhere. The old woman wasn't so old. She seemed to be taking a long time to go in if she was going; some people swam every day, all weathers. The woman took tentative steps, and the first clue was that she was still fully dressed except for the coat she'd discarded on the stones behind her. It took Maggie a while to notice Doug's car parked a way off by the roadside next to the beach. Clue two.

She called, *Hello?*, but not loudly because she hadn't worked it out yet and the woman was an adult, after all. She was in up to the waist, moving forwards very slowly, her arms out at each side like stabilisers. A charity swim, perhaps? When Maggie got close enough to be sure, the shock of it almost pitched her to one side.

'Amy?' She cupped her hands around her mouth.

Amy half-turned, her face lacking, the way you would draw a face before you started on the detail. She seemed to be scanning the water for something. She'd stopped moving. If she saw Maggie, she didn't seem to recognise her. Buster ran in manic circles, barking like an idiot at the edge of the water, confused by the shouting and by the person in the sea. It was the strangest experience, wading in, but what choice did Maggie have? Her legs wanted to bounce, astronaut-like, as her padded bodywarmer started to inflate. The water was so cold it was scalding.

'Amy? Can you turn round?'

Maggie was not a strong swimmer and was reaching that tipping point where she would have to start. She reached forwards and touched Amy on the shoulder, wary in case she spun round and thwacked her by mistake. But she didn't, instead she turned in slow motion.

'Maggie?'

'Let's go back now, shall we? Shall we go back?'

'Maggie, I'm so cold.'

Maggie got them both facing the beach. She tried to think of nothing as she put her arm around Amy's compliant back and guided her in. Once they were out, the water rushed off them and Maggie had no idea what to do next. Amy shivered and looked at her feet, awaiting instructions, her arms crossed over her chest. Buster barked and barked, and it was hard to think straight when he wouldn't stop barking.

It was what Doug called a dead instrument, the bass guitar. It had no soul and he was all soul. Unfortunately, the bass guitar teachers were all morons. He got Amy to ring and cancel his subscription to *Bass Player Today* magazine.

'Hit me,' said Grace.

Polina held up her glass of tonic water, making the ice clink. 'Seventeen months, two weeks and one day. Approximately.'

'So, you can't even have a beer anymore?'

They were perched on fishing stools on the prow of Aysha's houseboat, where pots of flowers and herbs took up almost all the space and grass grew up through the deck in stubborn tufts. Down below, Polina could hear Katie bullying Sam into a game. He hasn't got a hope, she thought.

'Nathan thinks we shouldn't all sit at one end in case the whole thing flips over,' Grace said.

'Let's test it,' said Polina. 'Get everyone down here, send him up the other end, if he flies over our heads, he was right.'

Sam sounded wretched. 'Can't you just play it by yourself?'

'You promised!' said Katie.

'Remind you of anyone?' said Polina.

'He'll have to man up,' Grace said, squeezing her own bicep.

'Like I did?'

'You didn't.'

'Is that apple juice?' said Polina.

'Don't say anything, I don't know how I feel about it yet.'

'You're not pregnant? Are you? You hate kids!'

'I know.'

'Does Nathan know?'

Katie was crashing up the stairs towards them. Grace shook her head at Polina.

'He promised!' said Katie, and she stood between them with crossly folded arms.

'That's what boys are like,' said Grace as she swilled the ice round in her glass. 'You'll get used to it.'

'What about I-Spy?' said Polina.

'What about hide and seek? You hide and I'll count to a hundred,' said Grace.

Katie was suspicious. 'I don't know.'

Sasha called: 'Katie, come down here and apologise now.'

'Oh-oh,' Grace said in a sing-song voice. 'Someone's in trouble.' To Polina, she said: 'At least I had Ed to protect me from my parents. Who did you have?'

—◊—

7.1: POLINA: FLASHBACK – NOT MANNING UP.

7.1.2: WHO'S PROTECTING ME PROTECTING YOU?

Polina had to get to them before the next big one because she'd changed her mind, but they were already out too far and every ninth wave was a monster. She swam their way, bobbing up and down.

'Grace!' Polina's voice got rammed down her throat by the wind. 'Hey! Grace!'

Grace was sitting on Doug's shoulders. She turned her head and Doug followed, struggling to keep his footing.

'Go back,' he called, shooing Polina.

'You won't like it,' said Grace.

'I love it!' said Polina, flapping her arms about to show them.

Rumbling with anger, a wave was drawing itself up and all Polina could do was laugh.

'Oh fuck,' said Doug.

'It's coming!' said Grace.

Doug waded towards Polina, but he was slow with Grace wrapped around him like weed. The wave was huge.

'I can't get – ' Polina said.

'Swim!'

He threw Grace roughly from his shoulders and lurched as

quickly as he could towards Polina, but he was too far away. The wave was deafening and it pushed her head down fast. She punched and kicked at the churning water and his hands scooped her under the ribs and lifted her clear into the air, gasping. He manoeuvred her onto his shoulders, but her legs wouldn't grip his neck properly because she'd gone floppy like a doll and she kicked him twice by mistake. She saw a flash of Grace's towelling bikini, her foot in the air.

'Grace?' Doug sounded like a bear, roaring.

'There!'

Polina pointed and Grace shot up in the air, propelled like a cork. She spun round looking for them.

'I did it!' she shouted.

They stumbled up the beach, Grace whooping. Doug had one of them either side, holding their hands, and was looking at Grace as though she was famous. He called her his mermaid; she shimmered. The sea was spent, and you might think they'd made it all up except for the cut under Grace's eye, a slit of red with tiny grains of sand stuck to it like glitter. They reached their towels. The dinghy oar that Doug had speared into the sand had fallen over. Polina smiled politely until her face hurt as Grace and Doug crunched into choc ices, Grace cupping a hand under her chin to catch the drips. Grace kept saying, I wasn't even scared was I, I wasn't even scared. Polina's eyes were stinging as she watched a little boy throwing pebbles at a seagull.

7.2: END OF BEGINNING/BEGINNING OF END?

Polina got the feeling that whatever she said next was going to zing with its own rightness like the sound you get when you run a wet finger round the rim of a glass.

'You sleeping with Jen probably saved my life,' she said.

If it was true, it was far too late, like a jigsaw piece you find behind the settee months later when no one's looking for it.

Grace said: 'Who?'

She looked so innocent it nearly made Polina spit out her tonic water.

'Are you kidding me?'

'I thought her name was Lou.'

'Lou was the girlfriend,' said Polina.

'The caveman?'

When Sasha came up to see what all the noise was about, she saw Polina, red-faced as she leaned over the side of the boat, and Grace holding her belly, sitting on the fishing stool with her head between her legs.

Polina said: 'Sasha, listen to this!'

'Shut up!' said Grace. She had tears streaming down her face.

Sasha looked at them both and then Polina heard her call down to Aysha: 'It's all right, they're only laughing.'

Acknowledgements

I have daydreamed for a long time about the luxury of actually writing this bit, and being able to thank the very many people who helped and supported me in writing the book. So here goes.

Love and thanks to Mum and Dad, Trev, Sarah and the boys for your love and belief in me. Thanks to Archie for making up 'Ladywell Fox', which I loved so much I used it as a band name.

Thanks to MMU and our MA online cohort – Jan, Leanne, Jackie, Surfy Dave, Pete, Dan, Bine – for the feedback and virtual support, and to James Draper and the tutors, especially Nick Royle, Robert Graham (who introduced me to *A Visit from the Goon Squad* and *Everything is Illuminated*) and Rachel Genn who I can't call Rachel (see below).

Thanks to BPP for part-funding the MA and especially to Leyanda for your kindness and for giving me some time, and Julian, despite the 3am call to Argentina.

Love and then some to my friends: Tori, for reading bits and pieces when they made even less sense than they do now, for listening, and for sleeping uncomplainingly with your head under a desk near a boules set; Claire, for lots of things including lending me your house to write in; Deb and Yvonne, who I've made sound like a couple, and who made work a total joy and supported me even when I insisted on eating sweet potatoes with hummus; Dan and Zoe for being calm and supportive in all weathers; Katie and Robbie for inspiring me (us), whether you know it or not; Jude, for reading the book in its early days and championing it, and me; Jo Avison, for the magic and the insight; Lucy Stone QC, for your kindness years ago and support ever since; the IOW crew, especially Ben Weedon, (all the best); and to others who are in my heart even though we only see each other once every hundred years – Emma, Ant, Mariana, Augusto, Paul and Jen, Rebecca. Lots of love and thanks to Len Genn (that's better) for so much valuable feedback in writing this book, especially the dialogue, and for making me laugh. Our trophy cabinet groaneth.

Thanks to super-talented Michael Brydon for the photos and to Smallbatch in Hove for the best coffee ever. A big thank you to Martyn and Mike at the Loud Shirt Brewing Company in Brighton for very generously providing (lovely lovely) beer for my launch. Buying beer? Buy it from them!

Huge thanks to Valley Press, of course, for being brave and actually saying yes to an unknown sitting on their submissions pile. I'll never forget the email from Tess as I stood in the fruit and veg aisle at Sainsbury's (other supermarkets are available) before quickly moving to the cold bubbly beverages aisle. Special thanks to Jamie, and also to my wonderful editor and all-round superstar, Jo, who's been so helpful and done a great deal for me with lots of humour, a light touch and no ego.

Thanks to our beautiful, chatty and funny son, Freddie. I'm afraid there are no tractors in this one but the next one will be called *The Tractored*.

And to Kate. I love you. Thank you.